BOUND SOULS

Forever Yours, Book 1

N.D. JONES

Kuumba Publishing

Baltimore, Maryland

Kuumba Publishing
1325 Bedford Avenue
#32374
Pikesville, MD
kuumbapublishing.com

Cover Design: Jesh Designs
Original Concept Art: Phu Thieu

Bound Souls/N.D. Jones. -- 1st ed.
ISBN-10: 0-9975293-5-0
ISBN-13: 978-0-9975293-5-7

DEDICATION

This book is dedicated to Brian Jones
October 13, 1965-August 12, 2015

Loved.
Remembered.

CHAPTER ONE

Hard Truths

Asiya Homeworld, 2295

"I'm not having this discussion with you," Lela said, face contorted in an annoyed grimace, voice echoing the same emotion. "You're being ridiculous, and I wish you would just calm down and think rationally."

"Rationally?" Zion followed her into their bedroom, slamming the door behind them.

Lela went to her closet and swung the glass doors open, trying her best to stay her anger. Zion had been on a verbal rampage the entire walk from the banquet room to their suite of rooms in the Hall of Concord.

"I should've knocked Ammon on his Paladin Band ass. He thinks he can seduce you to get your support for him on the Council of Magistrates. He thinks he's charming and virile and..." Her husband punched the closed door, his flesh no match for the metal. Skin split and blood oozed between his knuckles.

"God dammit." Zion pulled back his right hand to survey the damage.

Lela ran to him, grabbing a towel from the master bathroom first.

"Let it be," Zion growled when she took possession of his battered and bleeding hand.

Dropping onto the bed, he frowned when Lela claimed the spot next to him.

"Let me see." He did as she asked, although her low, angry voice came out more as a command than a request. With a delicate touch, she wrapped the towel around Zion's knuckles, holding it in place to absorb the blood. "You're acting like a complete maniac. Or perhaps jackass would be a more appropriate descriptor," she corrected, ignoring her husband's raised eyebrow at her uncharacteristic vocabulary choice. "And don't tell me I got it wrong because you've used that word enough times over the last twenty-seven years for me to know precisely the meaning."

Zion Grace, a human of keen intelligence and talented peace negotiator, possessed great impulse control. He was not a man given to senseless acts of hostility. Yet his behavior tonight wasn't the first time Zion overreacted to what he perceived as an insult.

"Lela," Zion started, "Ammon was flirting with you. It was as clear as the nose on his face, which I should've punched him in."

"There will be no more talk of punching or any other form of fighting. This isn't like you." Lela removed the towel to get a better look at his hand. "You're lucky, it doesn't appear to be so bad as to require sutures. A thorough cleansing, bandage, and ice should be all that is required."

Lela stood, narrowed her eyes at her husband and then walked out of their bedroom, opening the door almost as forcefully as Zion had closed it. He said nothing, and for that she was grateful. She hated his mood swings, and to her dismay, the occurrences between them had increased over the last six months.

Lela stalked into the kitchen, opened the refrigeration unit and shoveled two handfuls of ice into a bowl. She closed the door and sighed. Zion had always been a leveled-headed person, yet something was going on with him and Lela didn't know what.

She made her way back to the bedroom, Zion still sitting on the bed, nursing his hand, frown firmly fixed and unwavering.

"I can't believe you called me a jackass." Their eyes met when she reentered the room. "You never use that kind of language, and in defense of Ammon of all people."

Lela exhaled, indeed regretting her word choice. "I apologize, Zion," she said with genuine contrition before inserting his hand in the bowl of ice. "I was upset, and I shouldn't have spoken to you the way I did." She paused then, looking down at him. "Regardless of the word, however, the sentiment remains the same. I don't apologize for that part."

"What kind of apology is that?"

"An honest one and the only one you'll receive." She turned her back on her grumpy husband and returned to her closet. Lela removed her shoes, stockings, and purple evening gown. When she'd donned the dress, Zion had taken one look at the garment and said it reminded him of gowns from Earth's Victorian Era. She had no idea what he'd meant, but he'd pointed to her gown and said, "Victorian Gothic brocade, jacket with jacquard pattern, standard collar with pleat, buttons down the front, smooth matching skirt." Hands came to her waist, a smile on his handsome face. "All you're missing is the hoop skirt underneath." He'd kissed her cheek. "You look stunning, sweetheart."

And he'd looked regal in his Asiyan formal attire—form-fitting black trousers, a dark purple shirt with high-stand collar, antique buttons on the placket and a tie-hoop back, and a black frock coat with fabric-covered buttons and a notched lapel.

Slipping into a white robe, Lela sat on the opposite side of the bed, her front to her brooding husband's back. How had an evening that started with such promise ended on a sour note?

"Ammon was flirting with you."

"Asiyans don't flirt." Fates help her, the man was absolutely maddening.

A derisive snort followed her heated assertion. Zion shifted so they faced each other. "That's damn sure not true. I'll admit, your people are subtler than humans, using rituals to justify their actions, but the intent is the same."

Lela pulled her lean legs to her chest and gave her husband a long, considering look. "What's this really about?"

"What's wrong is that I don't like other men hitting on my wife. I don't appreciate you being eyed as if you're a piece of prime rib in a deli full of carnivores."

Even after so many years of marriage, Lela didn't always understand her husband's very human way of expressing himself, despite her own fluency in the English language.

"Whatever Ammon did that upset you so, I'm sure he didn't mean it the way you took it. We've known each other a long time. He's a friend. But you know that already. Before today, you've never expressed any ill feelings towards him."

Lela was taking a page out of her Verity training, yielding and redirecting a strong force with a seemingly weaker one. She didn't want to fight with Zion, especially not when he was in an irrational frame of mind, and she didn't understand the source of his anger.

"You're naïve." Zion swung his bad hand from the bowl of ice. "You never notice things like that. You think everyone is all good and light. Well, they aren't." Standing, he placed the bowl on the nightstand on his side of the bed.

"I'm not naïve. I just don't agree with your assessment of Ammon. I would know if he or someone else was interested in me in a romantic way. Perhaps there is some kind of miscommunication going on, and we simply need to think about it and figure it out."

Still yielding and reflecting his anger.

"Like with Bartek," he spat, whirling on her, bronze face set in granite. "How long did it take you to figure that little one out?"

Bartek, the Fates bless his departed soul, had been the best friend of Lela's brother-in-law. She'd known the man since childhood, thinking of him as a good friend and nothing more. Certainly not a romantic partner or a rival for her affections when her relationship with Zion had become public knowledge.

Yet Bartek had, for some inexplicable reason, taken Lela's courting of the human Zion as an affront to Asiyan men in general and him in particular. From there, well, their friendship deteriorated, with Bartek speaking against the Human-Asiyan pairing within the Verity Band, causing tension and dissension. As her band brother, she'd been angered by his selfishness and discrimination. As his childhood friend, Bartek's condemnation hurt.

In not recognizing Bartek as a prospective mate and choosing an off-worlder, Lela had, inadvertently, wounded his pride. But none of that made Lela responsible for his actions, no matter the regretful turn their friendship had taken. Worse, they hadn't reconciled before the Fates called him home, Bartek's soul one more star in the cosmos that birthed them all.

She still mourned him. The man he'd once been and the friendship they once shared, his bigotry toward Zion a shield that hid his pain at losing someone he thought to make his mate.

"No, Asiyans may not flirt, Lela, but they damn sure know how to squirm themselves into the lives of the person to whom they're interested."

Prudence and strategy gave way to anger. Lela moved quickly—shifting her position until she stood in front of her husband, thin finger poking him in the chest, chin lifted and set.

"Listen here, Zion Grace, you've been in a foul mood for the last six months, and I have no idea why. I've tried ignoring it and talking to you about it. Nothing works. You've just become angrier and grumpier as the days go by, and frankly, I'm sick of it. This isn't like you and if you insist on continuing this paranoia and disrespectful behavior…"

Lela trailed off, unwilling to issue the ultimatum she felt coming. In her husband's current mood, he would be just foolish enough to challenge her, and she was feeling just stubborn enough to follow through with her unspoken threat. "We both need time to cool off before we say something we'll regret. You can stay here." Lela moved toward the bedroom door. "I'll sleep in the guest room for the night. Perhaps in the morning we can have a more dignified conversation without insults and name calling."

Lela opened the door only a few inches before she saw a brown and bruised hand push it back into place. Zion's hand rested on the door above Lela's head, the front of his body pressed against the back of hers, his hot breath coating her ear.

"I overheard him," Zion said. "Six months ago I overheard Ammon ask your father if you would consider having an Asiyan after being mated so long to a human."

Lela stiffened, but Zion wasn't finished.

If possible, he leaned in even closer, his lips brushing her ear. "Your father told him he didn't think you would mate yourself to anyone else and Ammon said, unlike me, he had plenty of time. And in three years the Fates would take me, leaving you alone and without a mate. 'Lela Grace will be alone and lonely. But she won't have to be forever. Once she emerges from the requisite year of mourning, I'll be there to show her how much more living there is to do.' And that my naïve wife is an exact quote."

Zion pushed from the door and staggered to the bed, all but falling onto the mattress, his tall form closing in on itself in seeming defeat. He looked old, Lela thought. So much older than he had a few minutes ago. At least she now knew the reason for his uncharacteristic behavior. She thought knowing the source of Zion's anger would make her feel better, give her a better angle from which to deal with her husband. How foolish she had been. How utterly foolish.

Lela joined Zion on the bed, sitting next to him and grasping his unharmed hand in her own. They sat like that for long minutes, an uncomfortable bubble of truth having settled over them.

CHAPTER TWO

Forever Yours

It was true, Zion had only three more years left on his thirty-year life extension. He was tired and felt even more so as the days, weeks, months and years crept by. Zion spared a sidelong glance at his wife, whose head was down, eyes closed and hand still gripping his with a heartbreaking ferocity. She wasn't ready for the ride to end either, yet they knew it was slowing, preparing to grind to its final halt and he would have to disembark, leaving her behind.

This thing with Ammon had eaten away at him for the last several months. Yet Ammon was simply an outlet for Zion's anger, fear, and depression. He was growing older, his hair thinner and grayer, and his stomach… well, let's just say he'd had to use the services of a good seamstress over the years. Yet Lela remained as beautiful and as fit as when they'd first met.

Zion didn't begrudge his wife her slow aging or fine, alluring features. In fact, he loved that about her. What did bother him was that other men could see what he saw. Everything about Lela exuded intelligence, grace, dignity, strength, and beauty. Zion learned a long time ago that she couldn't see herself the way others did, especially men.

While Zion rarely entertained jealous thoughts before or cared much when he caught a man giving Lela an approving look, now he saw nothing but. Under the circumstances, the little signs of masculine appreciation for his beautiful wife enraged him.

"I'm sorry," Zion spoke into the quiet breach, lifting Lela's chin with his bruised hand.

Tears flooded her eyes. Even wet, they were still the most stunning eyes he'd ever seen. Picasso marble Zion thought the first time she'd looked at him—a combination of black, brown, gray, and white. Back then, they'd sparkled with intelligence and curiosity, now they glistened with pain. Lela wasn't ready for this conversation. How could she be?

"No, it's me who should apologize. I thought you were paranoid, seeing things that didn't exist."

"I acted like a jackass, a Neanderthal, damn near dragging you out of the banquet room before the function was over. Hell, I might as well have hoisted you over my shoulder and beat my chest like a caveman."

He rubbed his thumb across her right cheek, then lips. "You're an incredible woman, Lela." Zion paused, nearly biting his tongue on his next words. The ones his selfish heart screamed at him to not utter. "You'll live for a long time, probably another four or five decades. I only have three years left. For an Asiyan, you'll be in your prime when I pass on." His voice cracked when the held tears dropped from his wife's eyes. She knew where he was going with this, Zion realized.

"You'll have to go on without me, and I don't want you to spend the next fifty years by yourself."

"I won't be by myself. I'll have Xavier." Lela pushed off the bed and moved away from him. She walked to the window, refusing to acknowledge the true meaning of his words.

Zion followed, watching her stern but sad image in the window. Needing to touch and reassure her, he wrapped his arms around her waist and pulled Lela to him.

"The thought of another man being this close to you," Zion whispered, stirring tendrils of her long hair, "makes me want to commit murder. When I heard Ammon offering for you, it took all of my self-control to not take a laser gun to him. The only thing I kept thinking was that he couldn't have you. That you're mine and mine alone."

"Is that why you've been so angry these past few months?" She turned in his arms, resting her head against his resilient shoulder.

"Yes and something else."

"What else?"

Zion lifted her chin, compelling her to meet his eyes.

"I didn't want to acknowledge how selfish I was being." Leaning down, Zion placed a warm, soft kiss to her lips. "I want you to be happy in those four or five decades you have left, but I don't want you to find happiness in the arms of another man."

"I have no desire to mate with anyone else, or to take a lover," she reassured, initiating another kiss, a desperate embrace full of a wife's integrity and denial. "I can't imagine being with anyone other than you. I love you, Zion. I could never love another."

He knew she spoke the truth. He believed her, but she didn't understand. Zion did. He'd experienced the loss of a spouse.

"When Iman died, a part of me died with her. Like you, I thought there wouldn't be anyone else for me. And that was true for a long time—"

Lela shook her head in protest, not allowing Zion to continue. "Don't." A pained plea. "Don't say such things. There will never be anyone else for me."

Zion saw the near panic in her upturned face, her Picasso marble eyes glowing with resolution and despair.

"It's not the same. It just isn't."

It was exactly the same. Yes, what he felt for Iman was different from the love he had for Lela. But it was love all the same. Loving Lela didn't mean Iman ceased to occupy a special place in his heart and mind. A small, warm piece of her and their life together would always be a part of him. As he would always be a part of Lela, but she couldn't see it, not now. But someday. Zion didn't want to think about that and clearly, neither did his wife.

"Okay, sweetheart," he soothed. "Enough talk for tonight. We still have plenty of time."

"I don't need time. I know my mind, and it won't change. I won't have Ammon or any other."

Zion smiled at his devoted wife. She was indeed naïve, and blessedly so, the selfish part of him pleased at her defiance.

"Come to bed." Hand on the small of her back, Zion led her away from the window and the bleakness of the late night sky and their conversation.

He undressed in silence, Lela watching…studying him. He knew what she was doing, her rational mind battling her heart, considering his words and the long years ahead of her without him. She grimaced, turned away from him and hid beneath the improbable security of the comforter.

After tossing his clothing in the cleaning unit, Zion slid into bed, scooting until he was where he wanted to be. The perfect spot, body spooned against that of his wife's. Zion's left hand found Lela's hip and his mouth her bare shoulder. She'd removed her robe, leaving the woman beautifully bare. He caressed her hip with slow, practiced movements, creating an old rhythm and a familiar heat.

"Zion," she said, voice low and throaty.

"Shh, no more talking, no more thinking, no more anger, no more fear. Let's just enjoy each other while we still can. Please, Lela, I need that. I need you."

He did, so very much. Zion didn't want to think about the future any more than Lela did.

When they made love, it was slow, so heartbreakingly slow and exhaustingly delicious. Zion worshipped Lela's youthful body, whispering prayers and bestowing gifts, hording her essence, her light, for the dark, lonely journey to come.

Though exhausted, Zion didn't sleep. He watched his wife, the rise and fall of her chest, the anguished expressions that marred her features, telling him she wasn't sleeping peacefully. The poor woman was unable to let go of her anxiety over his impending death, even in her dream state.

Zion dug his fingers into her heavily coiled hair, finding sensitive scalp and massaging. He'd discovered, when they were courting, that

Asiyans held their tension in their head, unlike humans whose stress often found its way to their neck and shoulders.

After several minutes, Lela's tense body melted under his expert ministrations, taking on a more natural posture. Her breathing grew deep and heavy.

Zion smiled at his wife and wrapped himself around her, using his left arm to pull Lela close to him, claiming her as his. She was still his, he reminded himself. For the next three years and one beyond that, she would be only his in mind, heart, and body. After that… well, life went on, even for the most loving and dedicated of spouses. Zion was sure Iman had forgiven him for finding love and happiness with someone else. And he could…would do the same for Lela. But not now, not tonight, not yet. He still had time. They still had time. She was his. Yes, his and his alone.

*****

Three Years Later

Arbitrator Zion Grace awoke for what he knew to be his last time. After today, there would be no more sunrises for him. At the tender age of sixty-five, when most humans lived decades longer, Zion's body could no longer contain his soul. Thirty years ago, the three Fates of Asiya, in an act both merciful and shrewd, had breathed life into his ravaged body. On the smooth but oft traveled road to Willow Belfry, an ancient, towering edifice that housed meeting rooms and offices for members of the Confederation of Worlds on the planet of Ranbir, the multi-racial peace delegations' caravan came under fire. Once the screams of pain and hiss of laser fire receded into agonized groans of impending death, Zion found himself surrounded by shredded transporters and bloodstained hope.

After five years of battle cries, bloodshed, and prayers to whatever God would bring a quick and decisive end to a war that threatened to consume the cosmos, his time, like so many before him, had come to a vicious, grinding halt. Such was the way of warfare, no matter the century, no matter the rationale, no matter the hearts and beliefs of those who wielded laser guns and ionic bombs or those whose munitions of war were rhetoric and political policies. In the end, they all resulted in mass destruction and destroyed lives.

So it was, on that fateful day marked by glorious sunshine and terrorist bombs, the three Fates of Asiya appeared to Zion. One woman and two men, white cloaks like angel wings flowed and flapped around them. Faces the color of benevolent amber stared down at him, eyes focused in wizened concentration. Lips spoke in unison. "It is not yet your time, young one. You have much to do, much for which to live. She awaits. You know of whom we speak. Without you, without her, there is no us, no future, no hope. Build the bridge between her heart and yours, between her soul and yours, between your body and hers. Once done, Mother Cosmos will rejoice."

Zion, of course, had known to whom the Fates of Asiya referred. A beautiful peace negotiator from the Asiya Homeworld—Lela of the House of Asheema. They'd met, each representing their respective planets, neither willing to end talks until a compromise could be found that would end a tri-planet war that threatened to force the military hand of Earth and Asiya—neutral but concerned third parties. So they'd conversed and debated for a year, learning as much about each other as they did each other's race, dispelling stereotypes and preconceived notions that had made it difficult, in the beginning, to work together for the betterment of the people of the three planets at war with each other. Yet from harsh, distrustful beginnings, a friendship had taken root, blossoming in secret without the benefit of rainfall or sun rays.

"She is your other half as you are hers," the Fates had whispered. Their words, while soothing and warm, stung like a thousand pinpricks across his war-ravaged skin.

Inexplicably, Zion had known the first time they'd met that Lela, Chief Magistrate of the Verity Band, was indeed his soulmate. He hadn't needed the Fates to tell him. But their words, the confirmation that his heart had not betrayed his long dead wife, was a balm to Zion's conflicted mind.

"We return to you what has been taken, what has been spilled, what has been sacrificed." A partial truth, for not even the Fates of Asiya had the power to fully renew life. But they'd given of their own mystical essence, comingling embers of life with elements of death, forever altering Zion's genetic code. *Just enough.* He understood later. Yes, it had been just enough to create life where there should have been none. *Xavier, my son...our son. A child, a miracle, a symbol made manifest from our love, our want, our prayers.*

Those embers of life, a blessing for the dead, were finite, transitory, a wonder slowly seeping from Zion, leaving him as he'd once been. Dying and afraid, but no longer filled with regret. At least no more than any other man not yet ready to leave his wife and son behind, moving on to Heaven or perhaps what the Asiyans devoutly referred to as the Realm of Thuraya—a space of fathomless stars that connected all people and their Homeworlds. A majestic, serene existence not bound by time or cultural differences.

Eyes still closed, Zion rest quietly in his bed, not quite ready to face the end—a bleak eternity without Lela and Xavier.

Not wishing to wake his wife, Zion swallowed a sigh as he thought back to the words he'd spoken to his wife last night. *When we awake, let's not dwell on what we cannot change. Instead, let's remember the thirty years we were given. I don't want to leave you on talk of death but rather with hope that I'll see you again. In our next lifetime, Lela. In our next lifetime, we will meet again.*

A final wish, for anything less would rip his heart into jagged shards of sorrow, anger, and pity.

He shifted, turning onto his side so that he could see the sleeping form of his wife. Zion watched and listened, the strong up and down motion of her chest affirming her place on this plane of existence. The beat of her heart was always true, filled with an honorable determination Zion had admired in her long before his own heart had completely healed from his first wife's death. Over time and with the help of good friends and an understanding family, it had mended, becoming whole once more. But the journey had been a difficult one, a road he would've rather left untraveled.

Death, unbidden and unavoidable, it was now Zion's time to move on.

Unable to keep his lips from lifting, Zion smiled. He'd spent the last thirty years living among Asiyans. Ironically, on his last day, Zion only now realized how much he had grown to think like the people of his adopted home. Funny, funny indeed. So amusing he forgot about not waking his wife and laughed.

As he knew they would, sleepy eyes opened. A happy smile played around the edges of Lela's lips as her eyes focused and found him staring at her. The love his wife had for Zion never failed to humble him. They shone just as brightly as they did the day they'd taken their vows, pledging their eternal love and binding their souls.

Your request I will honor. How could I not? Lela's words from the night before. She would give him his happy day. Zion's last happy day. Heart in her eyes, her unwavering gaze spoke the words her mouth would not. An honest woman with the wisdom and cunning required to peacefully rule a planet, Lela Grace was unmatched. No matter how much grief she would endure when Zion left, she would honor her vow. For that, if possible, Zion loved his wife even more.

He reached for Lela, and she came, body still naked from when they'd made love last night. *The last time.* Or so Zion had told himself. Yet the way his equally nude body responded to Lela's nearness, he welcomed being wrong.

With a vigor that came from a reserve Zion hadn't known existed, he went about making love to his wife one last time. Knowing when they finished, when they exploded in rapturous, sensual glory, it would truly, inescapably, be the last time for Zion Grace and Lela of the House of Asheema.

When Zion reached his peak, when his heart raced, toes curled, and muscles clenched, there was only one thing he could say, "I love you, Lela. My heart is forever yours."

CHAPTER THREE

The Compromise

Seven Years Later

"Why are you still here?"

"I'm not going. I've changed my mind."

Sage joined Lela on the single bench on the balcony, a solitary spot until her sister-in-law chose today to invade her sanctuary.

"You can't just change your mind like that."

Lela could, and she had.

"We've gone over this before. You agreed, remember?"

Lela looked at her hand and the diamond ring that still sparkled upon her finger. "I'm not ready. I should've never allowed you to talk me into doing something I don't wish to do."

"Not ready?" Sage pivoted so that she faced Lela, before taking her hand in her own. Running a cool finger over Lela's wedding ring, she spoke in that gentle yet firm tone she used when Sage thought herself right and Lela stubborn. "It's been seven years."

"I know how long it's been. I don't need you to remind me." There was an unusual hardness to her voice, a reaction Sage didn't deserve but would continue to receive if she kept meddling in Lela's life. Yanking her hand, Lela tried to free herself from Sage's grip, but Sage only tightened her hold.

"You know what I mean and stop tugging like that before you bruise my shooting hand. You may be small of frame and height, but you're as strong as any male."

Lela glared at the statuesque beauty. Even now, after knowing Sage Grace for three decades, her nearly six-foot lithe form never ceased to amaze Lela. Humans were so varied in coloring—hair, eyes, skin, as well as in body type and size. They also spoke a myriad of languages and held various religious and philosophical beliefs. So unlike Asiyans whom, regardless of gender, grew no greater than five and a half feet tall, with thickly corded hair and skin the color of a sand storm.

For all their cultural and genetic distinctions, visually, Asiyans and humans were quite similar, closer in phenotype than other races. Yet Asiyans were stronger and lived considerably longer than humans. By the human lunar calendar, Lela was a decade older than Zion, but her slow aging gave her the appearance of a much younger woman. Yet another reason why Lela's father had urged her to not marry Zion. *"He'll die long before you do, my sweet daughter, leaving you alone and heartbroken."*

That Zion had. But the thought of not binding her life to his, her soul to his, was a fate Lela had no interest in living. So she didn't, accepting Zion into her heart, her life, her bed. Knowing their time together would be shorter still. The Fates the only reason they were given any time together at all. *The only reason we were blessed with our son.*

Smooth brown skin matched the brown hair that hung, uncharacteristically, onto Sage's shoulders, her too-severe bun the younger woman's typical style of choice. The warm look added a deceptively delicate softness to her features.

"Then release my hand and leave. I didn't invite you here. Do you make a habit of going places where you're not wanted? I didn't request a meeting with my High Star Chief."

Sage ignored Lela's inhospitable words, choosing instead to tighten her hold on Lela's hand, frustrating her even more. The woman knew perfectly well Lela would never hurt her just to have her way. Sage was as stubborn and persistent as ever, making her an excellent High Star but a most annoying friend.

"You can't get rid of me that easily, Lela. I don't even know why you try. You shut Xavier and me out when Zion first died. I accepted it then, but I won't accept it now. Hell, I should've never left you alone then. Except for Regent business, you became a near recluse."

"Asiyans must observe a year of mourning. You know that."

"I do, but you, my friend, observed two years of mourning. And would have gone on, for God knows how long, if Xavier hadn't gotten you to snap out of it."

"Yes, he thinks he's my father instead of my son."

"Xavier loves you and only wants to see you happy."

"I am happy. Can't you tell? I'm boiling over with happiness and mirth." Lela stood, which forced Sage to release her hand.

She walked to the edge of the balcony and looked out into the graying sky. Night approached, as did a commitment she made a month ago. A commitment she now regretted, a commitment Sage had talked her into.

Lela placed her hands on the cool railing, her shoulders and back perfectly erect and rigid. Was she happy? She'd used the word, but it was mocking, meant to push and annoy Sage. And while Lela knew Sage too well, Sage knew Lela just as well. This conversation, between best friends, wouldn't end without a concession made on both their parts.

Lela felt Sage's presence next to her. "He wants his mother back." Sage reached for Lela's hand again, but this time she simply placed hers overtop of it, rubbing a soothing finger across her tense knuckles.

"I've been right here. I've always been there when Xavier needed me, and I always will."

She had spoken the truth but only a partial one. Lela understood the subtext of Sage's words.

"You're very good at that."

Lela didn't bother asking the expected follow-up question of, "Good at what?" She didn't want to know or hear but, of course, Sage, being Sage, would continue whether Lela gave her an opening or not.

"Zion warned me. Explained a few things I needed to know if I was to help you get past his death."

"I don't want to know what my husband told you in the last days before his death."

"Too bad, you're going hear it anyway. You have a way of neatly sidestepping questions or issues you don't wish to directly address. Hell, all Asiyans do, I suppose. You tend to only say as much as is required and nothing more. And you have an amazing knack of appearing to appease a person while having offered very little, looking past the current predicament and planning long term. That's what makes you a great diplomat and Regent."

"Make your point."

Sage already had, but Lela wasn't in a conciliatory mood.

"Zion had more than thirty years to figure you out and only a few weeks to bring me up to speed. Otherwise, you would've had my mind spinning, burying me in partial truths, Asiyan logic, and tons of distracting paperwork, security details, and alien rituals."

"I'm pleased you feel that Zion adequately prepped you for the job as my babysitter."

"Babysitter, psychologist, friend, Lela, whatever you require. I'm here for you, you know that."

Lela turned to her sister-in-law, her face an emotionless mask. Yet it cracked around the edges, threatening to break if Sage kept pushing.

"You have Xavier and me. But you also have yourself. And it's high time you started taking care of yourself, started living beyond us, beyond ruling, beyond—"

Sage cut her sentence short, but she needn't have, for Lela knew the rest.

"Beyond Zion," Lela finished in a pained whisper.

"Yes, beyond my brother. He wouldn't want you to be alone forever."

He'd told her that, many times in fact, before he went to a place she could not follow. But Lela knew he'd only said those words for her benefit. He hadn't meant them—not truly. Hollow, empty words mean nothing to an Asiyan. Lela had told him she wanted no one else. She'd meant it—then and now.

Sage studied Lela, her eyes tender yet resolute.

"If you won't do it for yourself, then do it for Xavier. He may be a grown man, but he still needs his mother. In some ways, when Zion went on his space fly-about to die, Xavier lost him and a part of you as well. It's not fair, Lela, and you know it."

Sage hadn't learned that from Zion, for he would never go for her jugular the way her friend had just done. Yes, a dagger to her heart—effective and bloodless. Curse the woman.

"You're no better. You have no right to push this on me. You've never gotten over Nathan's death, a man who loved you but whose love you didn't acknowledge until his death. And yet you expect me to turn my back on thirty years of memories and simply move forward as if they…he never existed."

The words were harsh, deliberately so, but quite true, Lela's last defense.

Sage stiffened, her hands balling into fists, a faraway look appearing and then quickly disappearing.

"You're one hell of an opponent, and that almost worked. But my being a spinster has nothing to do with this, although I'm sure you'd love to turn the tables, put me on the defensive."

"We're not opponents, Sage, we're friends. Since Zion's death, you've become my best friend. I don't know what I would do without you."

Truth but also tactic. As soon as Lela saw Sage's smiling eyes, she knew her friend knew it as well. What had Zion told her? Curse them both.

"You know we can continue this duel until we grow older or come to a compromise."

Just as Lela had thought. "I don't trust any compromise that's preceded by that smile of yours. You may know me, but I know you equally as well."

"So you do." An easy concession followed by a smile of warmth and infinite respect.

"Let's hear it, Sage, before you threaten to call my son and have him bestow one of his famous Xavier Grace lectures, sounding too much like his father for me to argue."

Sage laughed. "I was saving that gem as my last ditch effort to get you to see things my way. And God knows, Xavier's got the Grace gift for long winded, over the top proclamations. Good thing he's good with a laser gun. Otherwise, I don't think he would've survived basic training."

"True." Lela permitted a weary smile. "Now, about this compromise of yours, what does it entail?"

Sage took a slow breath before she next spoke. "If you follow through on tonight's commitment, regardless of the outcome, I'll back off."

"What's the condition?"

Another slow breath. "You must give me your word that you won't try to sabotage the damn thing. You must go into it with sincerity and an open mind. Can you give me your word?"

Lela didn't want to give Sage her word, for that was how she got herself in this mess. Lela actually had no intention of not going because she had indeed made a pledge. In spite of that pledge, she also had absolutely no intention of performing the ritual in good faith.

"I'll go, that should be enough for you."

"Well, it isn't. I need a vow from you, Lela. I've never known you to go back on a vow, and I don't think you would, even to spite me."

"Did Zion tell you that about me?"

"He did, but I already knew that myself," she said with a smug wave of her hand.

Lela returned to the bench and took a seat, the sun having fully disappeared in the night sky, followed by a chill in the air and her heart.

"Fine," she said coldly, "you have my vow, and I have yours. When I return here tomorrow, I'll be free of you and your nagging. And we'll never speak of this again."

Sage took an audible sigh of relief. "You don't make my job easy, sister, I can tell you that."

"Easy, Sage, you have no idea. I just agreed to betray my marriage vows, my husband, and my beating heart."

She looked at her unmarried friend but knew she could never understand. No one understood, not even Xavier.

Sage took a step toward her, but Lela stilled her with one raised hand. "Go now. I think you've done enough for one evening. I'll see you tomorrow."

"But—"

"I'll be fine, just go. I need to pray before I leave and I don't need you hovering about with those guilty eyes of yours."

Sage moved, with reluctance, to the balcony door. "I'll have a transport sent for you with two High Stars. They'll take you there and wait until you're ready to depart the following morning or earlier if it isn't going well."

Lela nodded absently, mind no longer on Sage but on the pending ritual. She heard the balcony door open and close a minute later, then she was alone. So utterly alone. She cried, the darkness unable to absorb her pain.

C H A P T E R   F O U R

Truth

Lela sat in the transport, hands clasped firmly in her lap, back straight against the cushioned upholstery, face grim and heart heavy. She'd arrived nearly thirty minutes ago, and in spite of two gentle attempts by her driver to escort her inside, she remained still and utterly silent in the backseat.

She'd made Sage a promise, and while her body was committed to fulfilling said promise, it simply wasn't enough to get the mind to obey. When the mind refused, the body was forced to listen. And right now, Lela's mind was on strike, the body compelled to negotiate a new contractual agreement.

Lela closed her eyes, envisioning opening the door to the transport and getting out. The image was clear and vivid in her mind, her movements assured and dignified. Yet, she remained unmoved, feeling neither assured nor dignified. More like a scared, petulant child. She was being ridiculous, and she knew it.

One night, Lela. Just one night and it will all be over in the morning. If you don't, Sage will haunt your waking hours until one of us is forced to kill the other.

Lela sighed, resigned to her eight-hour fate. She peered out of the window and into the darkness. A two-story glass structure with multi-colored windows caught her eye. The home was breathtaking in its ancient Asiyan design and confluence of bright colors that, Lela speculated, created dancing lights in the sky when the sun rose from the east.

Odd, she thought. It wasn't what she had expected, perhaps something darker, rougher. It didn't matter really, she decided. It wasn't a place she intended to get to know well. Tonight would be her first and last visit. What did it matter that the home reminded her too much of a childhood dream? The type of dream that only children could imagine, places that held all their light, hope, and goodness. Naïve, short-lived thoughts the world quickly disabused them of, lest they find themselves victims to the ugly truth. Not all was light, not all was black, and even the gray could hold peril, heartbreak, and loneliness.

Lela gestured to her driver and once instructed, the High Star moved quickly, opening the door and bestowing a respectful bow before helping her out of the transport. Lela took his hand and allowed him to help her down. She straightened her purple-and-black Regent's robe, her pile of hair hidden under the loose hood that framed her tense face. A proper woman would've donned a more appropriate outfit, a lovely dress befitting the occasion. But Lela refused to act the part tonight of a proper courting Asiyan female, choosing the protective armor of professionalism her robe afforded her, hiding behind its dainty softness and silent imperial power.

She stared at the footpath with solemn eyes and proceeded to walk, two guards flanking her, slowing their strides to match her cautious, measured ones. While in no hurry to begin, Lela felt a shameful need for this night to end as swiftly as possible.

Standing in front of a towering door, she fought hard to compel her heart to slow and her knees to not buckle. She could and would do this.

An hour later, Lela's heart had still yet to settle, her mind counting down the minutes until she could end the evening with her honor and soul intact. Her promise to Sage a footnote they would never speak upon again.

"You've been quiet this evening. Did the meal not suit you…or perhaps it's the company?"

Lela lifted her head and blinked, her wandering mind snapping into place, her host's words interrupting thoughts she hoped her face and silence hadn't revealed.

"I apologize, Ammon," she said, feeling awkward and self-conscious. "The meal was very nice, as is the company."

He gave her a quiet disbelieving look but didn't challenge the depth of the truth of her words.

"If this isn't a good time, we can reschedule." A polite offer she didn't deserve, which made Lela feel even worse. She had already rescheduled—three times.

"That won't be necessary. I've made arrangements, and I'm already here."

"And your High Stars? Will they stand guard the entire night? Make sure I'm the perfect host, that I show the Regent of Asiya the proper respect due her station?"

Ammon's eyes laughed, although his mouth did not. Lela gave him a thoughtful look. His deep-set maple eyes shone with intelligence and warmth. With humbling honor, the mind-body contract solidified. She'd not only given Sage her word, but Ammon didn't deserve anything less than complete honesty. He was an upstanding member of the Paladin Band, respected by most, and feared by many. He was a political ally with Council of Magistrate aspirations but also her friend.

"They will stay, of course, not because I fear a lapse in your honor, but because their duty will allow nothing less."

She smiled at him then, genuine and unforced.

Ammon visibly relaxed, his broad shoulders falling from where they'd been hunched to his ears.

They lapsed into a comfortable conversation, centering around Asiyan politics, steering clear of the reason for her visit. It was nice, Lela decided, to have a quiet night out with an old friend. If she concentrated hard enough, she could almost forget the weighty expectation of the evening.

They moved from the small dining area to the spacious living room, Ammon leading the way, taking obvious effort to avoid invading Lela's space. Gray-black coiled hair fell past his wide shoulders, lean waist and almost to his ankles. Men of his band did not normally wear their hair down, choosing to keep it wrapped high on their head, a sign of might and power. Yet he'd worn it down tonight, for her, she knew. An act of humility for Lela's higher status but also an act of intimacy when a Paladin male wished to display a softer, warmer side of himself to the female he sought to impress.

Ammon's skin, darker than her own, his eyes streaked with red-and-maple bands of light, held the wisdom of his years and rank. By Asiyan standards, he was a handsome man in both character and form. While Lela had no interest in becoming his mate, even she couldn't deny what a man like him could bring to the life of an Asiyan female. And not for the first time, she wondered why Ammon had never bonded himself to another.

They sat on the couch, Ammon waiting for Lela to sit before he decided upon his own spot. The spot being two seat cushion lengths away. Looking at the intentional seating, a twinge of guilt started to form within her.

"You need not sit so far away, Ammon. If I recall, we are friends and have shared a meal and conversation before."

"This isn't the same, and well we both know it." His deep voice held a harsh edge of anger. But the anger was nothing more than a mask for his real emotion—fear. The enemy of every Paladin.

"I know it's not the same, but that doesn't mean we can't..." She couldn't think of the proper word. Lela wouldn't lie to him, but she didn't want to lead him on either.

"I don't want you here if you don't wish to be," he said, freeing her from the awkward pause. "Besides, this isn't exactly a ritual of the Paladin Band. We don't enjoy such displays. It puts one in a weak position, this soul beholding of the Verity Band. It's not natural. A man should win the woman by strength and courage not by an invisible soul the woman glimpses while he slumbers."

Lela almost laughed but knew better than to do so. Ammon's pride was on the line. In her own angst, she'd forgotten about his. For him, the Light of Nurzhan ritual was just as foreign to Ammon as it had been for Zion. Something about the similarity warmed and frightened her heart.

"I never said I didn't wish to be here, Ammon." Truth.

He gave her a knowing look, and she couldn't help but smile.

"No, you didn't *say* that, Lela, but then again, you wouldn't. You have too much sensitivity to deliberately harm one you considered a friend."

His insightful and gentle words shocked her. Tonight she'd witnessed a different side of Ammon, a softer, kinder side, a side that was less soldier and more man. If she had seen this side all those years ago, perhaps…but not now. She didn't want to know this side of him, the vulnerable, insecure man protected by a soldier's roughened shell. She wasn't going to have this conversation with him, no matter how hard he stared, or how patiently he waited.

"So, you would rather engage in a duel and possibly be harmed than allow me to gaze upon your Paladin soul?"

As the tale went, an Asiyan female loved two Asiyan males, who adored her equally in return. One male lived his life with truth as his core, seeking answers for self and others—even when the truth, sometimes, proved wholly unpalatable.

The second male cloaked himself in faith, his convictions, oftentimes, leading him down untraveled and dangerous paths. Not seeking answers but confirming what he knew to be true in his heart, mind, and soul—a singular purpose, an all-consuming obsession.

Unable to decide between her loves, the Asiyan female decided to spend one night with each male. When the male slept, she prayed for guidance, for insight, for the truth of her heart and his, holding onto faith that she would glimpse his soul and know what she should do.

At the end of the two nights, the Asyian female had indeed beheld the soul of each male, her prayer of purpose granting her wish. The women of the Verity Band, to which the Asiyan female belonged, adopted the practice, deeming it the first, if not the most important, of their courting rituals. For if a woman's prayer could not draw the man's soul to the surface or if the woman did not find compatible pleasure in the soul she beheld, then there would be no need for the male and female to begin the journey of bound souls.

The problem, with most ancient stories, was that one never knew the truth of the claim or, as in this case, the complete tale. Because, to many a Verity Band female's dismay, the tale never told which of the suitors the Asiyan female selected, which soul she bound hers to, if either of them. Yet the ritual remained, the beginning or, in some instances, an end. For Zion and Lela, the soul beholding had been a beginning. With Ammon…

Ammon paused, giving Lela his best intimidating glare, arms folded across his chest, chin up and head high. He waited, and so did she. He waited some more, and so did she. He huffed with impatience and she said nothing and smiled.

He frowned and said with indignation, "I would not be harmed, and if I were then I wouldn't deserve you. A Paladin must be able to protect his mate, his family." His tone softened, as did his body, and he moved one cushion length closer. "I would protect you, Lela. You know I would, you only need to trust me, open yourself up to the possibility of not living the remainder of your life alone."

Lela dropped her eyes, unable to look at his and see the depth of emotion there. She wasn't ready for this. She had known it in her heart. Ammon was a special man who deserved a mate who would love and appreciate his strength, his dedication, his kindness.

Zion had been right. All those years ago, he'd known when she did not. Even after what he'd told her about overhearing Ammon ask her father if he thought she would take another mate once Zion died, she still couldn't fathom Ammon's desire to bond with her. In fact, she found it difficult to believe that any Asiyan male would desire such a union, not after having joined with a human.

Interracial mating was rare on their planet, no matter that thousands of immigrants called Asiya home. Could so much have changed in the three decades since she mated with Zion, causing a furor among her people and within her band? If she were to believe Ammon, it had. And if she were to believe Sage, there were other Asiyan and human males who would reveal themselves to her if she took the time to "pull her head out of the goddamn sand and stop acting like Katherina." Lela had no idea who Katherina, William Shakespeare, or the shrew were, but she understood Sage's point clear enough. It was the same point Zion had made, the one she ignored then and tried to ignore now.

"Perhaps you should rest, Ammon. It's been a long, tiring day, and I have an equally long night ahead of me." She stood and smiled down at him, hoping he would push no further.

He didn't. Ammon stood, neither returning her smile nor frowning. Clearly, he'd also made a mind-body contract, resigned to allow the night to play out as the Fates intended.

"Come, Lela," he said, "let me show you to my room so you can begin the soul ritual. I think we've talked enough for one night. Perhaps, if my soul is pleasing to you, we'll have another dinner, more conversation, and another night of soul beholding."

He was still hopeful, and the thought of such blind faith made her heart sink. He was, after all, a dedicated soldier of Asiya. Did she really think he would crumble and surrender so easily? She did not. But Lela wished he would, for the alternative would be far worse for them both.

*****

Ammon slept soundly, the large, airy room illuminated to ten percent. Two hours had passed, and Lela hadn't taken one thorough look in the sleeping man's direction.

When she'd first entered his suite, Lela had made every effort to not linger on the big, comfortable-looking bed in the center of the room or on the ancient weapons of war mounted on his walls—priceless daggers and swords. Family Heirlooms, Lela knew, and weapons, despite being relics of a bygone era, Ammon had mastered by the tender age of sixteen.

A plush, royal blue chair, already placed by Ammon's bed served as a mocking reminder of the intimacy of the Light of Nurzhan and Lela's utter discomfort with the expectation. She'd sat in the chair until Ammon's eyes closed. Soon after, she'd risen and found a spot in front of his bay window. She stared off into the darkness, wanting nothing more than to join it—a star among many. She'd told Sage she was happy, but it was yet another partial truth. Her life had become full of partial truths, and she didn't know how to untangle the web that was slowly, meticulously strangling her.

It had been seven years since Zion's death. Yet, to Lela, it felt like only seven days. Sometimes, she would rush home with exciting news, run into the bedroom, open her mouth to call for him and realize she was all alone. How could she forget? Her heart still ached at the thought of her deceased husband, the other half of her soul. She wanted to weep for her loss and her present and future selves. Mating with Ammon or another wasn't the answer. But what was? That dangerous web was getting thicker, stickier and harder to fight.

Lela turned away from her morbid thoughts and back to the man she'd promised to pray over. She would speak the requisite prayer and search for his soul between the lyrical notes of the words. If recited with trust and sincerity, even if not hope and faith, Ammon's soul would rise for her, permitting Lela to behold it in all its diaphanous splendor. Prayer or not, hope or not, she knew what would be revealed to her. Lela also knew it would not matter, for it wouldn't be the soul she wanted…needed to behold and adore with a woman's awe and ardor.

She moved to the right side of his bed and looked down at him. His black sleep robe flowed from his neck to his calves, the bedclothes still folded neatly on the empty side of the bed, the warm summer night making it unnecessary for covering. He was indeed handsome, Lela already knew, in the classical Paladin sense, but that wasn't his most striking feature. Physical appeal and other such subjective notions could never reveal one's essence, one's soul.

Lela sidled closer, taking him all in, her eyes focused, discerning. What she saw surprised her, his sleep face different from what she'd remembered. Unconsciously, she leaned over and reached for him, her right hand moving to his cheek, the soul beholding prayer slipping, unbidden, from her lips.

Out it flowed, breathed words merging with the still darkness of the room. Lela felt the heat of them, her promise not one she would continue to forsake, so she didn't. And the prayer repeated, a woman's melodic lure cast out and into the sleeping man.

Her hand crept closer to Ammon's sleeping face, his soul moving to the surface, following the call of Lela's prayer. A petal soft glow and a responding hum of soul bells beckoned Lela nearer. Closer than she'd been to a man since Zion's death. So close. So. Close. The realization broke the enticing trance of the soul ritual. Lela's hand halted in mid-air—body frozen yet mind drowning in guilt and confusion. What had she been about to do? Why was she so close to him?

Ammon's eyes flew open. They met hers and time seemed to slow, shallow breaths stretching between them, invisible bands flowing outward. One of his hands reached for her stalled one and brought it to his chest, placing it over his throbbing heart. The bands coiled around her wrist, holding her in place. His other hand moved hesitantly to her hair, her scalp and then the nape of her neck. He caressed the soft curls there, his gently probing fingers knocking on doors Lela had long since boarded up and forgotten about.

"I've wanted to touch you like this for a long time," Ammon whispered, his mouth, his masculine scent far too close for Lela to think straight. And the bands tightened even more.

Move, she told her legs. Nothing. *For the Fates' sake, move.* Nothing. Apparently, the contract was no longer in effect, her body making the decisions, forcing the mind to comply.

"So beautiful." Strong fingers twined in her locks. "You're an incredible woman, Lela. I would battle a thousand Terrademons to reach your heart. But I cannot challenge or defeat an enemy that's already dead. I cannot fight for a heart that doesn't want to be won."

Lela opened her mouth to speak, but Ammon closed the distance between them, taking her mouth with his and pulling her to him. His kiss was warm, sweet and filled with forced control, Ammon's possessiveness and need for her bubbling so close to the surface she could feel his lips tremble from the effort.

While this man gave himself to Lela, cast aside his armor for her and willed Lela to do the same for him, all she could think about and feel was a sense of betrayal. It took every ounce of her self-control not to wrench her mouth from his and run from the room in tears, suddenly grateful that Asiyans didn't tongue kiss. That level of intimacy would undo her completely, Ammon's vulnerable lips and words already having done most of the job.

When she thought she could stand no more, it was over. Just like that, it had ended. No warmth, no tension, no passion, no guilt, nothing but bitter cold in the pit of her stomach remained. But she could move now, and she did so, straightening and walking, on shaky legs, to the other side of the bedroom.

"I'd forgotten what it felt like to kiss you. It's been a long time." Ammon lifted two fingers to his lips. "A long time," he repeated, a wistful breath of history between them.

Even in the tempered light of the room, Lela could feel his eyes on her, as much as she could still taste him on her lips. Finding a sturdy chair, Lela sat, and Ammon leaned back onto the bed, his eyes still on her.

"Am I being a fool, Lela, to think you could ever care for me the way you once did? Some of my band say that I am, that you are still too devoted to Grace to consider another. But I thought...I hoped...I had faith that..."

He stopped in obvious frustration, balled his hands into fists and looked more vulnerable than Lela had ever seen him.

"Would you like for me to leave?" She hated the way her voice sounded—soft and fragile.

Ammon cast his eyes upward when he spoke. "I would not like for you to leave. In fact, I would like to keep you here forever as my mate. But I think you should leave. No bloom will grow when it turns away from the sun and water droplets, preferring to wilt and disappear into nothingness."

With barely repressed tears, Lela stood and walked to the bedroom door. She opened it, took one step into the hallway before saying, "I'm truly sorry, Ammon. I wish I could be the woman you want me to be."

She took another step when a voice wafted through the debilitating night. "You are the woman I want you to be. The problem is that I'm not the man you want me to be."

With guilt and purpose, she strolled away from Ammon, the truth of his words having scorched her ears, her heart, her very incomplete soul. Tears threatened to fall and overwhelm her, but she refused to cry, not there, knowing when they finally did come, no one but the Fates or Zion could stop the flood.

CHAPTER FIVE

Memories

Lela walked briskly down the corridor, her white dress flowing about her, covering her purpose with its soft, delicate folds. She reached the end of the corridor, looked behind her, then to her left. Satisfied, she made a sharp right, her footsteps undetectable, her face set and determined. Two more corridors, another right and then a left. She stopped when a gray door loomed before her. She glanced about her for the third time since undertaking this dangerous mission. The passageway was clear, but she couldn't relax. Not until she was inside and out of sight.

She moved one step closer to the door, intentionally setting off the security sensor, alerting the person inside to her presence. Twenty seconds later, the metal door opened on a hush, forming a rectangle as each piece slid into its proper place, allowing Lela to enter. She stepped over the threshold, and the four pieces glided back into place, sealing her in with the smoothest of effort.

Darkness greeted her, save for three candles in the center of a low table in the middle of the room. She moved in the direction of the candles, arms outstretched in front of her, steps cautious so she wouldn't run into something. But she need not have been afraid of such conventional accidents, for a hand reached for Lela, pulling her deeper into the darkness, deeper into the forbidden.

One hand covered the mouth that threatened a scream, while the other took hold of her dress and pulled her along. She went willingly, her eyes wide and heart racing, the hands fully in control. Deeper and deeper into the room she went, her thin frame virtually carried by the set of strong hands. And when she was to the candles, the only illumination brave enough to shed light on this most improper of events, did the hand over her mouth release her and the hand on her back gentle.

"I thought you had changed your mind. You're late, and you're never late."

She reached and touched the cheek of her captive, and smiled sweetly up at him. "You need to have more faith, Ammon. Faith doesn't come from a weapon, but the complex workings of the heart and of the mind."

"Ah, such the philosopher, no wonder the Regent selected you. The two of you are alike in many ways—both dreamers. I, on the other hand," Ammon said, sitting on the couch and pulling Lela next to him, "prefer my weapons. They're reliable and not subject to the whims of the mind or heart. One can never go wrong with a well-placed laser blast to the head."

Lela sighed and placed her fingers to Ammon's lips. "Everything in life isn't about battles. What about peace?"

"Weapons bring about peace, Lela, not prayers. No one respects prayers, but everyone respects power."

"Paladins are as religious as any other band, yet you minimize the significance of prayer and narrowly define power to military might only."

"What other might is there?" he asked, his voice a gentle challenge.

The power of love she told herself. But she wasn't quite ready to make such a declaration aloud, for spoken words had meaning and a might of their own.

"Lights at seventy percent." Lela needed to see his face, his eyes, his deceptively wicked smile.

They both blinked for several seconds, allowing their eyes to adjust to the change in illumination.

"Ah, Lela, you ruined the romantic atmosphere."

What a childish-sounding complaint from her Paladin. She smiled at his frowning face. "I didn't think soldiers believed in romance."

"We don't," he said, his voice taking on a low, husky quality Lela's come to know and appreciate over the last several months, "except when we want to impress a very special female."

He bent his head to kiss her, and she accepted it with the same throat-tightening anticipation as she'd done the very first time they'd kissed. Wrapping her arms around his neck and pulling him closer, her body relaxed into the stolen familiarity. Ammon lifted her onto his lap, his sturdy arms supporting her, molding Lela's body to his own, causing heat to radiate from every pore.

They kissed, slow, sensual, and inexperienced. Lela toyed with the hair piled high on his head, while her other hand circled his right ear, enjoying the small shiver she felt run through him. Then it was she who shivered, Ammon gliding his hand from thigh to hip in an amazing display of blissfully torturous restraint.

"Lela, I don't know how much longer I can stand this." Ammon pulled out of the embrace. "I want to formally begin the courting rituals."

Lela sighed and slid from his lap. They'd had this discussion before, and each time they did she was left with a great sense of foreboding. Beyond the obvious obstacles, a sickening part of her knew that her destiny wasn't with the Paladin. Like her, he was young, untried and in search of self.

"You know we cannot. Neither your father nor Regent Etemaad will permit our joining."

"Because I'm Paladin and you're Verity." He nearly spat the words, his contempt for outdated traditions obvious. "We are of age, Lela. We can make our own decisions. We know our hearts. They do not. They keep us in the Hall of Concord to learn from them, yet they do not trust our good sense."

Lela knew the Regent did trust her mind. In fact, he placed much more faith in her than any member of the Council of Magistrates did in their own more experienced pupils. But she was only a few years out of

Sagacity, the Verity House of training for the next generation of planetary leaders. Lela of the House of Asheema, was a mere child in the eyes of some. The Regent, like her father, was far too protective of her and her future to ever allow Lela to make a life-altering alliance without their input.

"I'm a mere disciple, Ammon. Whereas, your father is Chief Magistrate of the Paladin Band. I cannot fathom any circumstance in which he would not wish you to mate with someone closer to your rank and who shares your band."

While Lela came from a high-ranking noble family, Ammon's family was second only to the Regent's in power and prestige.

Ammon snorted. "You belittle yourself, Lela and inflate me. The House of Asheema is a most respected family, and you are no mere disciple. You are the Regent's chosen. That's obvious to everyone, including my father."

Lela doubted Ammon's words, though not his sincerity. She didn't question her knowledge and skills in diplomacy, yet Lela's father and Regent Etemaad were of the same band and best friends. The Regent was more like an uncle to her than a ruler everyone gazed upon with awe. He and his mate had no children of their own, which placed Lela in the enviable yet awkward position of filling a role that rightfully belonged to a natural offspring.

As such, she'd received special privileges and training her entire life, including the upcoming diplomatic mission to the Walite System. She would accompany the Regent.

"As for me," he said with another self-deprecating snort, "I'm a second son whose only here because my father is afraid I'll get into trouble if left too long alone. He's training my brother to take his place on the Council of Magistrates, not me."

He looked away from her then and into the burning candle flames, his fire dying in someone else's shadow, unable to see his own self-worth, his true path. Lela moved closer and took him in her arms, wrapping him in her warmth of friendship and understanding. The cosmos may not intend for them to be together in the future, she thought as she moved to her knees and straddled his legs, but that didn't mean they weren't meant to be together now. Or for as long as they could.

"If I had known you would be so maudlin today, I would not have undertaken the mission to your chamber. I have a report to prepare for the Regent on the race known as humans. And if you insist on this path, then I'll just take my leave."

With mock effort, she made to disentangle herself from him, but strong hands held her down, and laughter rippled through the room.

"That's why I love you so. You're the only one in this monstrosity of a government complex who truly knows me, sees me…accepts me. Not even my father or brother can boast that claim."

He took her face between his hands and they kissed, Lela sighing into his mouth as she allowed him to claim her, his thigh muscles tense and rigid underneath her own. The heat between them swelled as it always did when they stole such time for themselves.

The Regent would remand her to her suite of rooms, or worse, sanction them both, if he knew what she'd been doing the last six months. Laws of propriety, subject to censure, explicitly forbade unsupervised meetings between young, unmated males and females. She knew, they both knew, but youth and the first blush of passion were hard to ignore. But something would have to give, Lela knew that as well.

That day came a year later and a month after Lela had been sworn in as Chief Magistrate of the Verity Band.

*****

She heard the beeping of the security system. Lela knew someone was on the other side of the door, but her mind couldn't register anything other than pain and anger. So much anger, so much blood, and no peace, only war and death remained. She'd seen to that, her bloodthirsty vote for war shattered her peace, her sanity.

The door beeped again, its incessant blaring angering her even more. She rose, located her laser gun and went to the door. With one fierce command, it hissed open, and she raised the gun for an attack, eyes black with unseeing rage.

"No, Lela, it's me."

Lela's finger trembled but stilled just as she began to press the button that would eviscerate the person on the other end of her weapon.

"Ammon?"

"Yes, love, it's me." He peeked from behind raised hands as she lowered her gun, allowing it to clank harshly to the cold floor. But nothing in her chamber was as cold as Lela's ravaged heart.

"Ammon," she repeated, her voice slurred. "They killed him. They killed the Regent."

Her voice was a low wail now, and her body started to follow the path of the fallen gun. But Ammon caught her up in his strong arms and walked until he reached her couch, and sat.

"They killed him," she cried into his black Paladin-in-Arms uniform. "The Lumerians said they wanted the Regent to help negotiate a peace treaty between them and the Amaka. He agreed in good faith. But the Lumerians used him to reach the Amaka leader."

Unidentified mercenaries had done the rest—murdering those in attendance, all except for the Lumerian Prime Minister, his entourage of bodyguards, and Lela.

"I know, love. I know."

Ammon didn't know. She could still hear the sizzle of laser fire around her, smell fear and blood in the air, feel the Regent push her to the floor and cover her body with his own. A protective hand slammed over the mouth that opened on a panicked scream, Lela more afraid of losing the man she loved like a father than her own life. He couldn't. He just couldn't.

More laser fire. Right above her.

Silence.

Dead weight.

No scream, no tears, just a young woman's blood boiling with fury and thoughts of revenge.

"Those Lumerians will pay. We will make them all pay. That I promise."

Somewhere in her delirium, Lela could hear the veracity of Ammon's words, feel the power of his intention, of his own righteous madness.

"We all heard your war call, and the Paladin Band will make it so. I will avenge him for you, for us all. Please don't cry, love, I can't bear it." Ammon wiped away her tears, then his own. "I vow, in the name of the Fates, Regent Etemaad will be avenged."

The pain-induced madness slithered through them like a venomous snake. It corrupted all in its toxic path, shedding what it was and giving way to a hardened and unfeeling self with a single purpose—death to all Lumerians.

Verity, principle, truth, gave way to vengeance and madness, and nothing mattered. There was no future, no bands, no propriety, only now, only this chamber, only them. She knew a glorious death would claim them soon, but not tonight. Tomorrow all of Asiya would know the decision of the Magistrates. Tomorrow, they went to war.

But tonight, Lela and Ammon gave their virginal selves to each other, reduced to their primal essence, their basic instinct to survive and find shelter with another.

That night, while Ammon slept, Lela spoke the words of the Light of Nurzhan ritual. His soul, drawn by her prayer and love, rose to the surface, revealing the depth of the man. But it wasn't the true soul of Ammon that emerged. Ammon, her Ammon, was a gentle, lighthearted young man whose soul was born into the wrong band. She'd always known that about him, no matter how hard he tried to convince his father and himself otherwise. But the soul she looked upon now held no gentle sweetness. Hard angles and grimness marred his poetic features, his pallor gray, the light and innocence gone. He was gone, and so was she. And all that remained was madness and revenge.

*****

"Earth to Lela," Sage said, waving her hand in the direction she believed her sister-in-law was looking, which, by the way, wasn't at her.

She'd spaced out for the third time since their meeting began and the initial surge of concern upon learning of Lela's early return from Ammon's home was now fully bloomed and about to burst.

"I'm sorry. I shouldn't have pushed. It's just…it's just you and Ammon seemed so well matched."

Lela turned too-dark eyes on Sage, and the horribly lost look had her stomach twisting. Her guilt meter jumped ten spaces, and a headache started to form. She'd crossed the line with her well-intentioned match-making. And, apparently, it had blown up all over Lela.

Shit, Sage. When will you ever learn to keep your big, fat mouth shut? She's a grown woman capable of handling her own love life or not, if that's her wish. Now you've gone and made things worse, and she'll probably retreat even deeper in her hole. Great, just great.

"You're not to blame, and neither is Ammon. You only did what you thought was right. I could've refused, but I did not."

"Do you want to talk about it? My advice sucks," she said with deliberate self-admonishment, "but I'm a pretty good listener."

Lela placed her hands on her desk and laced her fingers together and gave what Sage considered to be a scrutinizing look. After several tense seconds of piercing silence, Lela relaxed into her leather chair.

"He kissed me."

"And that's a bad thing?" she asked, trying to keep the sarcasm out of her voice. But Lela's raised brow told her she'd done a piss poor job.

"I thought you were only going to listen."

Sage raised her hands in defeat and nodded. "Go ahead, I'm all ears." Sage mimicked zipping her lips.

Lela gave a disheartened laugh and shook her head. "Zion used to do that, and I never understood how one could pretend to close one's mouth but was incapable of truly keeping it shut. Like you, he could never simply listen without expressing an opinion of his own."

She paused and gave Sage another considering look. "I think humans are uncomfortable with long silences and Asiyans too comfortable with them."

Sage reflected on that a minute and could see no flaw in her observation, so she agreed with a slight nod of her head.

"Was it a nice kiss?"

Lela's eyes dropped to an apparently very interesting spot on her desk. "It should've been."

"Why wasn't it?"

Lela paused, still enraptured by her desk. But Sage waited. She wasn't going to be the human who died a long, painful death at the hands of quiet air. Hell, not after what Lela just said. She could wait, she had some patience after all. She wasn't a Neanderthal, Sage reminded herself as the seconds ticked by like a festering boil on her skin.

"Because I wouldn't allow it." Lela raised her eyes after the admission. "I felt like I was being unfaithful to Zion. I know it sounds crazy, but that's how it made me feel."

Now Sage really was brought to silence. She didn't know what to say to Lela. She couldn't tell her not to feel that way. She was entitled to her emotions, no matter how debilitating. And Sage had to admit, she'd never loved anyone as much as Zion and Lela loved each other.

"Maybe it was Ammon," Sage attempted. "Perhaps having a good working relationship with someone and having them be attracted to you isn't enough."

"It should've been enough. We have a long history. I should've felt more…felt something other than a wife's sense of betrayal."

"Perhaps it was his soul that turned you off," Sage tried again.

Lela gave a weak but genuine smile, causing Sage to feel like she'd missed a fly ball.

"No, he has a wonderful soul. The one he should've had all those years ago, the one I robbed him of for too many years to count."

Yup, she'd missed something and was now standing in left field with an empty mitt and mouth opened looking into the blinding sun.

"So you liked his soul?" she said, determined to finish the inning, realizing all may not be lost on the romance front.

"Yes."

"Great, so what's the problem? He likes you, you like his soul. That's more than what most relationships start out with."

"I'm the problem," Lela growled in frustration. She stood, palms flat against the desk, eyes distressed. "Haven't you been listening? I'm the problem. Me, not Ammon but me. I'm incapable of feeling anything beyond friendship for any man other than Zion. And the sad truth is that I'm not sure if I want to because that would mean I have to give him up. I can't go back, but my heart won't allow me to go forward."

Lela fell back into her chair, her tiny body seeming to deflate from the emotional outburst.

"What can I do to help?" Sage posed the question, although she feared she knew her answer.

"Nothing."

Yup, the expected but unacceptable response and Sage was having none of it. She refused to allow Lela to implode. Zion wouldn't want her to live like this, to deny herself happiness and pleasure with Ammon or someone else. She'd been a good wife to Zion and was still a good wife to him, but he'd left her behind and Lela no longer owed him her loyalty and devotion. At least, Sage reasoned, not at the expense of her sanity.

Lela turned away from her, the back of the chair facing the desk, effectively ending their conversation. Sage stood, straightened her black, knee-length High Star cloak, then moved toward the door.

"I'll see you later." Sage expected no reply, and she received none.

Softly, Sage closed the door behind her and walked to what used to be Zion's study. Everything was as it had been since he died, Lela neither venturing inside nor permitting anyone to box up his belongings. While Sage loved and missed her brother as much as Lela, it broke her heart to witness the emotional battleship Lela had become since his passing.

Sage understood the spark of betrayal Lela had to have felt when Ammon kissed her. She felt the same when she slid behind her brother's desk, hit two buttons for the Asiyan com system and said, "Download residential address for Ammon of the House of Eetu to High Star Security Chief Grace's mobile unit."

CHAPTER SIX

Second Chances

Ammon rest on his bed, eyes closed and shielded against the sun streaming in from the east window. It wasn't the welcoming rays of the morning sun he was avoiding, but the bleak vastness of his empty bedroom. The shadows of a failed night of soul beholding hovered in the corners, peering at him with sympathy and remorse.

Slowly and reluctantly, he opened his eyes. Unable to stop the impulse, his orbs darted to his right and settled on the vacant chair beside his bed. Like the shadows, the chair taunted him with his failure, his inadequacy. He'd long since ascended to the rank of Commander of the Paladin Band, a great personal and family honor. Through his actions, warrior spirit, and intelligence, he'd obtained his life's dreams, except two.

After all these years, Ammon desperately sought the ultimate approval and recognition from his father and knew only one accomplishment would do. He must become Chief Magistrate of the Paladin Band. He'd coveted the position for so long, he now wondered if it was ever his true dream or simply the aspiration of a man-child seeking love from a father who had no idea how to relate to a son who preferred art, music, literature, and prayer to battle drills and strategy sessions. Ammon learned, as a child, that his interests were not valued by his band. In fact, they were often viewed as weaknesses. So, Ammon buried that part of himself, becoming the cold-hearted soldier his father wanted, the soldier Asiya needed against the Lumerians. But he wasn't that anymore either. Yet, old ambitions died hard, and Ammon still dreamed of becoming Chief Magistrate.

He leaned up in bed, still staring at the depressingly empty chair, remembering his second unfulfilled dream. Lela of the House of Asheema, now Lela Grace, haunted his waking and sleeping hours. She was of the past, he'd told himself when she took an off-worlder as mate, bearing him a biracial child and daring anyone, including her band and political leaders, to judge her decisions. For many years Ammon pushed thoughts of her from his mind, relegating Lela to the same dusty prison where he'd banished his love of music and literature and all things gentle and comforting. But that too changed, and he found himself wishing and dreaming and opening himself up to the possibility of love, of rekindling a long dead flame.

Ammon swung his legs over the bed and groaned. The glimmer of hope he'd been nursing, he admitted on another grunt of disappointment, had disappeared through a wormhole of lost love.

Who knew a kiss could be an exit instead of an entrance? Fates help me. I need your guidance, your wisdom, your strength. What am I to do? How can I bridge the chasm that separates my soul from Lela's? What do I need to do to help her rebuild her heart?

Ammon stood, and as he did so, pain shot through his head, entering but finding no exit. He'd experienced sudden bouts of cranial pain before, but never like this, never this strong, this excruciating. Reflexively, he grabbed both sides of his head and closed his eyes against the blinding pain that started somewhere in the hollow of his inner ear and ended in his cerebral cortex. Ammon grunted, fighting to swallow the pain but unable to do so. In a vain effort to stay upright, he meant to reach back for his bed. Instead, his body tumbled forward, collapsing onto the hard floor. As darkness and agony overtook him, he could hear an unfamiliar yet reassuring voice whisper answers to his questions.

You cannot bridge the chasm that separates your soul from the one you desire. You cannot rebuild my child's heart, for you are not the one who holds it captive. That isn't your fate, your responsibility. But there is a way, there is a way, Ammon of the Paladin Band.

*****

Ammon lay sprawled on his back, eyes open and unfocused. The throbbing ache in his head was gone, but the one in his heart remained. He rolled onto his right side, using his arm to support his weight. Slowly, very slowly, he extended his arm, searching for the bed and pulling himself upward. To his surprise, his wobbly legs held his weight.

He looked down at himself, his black silk robe covering him from neck to ankles. Ammon glanced about his bedroom, narrowing in on a slightly ajar door.

The bathroom.

With caution, he walked to the room, keeping his movements steady and unhurried. The pain may have receded, but his equilibrium wasn't restored. Once he reached the door, one hand lifted and pushed it further open. A midsize washroom loomed before him, clean and efficient. But Ammon only had eyes for one feature—the mirror.

Moving like a man unsure of his fate, Ammon squared his shoulders and made his way to the full-length mirror. He stood in front of it but only saw his toes. Head hung improbably low, Ammon inhaled deeply, shored up his nerves and lifted his head. The reflection was of a well-built, middle-aged Asiyan male with red-brown eyes and a grim expression.

Disgusted, Ammon turned from the image and swore. This wasn't what he'd expected, wasn't part of the goddamn plan. It wouldn't do. It simply wouldn't do.

Ammon made his way from the bathroom and back into the bedroom, eyes searching every part of the room. Fueled by rage and annoyance, he shrugged off the remaining tendrils of discombobulation and ran out of the bedroom and down the hall. He searched every room he encountered but saw no one, nothing. Nothing but silence and the solemn face that met him each time he glimpsed his reflection.

He ran back into the bedroom, skidding to a halt when the one he sought stood before him.

"I didn't agree to this," he said, waving a hand over his body. "Not him. Anyone but him."

"There is no other and time is of the essence." Her voice was gentle, words uttered slowly in a way too many adults had of speaking to children when they mistook a child's disagreement with confusion. "He is the right one, in the right place, at the right time. He will do, Zion, and you will make sure he succeeds."

Zion Grace glared at the Fate of Purpose. Slim of form, ethereal of beauty, the ageless creature's eyes glowed as white as the hair flowing down her back and onto the floor, a ghostly train of unexplainable magic and power sparking through the thick locks.

"You should've warned me." He felt blindsided. "Out of all the men in the cosmos, hell on Asiya, you had to drop my soul into the body of this asshole."

The Fate of Purpose raised one long, thin finger, as if to scold but then lowered it, shaking her head instead. "I hoped you would be able to look past the body and focus on the mission."

That voice. Yes, Zion recalled the voice. She'd returned to him, along with the other two Fates, his life. Back then, he'd been grateful, her voice the sweetest melody he'd ever heard. Now, well, now it didn't sound nearly as sweet to his ears.

"The mission is all that matters, not your opinion of your host. Without him and his relationship with Lela, you would not be here."

Zion frowned. He knew the Fate spoke the truth. Yet he wasn't ready to think about what type of relationship existed between Ammon and Lela. As far as he was concerned, she was still his wife, and Ammon nothing more than an opportunistic interloper.

Nervous and angry, Zion lifted his right hand to run it through his hair, stopping when his hand met layers of thickly coiled locks.

"Dammit, I can't do this, Purpose. I don't know the first thing about being Asiyan. Hell, after thirty years of living among them, I still never managed the accent. And I don't know a damn thing about Ammon's life."

"You have his memories. Everything he is and was resides inside of you. All you need to know to complete your mission is right there." The Fate lifted a shimmering hand and pressed it to Zion's chest…Ammon's chest.

From the point of contact, an indescribable pulse of cold heat bloomed around the Fate's hand, thrumming in purposeful waves of patience and wisdom.

Zion didn't want to know the man better, but stubbornness and complaints weren't effective strategies, so he closed his eyes and focused on the Paladin soldier. No more than mere seconds passed before images, facts, events, and more flooded his mind. His head swam with knowledge, Ammon's knowledge and personal experiences.

Zion didn't like it, but he also couldn't stop what was happening to him, a swirling wave of thoughts and emotions that felt both foreign and familiar.

When he opened his eyes, Zion struggled to place his weary soul in a chair, the power of the images overwhelming and enlightening. He had no idea.

"I was wrong about him."

"Yes, we know."

Zion ignored the plural, his head still reeling from being plunged into the mind of another.

Closing his eyes once more, Zion breathed deeply, laid his head against the rise of the chair, and began searching. Several frustrating minutes later, he opened weary eyes and met the stoic ones of the Fate.

"The memories of Lela are sketchy. The others were vivid and detailed, but not the ones of her. Why is that?" He sat up, clear of head but not of heart.

The Fate of Purpose gazed at Zion with a depth of wisdom no being should possess—an unnatural and utterly inhuman perception that saw all, knew all.

"One body. Two minds. Two souls."

"You mean to tell me Ammon is still in here?" He pointed to his temple.

"Yes. He's submissive to your dominant. But he still exists."

"If I'm dominant, why can't I see everything about Lela?"

The Fate paused, seeming to give his question serious thought. Odd. Perhaps the Fate did not know all, which discomforted him even more than the thought of her being omniscient.

"You must understand, we've never done this before, so we have no precedent from which to judge. But it's reasonable to assume that the submissive host retains a certain amount of control, at least when it comes to the information he wishes to share."

"Are you telling me," Zion said, getting to his feet, "that Ammon is deliberately withholding information about his relationship with Lela from me?"

"That would be the most likely conclusion, yes. However, the longer you remain in his body, the weaker his will becomes and the stronger yours will become."

"Meaning, in time, he'll spill whether he wants to or not?"

The Fate of Purpose nodded. "But you will not occupy his body long enough for that to happen. Remember, you are not here to stay."

Yes, Zion didn't need to be reminded of that little fact. He was given this second chance to save himself.

"Explain it to me again. I need to understand everything."

The Fate inclined her head again with a patient indulgence befitting a being of her status. Yet the Fates of Asiya were unlike any supernatural or mystical being Zion had ever read about or heard of. They possessed godlike powers, true, yet they did not keep themselves entirely apart from the people who believed in and worshipped them. As far as Zion knew, god-like creatures did not play an active role in the lives of mortals. Hell, none of what Zion had seen or experienced could be explained by science, no matter the scientific field.

"You and Lela share one piece of the other's soul. You complete each other, make the other whole. That bond is special, but it doesn't come without caution."

"Caution?" Yes, this was the part Zion needed to be explained to him again. How could his bond with Lela be bad?

"Seven years ago you died, but you haven't moved on. Your death was merely physical in nature. Your mind, heart and all you were or ever wanted to be are still here, on Asiya, with Lela and Xavier."

"They're my family, for God's sake." He was angry. The being had no clue what it meant to be mortal, to love, to die. The Fate couldn't understand what he'd given up, what he'd left behind. Zion had a right to his memories, to his thoughts of Lela and home.

"Of course," the Fate of Purpose agreed, yet the response sounded devoid of emotional understanding. "But your refusal to leave the old and accept the new is slowly killing you."

"I'm already dead, Purpose, or have you forgotten?"

"There are many facets of death. Seven years ago, you only experienced a physical cessation of life, but now you risk dying metaphysically, spiritually even. Without this body, you are nothing more than electrical energy. That energy, in its complete, conscious state, can only stay as such, on this side of the cosmos, for a limited time. And you have virtually exhausted that time."

"Meaning?"

"It means you must travel to the Realm of Thuraya in order to live. For that to happen, you must shed your former life and embrace your new one."

"I'm not a dog. I don't shed, and my family isn't inconsequential hair to be swept into a pile and discarded."

"No, but if you ever want to see either one of them again, you must release them. They will be returned to you, Zion. But if your remaining life essence burns out and is absorbed back into the cosmos, you are lost to them forever."

Forever? That word echoed in his head like a horrible scream.

"What do I need to do?"

"You need closure."

"How do I get closure?"

The Fate of Purpose paused again, and Zion knew whatever she was mulling over wasn't something he wanted to hear. But he would listen, because there was no way in hell he was going to ruin his opportunity of eternity with Lela and Xavier.

"You must," the Fate started, and Zion stiffened at her grave tone, "free Lela from the binds that bond you. You must let her go."

Let her go?

He then remembered into whose body his mind and soul now resided and his face darkened with fury.

"You mean I have to convince her to accept another man, to accept Ammon as her mate and to forget about me?"

"Yes, it's the only way."

"Like hell," he yelled. "I may be inside his body, but it's still *his* body. If he couldn't convince Lela to open up to him, I damn sure won't help him. What kind of husband do you take me for? I won't help any guy get my wife into bed. Hell no, out of the question."

His words were final, but the look in the Fate's eyes said the conversation wasn't over.

"In order for you to release her and save yourself, she must also release you. The only way she can do that is by opening herself up to the possibility of new love."

"Lela doesn't love Ammon. She loves me."

The Fate of Purpose said nothing, yet her small, round eyes spoke volumes. She was withholding something. Zion could sense it. What was it? Hell, Fates could be such a pain in the ass, cryptic and damn frustrating.

"You have two months and not a second longer. She beheld his soul once. She must finish the ritual and complete the Unity of Hearts with Ammon. If she doesn't, you'll be lost to each other forever."

"But—"

The Fate of Purpose disappeared, no cloud of smoke, no crackle of magic, no glow of power, just there and then gone. Perhaps the disappearing act should've surprised him, but seven years without a body had a way of making a man see the physical and metaphysical world in an entirely new light.

No, the Fate disappearing into thin air hadn't shocked him, but her words of, "She beheld his soul once" had.

But it couldn't be true. Lela would never... An unbidden image crept into his consciousness—a kiss, in this room and on that bed.

Zion glared at the bed and then his eyes settled on the chair beside it. It was true. Lela had beheld another man's soul. She'd wanted to see what lay within the Paladin. Zion gave a disgruntled laugh—harsh, brittle, and laced with pain and loss. Lela was no longer his. He had to give her up to get her back.

Zion strolled back into the bathroom and to the full-length mirror. He stared at the reflection with contempt. This was the man he had to use to woo Lela, to convince her to sever ties with him and forge new ones with Ammon. He cursed the Fates and Ammon. Angry, the mirror didn't stand a chance, the broken shards a subtle metaphor for the current state of his heart.

Seething and breathing hard, a consistent and annoying beeping drew him from his melancholia. He didn't have to question the source of the sound, for Ammon offered up that bit of information. How kind of him. It was the security gate. Someone had come for a visit. He wasn't ready to begin the lie, wasn't ready to pretend to be the man who would steal Lela's heart away from him. But he had no choice. Like Purpose said, he had to give her up to get her back.

Zion moved to the security screen on the other side of the living room. He punched one button, and an image of the front of Ammon's home came into view. A familiar, unsmiling face waited impatiently for him to answer.

"My God, Sage."

CHAPTER SEVEN

Her Men

After having Ammon's housekeeper, a woman who seemed to have appeared out of thin air, because Zion damn sure hadn't spotted the cheery woman when he'd staggered through the house earlier, admit Sage, he took a quick shower. Once he'd disrobed, Zion couldn't help but look at the body he now occupied. It was definitely odd seeing a man other than himself nude. But that wasn't what disturbed him the most. What grated on his pride and dignity was the obvious fit state of the Asiyan. There wasn't an ounce of body fat on the man. He was lean, muscular, and damn strong. And Zion had to admit that Lela's last image of him was of a man with a growing midsection and graying hair. He could now concede that he'd unconsciously let himself go, mild depression riding his last few years of life. What was the point, right? What would it matter what he ate or whether he exercised? He had no future.

Taking in the fit specimen before him, Zion wasn't so naïve or arrogant to believe that Lela couldn't or wouldn't find him attractive. Asiyans may not be as obsessed with physical looks as humans, but he knew from experience that they did find strength of body appealing. Lela was no exception. She was a woman, and what woman wouldn't rather have a rock hard man of steel in her bed than a flabby, aging dinosaur? And Zion didn't even want to think about the most obvious comparison. Not that he ever lacked in that area, but the thought of Lela seeing Ammon naked and fully erect was more than he could handle.

If it were just two more nights of soul beholding, Zion thought he could manage that without too much distress. But there was the Unity of Hearts—the most intimate of Asiyan courting rituals. Zion shook himself at the thought, finished dressing and made his way into the living room where the housekeeper had asked Sage to wait.

Zion paused at the threshold and simply watched his younger sister. She stood at the floor-to-ceiling window, her back to him. Her hands were clasped behind her back, hair pulled up into a neat, conservative bun. And she was a blessed sight to his homesick eyes.

God, he missed her. He hadn't known how much until he saw her standing there, tall and proud. Sage, five years Zion's junior, had come to Asiya a month before his death. Not only had she come to be with him in his final days, but she'd also agreed to stay. While, on the surface, his request may have seemed selfish, asking his sister to uproot her life on Earth to watch over his wife from another planet, but it hadn't been.

The Graces had always been a small family. Distant cousins were all Zion and Sage had left after the death of their parents. And Sage, well, she'd never been one to make friends easily or to give her heart and trust just to anyone. Yet she'd taken to Lela when Zion had brought his bride home to meet the family, as did his parents. And that was the beginning of Lela and Zion's annual visit to Earth, spending time with the Grace family each year, even after the death of his parents and Lela's ascension to Regent.

Yet the last year of his life, Zion knew he wouldn't live long enough to see Earth one last time. So Sage had come to him, pulling up stakes and leaving her old life behind. A handful of friends and a job she'd retired from were all that kept her in New York and on Earth. Zion had known, although Sage would never admit the truth. She'd been so lonely since their parents' death, aching for the husband and children she'd never had and the man she let get away.

With his death, Sage would have no one. So Zion had given Sage his family—a sister and a nephew she loved, a family she could take care of in that tough Grace way of hers. Knowing Sage, Lela, and Xavier would be together, loving and protecting each other, had made the passage from life to death an easier journey to undertake.

"High Star Chief Grace, I apologize for keeping you waiting." At his voice, she turned, and Zion fought every muscle in his temporary body to not stride to his sister, take her in his arms and hug her with a fierceness she would neither understand nor appreciate. Older than he remembered but still beautiful and bold, their mother's eyes stared out from his sister's face—wise, honest, discerning.

She watched him watch her. Her posture was rigid and face all too serious. Zion itched to pick her up into a big bear hug, swing her around the way he used to when they were children and Sage was being uptight and Zion silly. He laughed to himself thinking how she would react if Ammon of the Paladin Band did that very thing. Then he had to bite back the unbidden thought of Sage kicking Ammon's very distinguished ass.

She bowed slightly but respectfully. "Commander Ammon, I should be the one to apologize for coming to your home unannounced and without an appointment. Forgive my intrusion."

For the second time in less than two minutes, Zion wanted to howl. Had the former New York Sentinel of State Defense turned High Star Chief of Regent Security been tamed? Surely not, Zion chuckled to himself. Oh, but his sister was on her best behavior, Sage's serrated edges nicely hidden behind proper Asiyan manners. Sage Grace, a product of Lela's School of Asiyan Etiquette. Ah, he knew it well, the one founded for her culturally tactless human of a husband. Her tips had saved his political ass on more than one occasion.

"No intrusion at all. I assume it must be important for you to come to my home."

"It is," she agreed, showing the first signs of discomfort. "My visit is of a personal nature."

He assumed as much.

"It's about Regent Grace… Lela."

Zion knew that as well.

He considered offering her a seat, returning her manners with some of his own. But he knew Sage very well and when she was nervous, and about business, the last thing she wanted to do was sit still.

"Did she ask you to come?"

A small smile played across her elegant features before she furrowed her brows. "I suspect by the end of the day I may find myself unemployed. No matter," she said, waving the thought away.

"Lela would never do that."

"Of course she wouldn't, but she won't be pleased with me, which is worse than losing my job."

Yeah, Zion knew that side of his wife. The side that never had to raise her voice to make a person quake in their boots. How he'd missed her.

"This is about last night… the Light of Nurzhan ritual."

He was very interested in what she had to say, Ammon none too forthcoming about the events of last evening. Besides the kiss, the Paladin had revealed nothing more to Zion. Strategy told him to wait for her to elaborate, hoping she would fill in the missing pieces without realizing he was a blank slate. But his instincts also told him that Sage wouldn't have appeared on his doorstep so early in the morning if the ritual had gone well.

"How is she?"

She didn't answer right away, which meant his sister wanted her words to deliver the right message and have the desired impact.

"You've been a very good friend to her, and I hope that will continue," she said diplomatically, conveniently sidestepping his question.

Yes, Lela had taught her well.

"Do you see any reason for that to change?"

Something happened last night between Ammon and Lela, Zion could feel it in his… well, his host's bones.

Come on, Sage. I need more than Asiyan vague speak.

Zion knew he couldn't ask a direct question like, "What did she say happened last night?" or "Is she planning on coming back for a second night of soul beholding?" Asiyan training or not, Sage Grace would never betray a confidence.

"I have no intention of severing our friendship, if Lela still wishes my companionship." He gave a strategic pause, then asked, "Does she?"

"She does," Sage answered after a pause of her own. "She would enjoy your company at dinner tonight."

Tonight? Hell, Zion thought to give himself a day or two to iron out a plan of attack. He had no idea how to accomplish his task or whether he truly wanted to. Winning would mean losing. Winning would mean watching his wife fall in love with Ammon and out of love with him. He needed time, but he was also too smart to allow an opportunity to slip through his fingers.

"Dinner sounds like a fine idea. Will you be there as well?"

"Unfortunately yes, as will Xavier. He has a few days of leave and will spend most of it with his mother."

Xavier.

In the madness of the last couple of hours, Zion hadn't considered the possibility of seeing his son. And now he was just given a chance to spend an entire meal with him and Lela. This was a dream he hadn't dared have.

"I would be most honored to have dinner with the three of you. What time?"

"I'll have a transport pick you up around 1700 hours, and I'll meet you at the hall. We'll go in together, and when you're ready, a High Star will return you home."

"Sounds like a plan."

Sage's right eyebrow rose, her discerning eyes narrowing.

It was a slip, and he had been doing so well. If he were to fool his family, Zion knew he would have to do better.

After excruciatingly long seconds, Sage shrugged off whatever had bothered her about his statement, and gave him a polite nod.

"Thank you for your time, Commander Ammon. I'll see you at dinner."

Sage turned to see Ammon's housekeeper waiting in the foyer right outside of the living room. She bowed once more and allowed the housekeeper to see her out.

Zion had eight hours to prepare.

Dear God, my seven-year wish is about to come true.

He collapsed onto the sofa, suddenly very tired. His heart, Ammon's heart, raced with frightened anticipation.

*****

Zion followed Sage to the Regent's personal wing in the Hall of Concord as if he hadn't made the trek a thousand times before. His first day as a born again blood and flesh man was but a blur. Ammon's memories told him what he should've done today, but there was no way in hell Zion could manage to follow such a strict routine without giving everyone the impression that Ammon was in desperate need of a mental health professional. Two months wasn't much time, and he'd be damned if he wasted a minute of it. He would do just enough to get by, to convince everyone all was as it should be, and no mystical hocus-pocus was going on.

During those eight hours, Zion formulated a rough plan. In mapping out a plot to woo his wife, he'd reached a startling conclusion. Zion had absolutely no idea what he'd done the first time to get her to fall in love with him. He assumed he'd done something right. But for the life of him, he couldn't figure out exactly what. One day they were friends, allies, and the next... much more. How in the hell had that happened without him noticing?

And Ammon was no goddamn help, still refusing to share his memories of Lela. Zion needed to know what the man had already tried, so he wouldn't duplicate wasted effort. He knew whatever the Paladin had attempted hadn't worked. If it had, Zion's bond with Lela would've been severed, and his soul would now be somewhere on the other side of the cosmos. Ammon may not be the conceited, power hungry Paladin

Zion once thought him to be, but when it came to Lela, he was still an asshole who coveted another man's wife.

Sage keyed in her security code, which had the heavy doors to Lela's private quarters sliding to the left and right, then disappearing into the walls. Once inside and the doors closed behind them, they walked down a hall, made a right and turned into the main dining room. The table was already set.

For three.

She's not expecting a guest. What the—

In the time it took Zion to see there was no fourth place setting, was the same time it took him to notice the man sitting in the first chair to the right of the head of the table.

"Xavier," he breathed.

His son rose, tall frame sliding away from the table and around his chair. He was taller than him, or rather taller than Ammon by a good six inches. Zion started to speak, feeling his mouth open but unable to utter a single word.

Xavier Grace was no longer a boy, no longer a gangly young man just beginning Paladin training with pimples decorating his forehead. He was a solidly built man of twenty-six whose Picasso marble eyes, Lela's eyes, were looking past him and at Sage.

"What in the hell are you thinking?"

"That's no way to address your superior officer," she chided, Sage's voice lacking the power of her words.

"In these quarters, we're family. We drop the titles at the door, and you're just Aunt Sage to my Xavier, or Little X if you want to go there."

"Where's Lela?" she asked.

"A'bra is taking a call in her study."

"Good, that gives us a few minutes to talk."

"About the fact that you brought Commander Ammon here without asking or even warning her."

Xavier turned his attention to Zion then and bestowed a low bow of deference.

"No disrespect, sir, but my mother doesn't like surprises. And your presence will be a—"

"Unwelcome surprise?" Zion questioned.

"Not unwelcome, just a surprise."

Xavier gave Zion a long, disapproving look. "She told me about last night."

"She did," he said, wondering what Lela had told their son and whether Ammon had done something that would give Xavier cause to avenge his mother's honor.

"Aunt Sage and I only want the best for her. She hasn't been the same since my father died. You've known her for a long time, I'm sure you've noticed."

Zion nodded. He didn't know what else to do. This was all news to him, and the smallest embers of guilt started to form.

Xavier looked at Sage again, his eyes inexplicably sad and angry. "He didn't do the right thing before he left, and now she suffers because of his—"

"This isn't the time, Xavier, and I didn't ask Ammon here for this."

Zion felt lost. He was missing something huge and had a feeling it was the key to completing his mission.

Xavier turned his eyes upon him again. "Unlike my aunt, I'm not interested in promoting a romantic relationship between you and my mother. But there's something about you that appeals to her… something she won't share, even with me."

"We're friends," Zion replied, echoing what Lela had said about Ammon all those years ago.

"True," Xavier agreed, his eyes critical, suspect, "but there's more. She won't tell me, and I respect her privacy too much to push."

More? What more could there be?

Zion found himself grinding his teeth. He didn't like this. He didn't like it at all. Lela was his, not Ammon's.

"You may stay for dinner, and you're welcome in our home but," he stepped back and glared at Zion and Sage, "neither one of you will push her into another night of soul beholding. She knows her mind, and if she desires to see your soul for a second night, she'll come to that conclusion on her own." He pointed at them. "Without interference from either one of you."

This mission had gotten exceedingly more complicated, but as Zion took in his grown son, a well of pride sprung forth. The urge to wrap his arms around Xavier's wide shoulders was almost unbearable. Xavier Grace had claimed his father's place in the family, taking on the role of his mother's protector. It was a role Zion held for three decades, until his fly-about and his death.

"I have no intention of offering Lela anything more than friendship."

"But you'll take more."

"Of course. Lela is a wonderful woman. She knows and respects fear but never lets it control her, she loves fiercely and passionately, she's a philosophical and political warrior who understands that force is sometimes necessary, and she's a dreamer of the highest caliber with faith bright enough to light this entire planet."

When the flood of words stopped, Zion realized it was Ammon who'd formulated them. He realized one other thing.

He loves her. Ammon truly, deeply loves my Lela.

Temporarily appeased, Xavier released Zion from his hard glare and turned it on Sage.

"She's going to have your High Star insignia for pulling this stunt, and don't expect me to intervene."

"You're such a brat, and I'm not afraid of your mother." Sage stepped around Zion and faced Xavier.

She punched him in the arm and then hugged him fiercely. "I've missed you, kid. Try not to be away so long. Your mother drives me crazy when you're not around."

"She misses me. I'm her baby."

"Baby my foot. You're a pain in my—"

"Xavier, is that Sage I hear in there with you? Give me another minute, and we can sit down for dinner."

Zion's knees buckled when he heard the familiar voice. His hand went to the nearest chair, steadying his frame but not his thudding heart and racing mind.

CHAPTER EIGHT

Faith Manages

Zion's throat tightened, and his heart shoved against his chest, trying to escape, to free itself from its confines. It wanted to run and hide, and he wanted to shout for the Fate of Purpose to rescue him from himself. And his brain, dear God his brain flickered on and off, teetering on the edge between sanity and lunacy. He licked dry lips and wondered if it was too late to decline the dinner offer. And no, he didn't need Ammon to tell him that leaving now would be a serious breach of Asiyan etiquette.

The part of his brain that still functioned heard Xavier and Sage discuss his son's recent appointment as captain of a peace-class escort ship. While fatherly pride served as a formidable opponent against his panic shrouded brain, it was no match for the ringing in his ears. Zion felt as if he would go blind and death. His eyes filled with an indescribable haze, ears full of ice cold air that pushed against his cranium, causing his mind to nearly shut down from the effort to focus. Focus on the small *tap, tap, tap* of heels on the wooden floor. She was coming, and he was going to pass the hell out.

A second later, a jolt of awareness sizzled through him. He could feel her presence, although her sight was obscured from him. Sage and Xavier stood in front of Zion. Hiding him from her, he didn't know. Yet the small logical part of his brain knew it wasn't intentional, merely coincidental. But the few seconds more gave him time to harness his thoughts and calm his nerves so he wouldn't come off as a drooling, braindead idiot in front of his wife.

"Chayna will serve us as soon as we're seated," Lela said. "She's gone to such trouble to make a special meal for Xavier and refused to listen to a word I had to say when I told her she needn't make a fuss. Xavier has never been a particularly picky eater," she said, a hint of laughter in her voice.

Zion could've drowned in the sweetness of her voice alone. The melody of it held him rooted to the floor, his hand bearing down on the dining room chair, his heart reaching out to Lela's, but finding dead air.

Xavier laughed. "I guess that's your way of saying I eat like a fat cob roller."

"Well," —Sage slapped Xavier's back— "if the stomach fits."

The three of them laughed, and Zion wanted to laugh with them, be one of them. But he wasn't, not in this body, not as Zion Grace, the husband, father, and brother. He would never be that to any of them ever again. For the time being, he was Commander Ammon, leader of the Paladin Band, a peripheral friend of the family with delusions of much more. It would have to do though because he had nothing else to offer himself or them.

Like the parting of the Red Sea, Xavier and Sage moved aside. Across the Egyptian desert of loneliness, fear, and grief stood Lela, his Mecca, his holy land, his soulmate. If it were possible for the heart to cease its pumping of blood and the lungs to halt all oxygen circulation and one to still be alive, Zion would've been just that—a zombie fixated on one thing.

Lela's eyes flashed to Sage, her face suddenly flushed. Anger then annoyance flickered just below her poised surface. Despite Sage's words to Xavier that she wasn't afraid of Lela, she took two steps back, her palms going up in explanation.

"I thought it would be a good idea to have Commander Ammon to dinner so we could discuss the recruitment of additional Paladin-in-Arms pilots. The new line of warships will require specialized weapons training and highly skilled aviators."

Sage continued to plead her case, using Asiyan planetary security as her sole reason for inviting Ammon to dinner. Of course, it had nothing to do with her playing matchmaker. Yeah, right.

At some point during Sage's lengthy monologue, Lela's eyes had settled on him, or rather on Ammon. Zion felt naked under her penetrating gaze. Those gorgeous Picasso marble eyes of hers bore into him, as if she saw through Ammon and to the soul of her husband within. Impossible, Zion knew, but he couldn't help the desire for Lela to see him as the man he'd been, the man she'd fallen in love with.

And like a braindead zombie drawn by an indescribable impulse to feed, he was pulled to her, unable to control the overwhelming force of her magnetic field. Zion leaned in and embraced Lela. She felt heartbreakingly soft and warm, smelling of lavender and home, the way he remembered. Zion buried his face in her long, thick locks of hair, his own wrapped high and tight atop his head. It was all he could do to keep himself from weeping, allowing her mane to absorb his tears of joy, tears of pain.

Just when he thought she would politely but firmly extricate herself from him, or worse, Xavier haul his ass away from his mother, she circled her arms around his waist. It wasn't a passionate or even romantic gesture, but there was an undeniable emotion in her light embrace. For Ammon? He didn't know, and honestly, it didn't matter, not now. Perhaps later, but not now. He would take whatever she was feeling that had Lela returning his desperate hug. Oh yes, Zion would take it all.

"I'm sorry," Zion croaked, and Lela gave the barest of nods.

He was sorry, but not for what happened between Lela and Ammon last night, or whatever Lela thought Ammon had to be apologetic about. No, Zion was sorry for dying, for leaving her alone, for her pain, for… God, he didn't know. But one thing he was absolutely certain of was that he had to say the words and have her in his arms, no matter how awkward, inappropriate, or fleeting.

*****

For the next hour, Zion simply enjoyed having dinner with his family. He knew he must look like a complete idiot, a huge grin having taken up permanent residence on his face.

Every taste, every sound was delicious to him. For seven years, he existed only as electrical energy. In that form, time ceased to exist. He was gone, but not quite. His body was God knows where, but his thoughts and memories were still his, still sharp. However, there were times he wished otherwise. A body without a mind had to be better than a lifetime of memories without a body. If he could define his experience in those seven years, he would sum it up in one word—torture.

As much as this unexpected respite meant to him, Zion couldn't imagine going back to that existence. Sometimes, ignorance really was bliss. His smile faded then, replaced with a longing he didn't know how to fill. Correction, he knew how to fill it, it just wasn't possible. He had no body, and he couldn't stay in Ammon's forever. It was on loan to him, and in two months, he had to give it back.

That was all he had—two lousy months. It would have to do. He looked down the table and at Lela. She was speaking to Xavier about his recent promotion, and he was telling her about his first mission as captain of a peace cruiser. He realized the cruiser had been Zion's.

When he'd gone on his fly-about, he'd set the autopilot for Earth. He'd wanted to see the planet of his birth one more time. Zion hadn't made it that far before he died. Apparently, the advanced system had overridden his command code when he failed to reconfirm the destination twenty-four hours later, per security regulation, and returned to Asiya—no Zion Grace inside.

The news shocked him, and he had no explanation. From the looks of his family, neither did they.

Zion didn't know if it was morbid or a crazy way for Xavier to connect with a father who'd died when he was just coming into manhood. A father who would never see any of his accomplishments, a father who'd left him a flying coffin of disembodied misery.

When the Fate of Purpose had come to Zion in a dream, a week before his fly-about, she'd asked if he were ready to travel beyond the cosmos. His dream-self had known it was time, so he'd nodded, accepting his fate. It was a lie. The biggest lie he'd ever told in his life. Yet the truth would've done him no good. Would Purpose had simply said, "Okay," and granted him another thirty years? Of course not, so what would've been the point of repentant honesty? His time was up, he had to go. No arguing, no bartering, no whining, no tears. His time was simply up, and his body agreed.

That should've been that, but it wasn't. He had stayed. He didn't mean to. Zion wasn't trying to be defiant. He merely couldn't will himself to go to the other side. He looked at Lela again, she was giving him an odd little smile, but her eyes dropped when he caught her gaze. She was the reason. Purpose was right. He was still bound to this place, to her, and he had to give Lela up so his soul could be set free and survive in order to reconnect with his beloved many years from now.

Yet, as Zion watched his wife, he didn't care about any of that. He wanted to be with her now and for however long he had. Hell, he didn't even know what Purpose meant about severing their bond. How could he be expected to do that in such a short amount of time? And what was up with the two-month time limit anyway? If she hadn't cut their bond during the last seven years, what in the world did the Fate expect him to do in eight weeks?

When Lela lifted her head, she gave him that odd look again. He frankly didn't know if she were glad to see Ammon. Well, that wasn't exactly true. Lela had definitely been upset at Sage for inviting Ammon to her home without first clearing it with her, but she'd eventually relaxed into the idea and seemed to genuinely enjoy his company. Zion would've liked to believe that it was his personality that was coming through that she found interesting, perhaps even appealing, but he couldn't be sure. In fact, he was almost positive she recognized none of him in Ammon. So, those odd little smiles she kept giving him was for Ammon and not a man who reminded her of her long dead husband.

The thought disturbed Zion, causing him to frown at one of the moments Lela decided to turn her beautiful eyes his way. She gave him a questioning look, then answered a question posed by Sage about her High Star's security budget.

The remainder of the dinner, he nodded, spoke when spoken to, and shoveled Chayna's well-prepared dinner down Ammon's throat, curbing his desire to yell, "It's me, Zion. I'm back. I've missed you, love you. Love me." But he said nothing. His eyes threatened to water, nerves felt raw, his heart confused, and mind tempted to fracture into tiny bits of self-pity.

As the dishes were cleared, Zion wandered off, surprised to find himself on the balcony. He stood by the railing, peering over the compound grounds. It was beautiful at night, the multicolored buildings glistening in the blackened sky like lights on a Christmas tree. Standing there, taking in all around him, an absorbent sponge of senses, Zion realized he hadn't remembered it all.

The strange but peaceful singing of Tolurs in the trees below the balcony.

The incessant yet melodic whistle of air cutting through walkway bridges that connected one wing to another.

The satisfied contentment of a full stomach.

Zion had forgotten more than he knew. Death the greatest thief in the cosmos.

"They're beautiful."

Zion turned to see Lela standing behind him and pointing at the stars circling the moon.

"Beautiful," he repeated, his gaze on her and not the night sky.

Lela moved to stand beside him. She didn't speak, and he was too afraid to say the wrong thing. He'd wanted to be alone with her during the entire meal. Zion had shamelessly stared at Lela, causing Xavier to shoot daggers his way. But now that they were alone, Zion didn't know what to say, where to begin.

"Lela..." he started but stopped, his mind going blank.

She looked up at him expectantly, her mouth open, but no words came out. He guessed he wasn't the only one nervous.

Why would she be nervous?

The silence stretched between them, and Zion grew anxious. Perhaps Xavier was right. Perhaps there was something between Lela and Ammon other than friendship. They had known each other for a long time. But Zion never asked about the context or extent of their friendship. And frankly, he never cared. Ammon was a non-issue. Yes, he'd been angry when he found out about his romantic interest in Lela, but he was never truly threatened by him or their friendship. Lela had never given him any reason to doubt her fidelity, and he didn't doubt it now.

Zion reached down and grasped Lela's right hand in his left. He held it, gently caressing, Lela silently accepting his touch, his affection. Feeling bold, he lifted her hand to his mouth and placed a soft, chaste kiss on her knuckles. Her eyes widened at the gesture and Zion kicked himself. Asiyans didn't hand-kiss. That was a human custom.

Lela politely extracted her hand from his hold, her eyes quizzical. "You are different tonight," she finally said, stowing her hands in the side pockets of her purple-and-white dress.

Was she trying to give him a subtle signal to not touch her? He didn't know, but Zion wasn't about to let a little thing like propriety or good sense stop him. He wanted to touch her. Correction, he had to touch her.

He moved to stand behind her, cautiously placing his hands on her waist and his chin on the top of her head. Zion felt her stiffen, but he didn't release her, and she didn't step out of his loose embrace. It wasn't the greatest first move he'd ever made, but he knew Lela well, and his wife liked to be held, reassured through touch that all was right in her world. He may not know what he'd done to have her fall in love with him all those years ago, but he knew the woman, and that was much more valuable.

"The grand reopening of the Botanical Gardens is tomorrow," he said, moving to phase one of his plan. "Would you like to attend? I know how much you enjoy the sight and smell of flowers."

The body that had slightly relaxed stiffened once again, her response slow to come.

"That… would be lovely. I have missed the gardens. I would very much like to see the additions. I'm told the Horticulture Institute imported several species of flowers from other worlds that can live and thrive on our planet."

She paused, relaxed again and then said, "I'm pleased to see your renewed interest in aspects of Asiyan culture that doesn't involve battles and weaponry." She took two deep breaths, her voice going lower, taking on a regretful tone. "I thought that side of you was lost forever… that I'd stolen such pleasures from you."

Now it was Zion who stiffened. He didn't know what to make of her words. They definitely had a past, conceivably a bit deeper than he'd imagined. And Lela felt guilty about that shared past. But why and about what? Hell, he really didn't want to know. Then again, he reasoned, Lela had lived a long life before they met, much of which she never shared during their marriage, and he never asked. It just never seemed that important. Did it now? He didn't know.

She turned in his arms, leaning back, giving herself space, her hands low and not touching him.

"What I said last night is still true today, Ammon. I don't think I can give you what you want, be who you want me to be."

Her voice was thick with sorrow and pain. She hadn't let go of him. He could see that clearly now. He could also see that she had feelings for Ammon that went beyond mere friendship. Yet, she denied herself even the slightest possibility of a second chance at romantic happiness. And while Zion thought that her eternal love for him would be wonderful, he couldn't deny the pain it caused her.

The pain it caused him.

But she didn't have to give him up, he reminded himself. He was right there in front of her. She could still love him and Zion her. His plan could still work. With a bit of fine-tuning, it would work and to hell with the Fates of Asiya.

"I won't push." He spoke as if he had all the time in the world. "I just want us to spend time together."

"I can't guarantee another night of soul beholding," she said, running a nervous hand under her hair and over her neck.

"I know… just don't rule out the possibility that you may want me to behold your soul."

That was how the ritual worked. The female went first, beholding the male's soul. If she approved of the soul revealed to her, she would then invite the male to behold her soul. In turn, if the male felt the same about the female's soul, they would engage in a third night of the Light of Nurzhan, taking turns praying and seeing each other's soul, making sure they were indeed pleased before moving on to the Unity of Hearts ritual.

He was pushing it, bringing up the soul beholding ritual. But he had to either roll the dice or pass his turn. Zion would be damned if he passed his turn.

She nodded and turned her back to him again, his arms still wrapped around her waist. She was so tiny, but he'd learned a long time ago that there was much strength within Lela's delicate frame.

"You're different tonight," she repeated, her voice a meager whisper in the dimness of the night.

"Is that good?" He leaned down to speak the words into her ear, the urge to kiss her there powerful.

She didn't answer. Lela didn't have to. He knew. She accepted his invitation to the gardens—a date—and he was holding her. *He* was holding her, not Ammon, but Zion Grace. That was the lie he consciously told himself, and he would live every minute of it until the Fates ripped him hollering and screaming from Ammon's body. Zion admitted that to himself as well, for that was the only way he would ever allow himself to be separated from Lela and Xavier again.

I love you. A silent confession and one he wished he could speak aloud. Instead, he said, "Life is never as it seems, Lela. When one star dims and disappears, another is born to replace it. You must have faith. Have faith and believe in me, in you. I'll see you tomorrow."

Forcing his hands to release her, Zion left before she could respond. He had no idea where those words had come from, but he'd suspected Ammon had something to do with them. But like the first time Ammon had reared his supposedly submissive head, Zion wholeheartedly agreed with his statement. He didn't like it. He didn't like it one damn bit. There could be only one captain, and as far as he was concerned, he was it. No mutinies allowed and definitely no sharing of the spoils.

CHAPTER NINE

Past, Present, Future

"Come back to bed, Lela."

She turned away from the comfort of the burning candle flame and rejoined Ammon, her mind too jumbled to allow for a peaceful rest.

"You haven't slept more than a few hours in a week. We have a war upon us. You and the other Chief Magistrates must lead us to victory, my love."

The pending war was the reason for her sleepless nights and inability to meditate. How could one meditate with the screams of war and revenge as a backdrop? Her screams, her revenge, her war.

"Am I?" Lela asked, rolling on her side to face Ammon.

"Are you what?"

"Your love? Am I?"

He laughed, then pulled her closer, wrapping his right arm around her waist, eyes a fathomless shade of cornelian—a maple-red mineral found in the northern mountainous region of the planet.

"You are. I love you."

He kissed her, mouth warm and soft. She wished they could hide in her bedchamber forever, forgetting about the outside world and the ugliness to come.

"Then stay here with me. Don't go."

Ammon leaned back from her, a slight frown beginning to form.

"It's my duty to go. It's what I've been bred to do, to protect our Homeworld and our people from those who would do us harm. The Lumerians have done us a tremendous harm, and they must pay."

"We've already caught and killed the hired assassins. Is that not enough?"

"No, it isn't." His voice rose in anger. Frown deepened. He sat up and peered down at her. "The assassins were mere tools. They didn't have to slaughter everyone, including our Regent, to murder the Amaka leader. The Lumerians wanted to send a message to anyone who would dare interfere in their political affairs. They're bullies who won't stop until someone bigger and stronger brings them to heel. They will come after us again, Lela, don't doubt that. They think, because we're peace-keepers, they can intimidate us into submission." Ammon's growl sounded no less bestial for all that he was a man. "We will prove them wrong."

She knew this would be his reaction, but she had to try. Lela placed a firm hand on his shoulder, encouraging him to lie back down. With reluctance, he allowed the gentle persuasion.

"I asked you to stay not because I doubt your honor or your warrior spirit. My reason is much more selfish."

His eyes softened at her honest words and the beginnings of a smile started at the corners of his mouth. Lela cradled his face in her hands and ran her lips over his, savoring the feel and taste of him.

"I fear for your safe return."

"Those Lumerians can't harm me. A Paladin does not fear death, for the Fates have blessed our souls and watches over us when we rejoin Mother Cosmos."

She kissed him again, a slow, sweet embrace that heated her body, her heart a whirling vortex of emotions. Breaking the delicious kiss, she smiled at Ammon and hoped he would understand her next words.

"I fear for your soul, Ammon, your personhood, not your physical form. I believe you will return to me, but not as the man I know, the man I love."

He tried to pull away from her then, but she held him close, refusing to let him go.

"I can see the change in you already. Ever since the attack, something in you has hardened or perhaps even broken. I feel the same in me, and I don't know how to free myself from its malicious web. But this war isn't the answer."

Ammon managed to remove her hands from his face and hold them firmly between his own.

"War is never the answer, but it must be done. I can't be the soft Paladin who recites poetry to his mate or the warm-hearted soldier who brings you flowers at the end of a tiring day. I can't be that male and fight this war. That type of warrior ends up on the wrong side of a laser weapon, my love. I won't be one of them. I will return to you. Trust me."

She did trust him, but this wasn't about trust. He would lose himself in the war, become something dark, something unrecognizable. They all would, including herself. This she knew. This she feared. What could be done? Their fate sealed with one senseless attack and an even worse vote for war—her vote, her vengeance, but everyone's blood.

Ammon's soul.

"Will you wait for me? Can we begin the courting rituals once the Paladins destroy the barbarians and I return home? You deserve better than all this sneaking around, and I want to make a public declaration to our houses and bands."

Tears burned her eyes, forcing them closed. They weren't meant to be. Ammon would never be her mate. She felt it with the same certainty she had about the war. It would be long, hard, and bloody—no winners, only losers.

Lela wrapped her arms around Ammon's neck, a desperate need to be with him surging through her. She removed his sleep robe, taking no care for the force she used to do it or where it landed. Lela needed him now—his strength, his love, his masculine hardness.

Being together like this, without having progressed through the Light of Nurzhan and Unity of Hearts rituals, was a sin, regardless of the band to which one belonged. Yet, Lela cared nothing for propriety or her honor. All she cared about was Ammon and the way he made her feel. Her heart would surely crumble when he left, for he would leave and they would never be like this again. Tonight was all they had, for tomorrow Asiyan warships would depart for the Lumerian Homeworld.

War.

Blood.

Death of the soul.

Ammon didn't understand, even if she had the perfect words to explain it to him. But Lela could love him and permit Ammon to love her, one last time—a clandestine Unity of Hearts ritual, joining of the body no one would ever know.

Except them. Only ever them.

*****

"Come in," Lela said, forcing her mind to the present.

Xavier entered her office, and she smiled. She still couldn't get over how much he resembled his father—tall and lean and unaccountably handsome. One of many defining features of the Asiyan people, their locks, coiled from birth, grew long and thick with age, an intricate web of genetic embroidery unique to each house. The House of Asheema's locks descended in waves of pure, uninterrupted ivory. Unlike pure-blooded Asiyans, however, Xavier's hair, like his father's, was dark-brown and short against his scalp, revealing a perfectly shaped head and oval face. His black captain's uniform, with a purple sash around his waist, fit his slender yet solid form in a way that reminded Lela that her son had grown into a powerful, confident man. Intelligent and capable beyond his years, she couldn't imagine a mother prouder of her son.

Their son.

"I thought I would stop by before my ship departed. I'll be gone for about a month, maybe a little less."

"I know." Lela rose and walked around her large desk.

She gestured for Xavier to join her on the beige-and-green office couch. They sat, and she couldn't help but reach up and run a hand through his short, wavy hair.

After a few seconds of indulgence, Xavier removed her hand and placed it over his heart.

"You always get like this when I have to leave."

"I know. You're too old for me to worry so."

"I don't believe there's an expiration date on motherly concern." He smiled, kissed the hand he held and then placed it on her lap. "I think we should have a talk."

"About your mission? It should be a simple one. Your crew need only escort the cargo ship to Kear space, making sure to keep an eye out for pirates."

"No, A'bra, this isn't about the mission. Aunt Sage has already briefed me."

"Then what?"

"Commander Ammon."

She should've known. He'd been uncharacteristically quiet on the issue, allowing as much as two weeks to pass since Ammon joined them for dinner.

"How were the Botanical Gardens?"

"Beautiful."

"What about the Lelo'ur Festival?"

"Entertaining."

"What about the—"

"Get to the point, Xavier."

Her son appeared a little uncomfortable, his eyes casting down and away before rising to meet hers once again.

"Ammon's a nice enough man, I suppose. He definitely seems interested in you."

He gave her a considering look, then retook her hand, this time placing it on his knee.

"I worry about you living in that big wing by yourself."

"I'm fine. The guards are always there."

"That's not what I mean and well you know it. You spend far too much time by yourself. I like that Ammon has encouraged you to leave the hall lately. He's good for you."

"You think so?"

"I'm not suggesting you marry the commander, but he's brought a smile to your face that I don't see often enough."

"Has he?"

"By the way, I hate it when you answer me in three words or less. It usually means you're not listening to a word I'm saying or hell-bent on having things your way."

Lela scowled. Looks weren't the only thing Xavier inherited from Zion. He knew her far too well. She removed her hand from his knee, using it to run along her neck. Reclining against the plush cushions, she observed the tense set of her son's shoulders and the intensity of his multicolored eyes.

"I have no intention of marrying Ammon. We have a lot in common, and he's enjoyable to talk to, but nothing more will come of our relationship. He's just a friend."

She closed her eyes, seeing the image of Ammon in his Paladin-in-Arms battle armor, boarding a war cruiser, destination Lumeria.

Lela felt the couch sink a bit deeper. Xavier had mirrored her position. He reclaimed her hand, much the way his father did when he decided to push his point, not allowing her to retreat.

"You have to let him go, A'bra. You can't go on like this. It's been seven years. He doesn't deserve your devotion."

She refused to open her eyes and look at Xavier's, unwilling to see the familiar sad anger in them. They'd had this discussion before, and Xavier still hadn't forgiven his father. She wished he would, for both of their sakes.

He ran a gentle thumb across her knuckles, the callous from his hand-to-hand training a subtle reminder of his warrior's heart, his protective nature.

"You were alone when he died—when he decided to have his fly-about. A last trip to Earth, which he damn well knew he wouldn't make. He should've stayed here instead of leaving you alone to deal with the aftermath."

"Sage was with me."

"*I* wasn't with you," he yelled, his body bolting upright, forcing her to open her eyes. And she saw them, dark-brown with a son's anger, a son's grief. "He should've called me home. Told me how close he was to death."

"Xavier, please, don't," she pleaded, reaching for him. He stood, unwilling to be cajoled.

"No, he left you by yourself, and there's no excuse for that. By the time news reached me, you'd been living with his passing for a month. A whole goddamn month. And what about me? Did he ever once consider my feelings?"

"Zion didn't want to burden you. He didn't want you to see him withering away, one wretched day at a time. Your father wanted to be strong for the both of us."

"That's a load of bull. He may have been the one dying, but he wasn't in it alone. We lived every dreadful day with him. I cursed every year I got older because I knew that was one less year my father had. Can you imagine, a kid loving and hating his own birthday?"

She didn't have to imagine, her wedding anniversary affording her the same mixed emotions—happiness and regret.

She grabbed his arm. "You must stop this, Xavier. Your father did what he thought was best for the both of us."

"No, he did what was best for him. I don't think either one of us factored into it. He did the wrong thing, A'bra, and now you can't bring yourself to move on."

"That's not true. He didn't know of the ritual, and I never told him that part."

"He lived on Asiya for thirty years, for the Fates' sake. There's a ritual for every major life event from birth to death. You mean to tell me it never occurred to him that there was a ritual for what was to come. He could've set you free. Instead, he left you in a state of limbo, unable to go back or forward."

"You must stop blaming your father." Lela tightened her hold on his arm. "I never told him about the ritual."

She couldn't, especially not when he'd been so upset after overhearing Ammon and her father. How could she then, in good conscience, bring up the ritual, confirming Zion's fears and insecurities?

"And he never asked. He should've known. He only thought of himself. Ab'ba never thought how you would manage without him, what it would mean for you to be alone for so many years."

She turned from him then, not wanting Xavier to see her cry. Lela didn't blame Zion. She could never blame him. She hadn't wanted the Dissolution of Fidelity ritual, so she'd said nothing to her husband. The ritual would have indeed "set her free," if that had been her desire, to find love with another while remaining soul bound to Zion.

Did she feel the same now, willing to forego a woman's desire for male companionship for the rest of her life? She didn't know. But she did need to begin to plan for her future in a way she refused to do before or after Zion's passing. There was, after all, Ammon, her past. Could he be her future?

She didn't know.

Lela felt two strong arms on her shoulders, then loving lips on her cheek.

"I'm sorry. I didn't mean to upset you, to yell. That was disrespectful, and I apologize for my crass behavior and words." Warm, apologetic lips kissed her other cheek. "I didn't seek you out for this. It's just… just… I hate to see you unhappy, and I think Ammon could make you happy if you would give him a chance. You don't have to admit it, but I know there's some old business between the two of you. If you ever cared about him as a man, even a little bit, maybe it's worth pursuing, see what the cosmos has in store for the two of you."

He squeezed her shoulders, his embrace firm but gentle.

"I know I blow my top when it comes to Ab'ba and his final weeks and days, but I miss him too. I'll never forget him. So much of who I am today is because of him. Whenever I feel a sense of loss or am far away from home, I read his virtual diary."

From the day they learned of Lela's pregnancy, Zion began a diary, chronicling his thoughts and feelings on fatherhood. Without fail, Zion recorded every day as a father, from Lela's morning sickness, to Xavier's first tooth, to Zion's last Father's Day. Zion had recorded it all, unwilling to forget one moment he had with his son.

Lela turned to face him, no longer concerned with hiding her stream of tears.

Xavier stroked her face, wiping away her liquid defeat.

"For once, accept my wisdom. Keep Ab'ba in your heart, cherish your memories of him, but perform the ritual and set yourself free. Not for Ammon, not for Sage, not even for me, but for yourself."

He covered Lela with his tall, solid frame, his resilient chest absorbing the tears she hated shedding. Lela didn't know if she could do what he asked. But for the first time in seven long years, she prayed for the courage to do what needed to be done.

"It's time we had his funeral."

She nodded. "When you return."

"Good, that'll give you a month to prepare."

"I'll be ready."

He hugged her once more and then stepped back, his features as solemn as her own.

"We can do this," he assured, moving to her office door.

Lela wiped the remaining moisture from her eyes, feeling emotionally spent.

"Be safe, Xavier," she said when he pushed the door further open.

Blowing her a kiss, the way Zion's mother showed Xavier when he was but a boy of three, he smiled before gracing her with a respectfully low bow. A soft, "Love you, A'bra," floated to her ears, warming the air as he made his leave.

Love you, too, son. My heart, my soul.

*****

Zion staggered away from Lela's office, his mind unable to focus. He'd wanted to take Lela out for lunch. In fact, he'd been looking forward to it all morning. The last two weeks had been nothing short of wonderful. He'd not only taken her to the Botanical Gardens, but she'd accepted his invitation to one of Asiya's festivals, which came after a romantic dinner the night before.

His plan was proceeding nicely, the tension he'd felt from her the first night was slowly, cautiously abating. He was hoping to use today's lunch as an excuse to bring up the possibility of a second night of soul beholding. Then he'd overheard them.

He hadn't meant to pry. After being cleared by the High Star on duty, who'd opened the door to the Regent's waiting area, he'd strolled inside, walked past the desk of Lela's administrative assistant, who wasn't present, and down a long hall to Lela's inner sanctum.

In hindsight, he should've waited for the assistant to return, who would've informed Lela of his presence. But Zion, accustomed to not having to go through normal protocols when he visited his wife, hadn't given it a moment's thought. He should have, though.

Zion intended to knock on her office door, but it was already ajar, voices wafting into the deserted hallway. He never realized, but Asiyans had excellent hearing, far superior to humans. Yet, he'd give anything to have had normal human hearing at that moment. It would've spared him. He had no idea.

My son hates me.

Deep in thought and eyes cast down, Zion rounded a corner. And ran straight into—

"Ouch."

He looked up, and an annoyed High Star Chief Grace stared down at him.

"Ah, sorry, Sage, I didn't see you there."

"Obviously." She glanced around. "What are you doing in this wing of the Hall? Wait, stupid question. You're here to see Lela."

"Actually," he said, straightening his black-and-purple cloak. "I'm here to see you."

"Me?"

"Yes, I need to talk, and you're my best and only option."

"Me?"

"You're repeating yourself, Sage."

She frowned at him then, crossing her arms in front of her chest, eyebrows arched.

"Since when did you start referring to me simply as Sage? We're not exactly friends, Commander. Your familiarity is a bit off-putting."

Zion didn't have time for this little bout of defiance. He needed to talk and for his sister to shut up and listen.

"You were born in Brooklyn, New York in 2230 to Elijah William Grace Jr. and Jasmine Wright-Taylor. Elijah was a respected sentinel detective but retired early after he found the lair and burial ground of a child serial killer and rapist. He was never the same after that, unable to get the images of so many abused and dead children out of his head. You followed in his footsteps, having as big a heart as him but a stronger stomach for the cruelest nature of men and beasts. You had one sibling, Zion Elijah Grace, who died seven years ago.

"You fell in love with Nathan Evers, your sentinel partner. But you put the job before your heart, thinking that was your father's weakness when he was in law enforcement."

Her face dropped, as did her mouth.

"Do I need to mention what you did and how you felt when Nathan was killed in the line of duty or can we go to your office now and talk?"

Anger then confusion flared in her eyes, but she held her tongue, black combat boots silent when she turned in the direction of her office.

Good, I've got her attention. Now what?

CHAPTER TEN

Eyes to the Soul

Sage sat behind her desk, fingers laced and eyes tracking the nervous Asiyan. She wished he would just sit down and tell her what's on his mind instead of giving her a migraine with his silence and pacing. She hadn't liked the familiar way he'd addressed her earlier, and she most certainly hadn't appreciated the knowledge he had of her family and the way the Paladin used it to weasel his way into a meeting with her.

The commander's strange behavior lately hadn't passed her perceptive eyes and his actions today only served to raise her alert level to red. This was the man she'd convinced Lela to spend more time with, to consider as a possible mate and husband. Had she judged him so incorrectly, she wondered, glaring at Ammon as he circumnavigated her office for what felt like the thousandth time, mumbling to himself.

It had taken her awhile to get used to living and working among Asiyans. Their rituals, customs, and beliefs could be complex, but underneath it all, they were a very straightforward people, who rarely deviated from their assigned roles in society. Everyone had a place, and everyone knew their place and acted accordingly. A complex society with uncomplicated people, so very different from Earth and humans.

Yet she'd come to love the planet and its' people as much as Zion had. This was her home, had been for the last seven years, Lela and Xavier her family. And if Commander Ammon thought to disrupt her little piece of heaven with his strange behavior, he could just think again.

"Why don't you tell me what that little show you put on in the hall-way was all about?" she said, her voice sharp, agitated. Sage wanted clarity, to know if the man she'd thought so perfect for Lela was a head-case who couldn't keep his shit together. Perhaps that was why Lela had been taking it slow with him. Maybe she knew something about the Paladin that Sage didn't. Or maybe something else entirely was going on there.

Commander Ammon gave her a dubious look, his wildfire eyes scorching her with their intensity and making Sage feel as if she were gazing into a solar eclipse.

He made one more trek around her office and then sat, claiming one of the plush white chairs in front of her desk. Glancing around the room, his eyes settled on every inch of her office, nodding with indefinable appreciation.

"You haven't changed the place much. The colors are more subdued than I last remembered, white and light-blue instead of purple-and-black, which Asiyans are so fond of."

He surveyed the room again, another agreeable smile reaching his lips and eyes.

"The light, airy colors suit you, Sage. When you agreed to serve as Lela's High Star Chief, I assumed you would put your personal stamp on the place." Ammon pointed to the picture on the wall behind Sage. "That's also new. Well, not exactly new, I suppose, seven years ago now. But I've never seen it before." A slither of a smile crossed his face, which made no sense at all because, if she weren't mistaken, it was a smile of pride. "You look happy in the picture, accepting your gold star from Lela. You've carried on the Grace name well."

Okay, now this was getting really weird. The thought of calling in a psychiatrist was looking like a good idea. How could she have mis-judged him so completely? If he wasn't already crazy, Ammon was flying down that road at full throttle. And Sage would be damned if she allowed him to take Lela with her. She'd really screwed this one up, and now she had to fix it. Paladin Commander Ammon had to go.

"I don't appreciate having my family history dug up and thrown in my face," she said, going for calm, but the tapping of her fingers on her glass desk betrayed her.

Ammon settled deeper into the chair, his lips no longer twisted in that discomforting little smile of his. "I could think of no other way, Sage, for you to take me seriously. Perhaps if my mind wasn't so confused, I could've approached this whole thing differently. I don't know." A sigh, which Sage could only describe as anguished, escaped the Paladin. "I don't know anything anymore. I thought I could do this, that it would be easy. I was wrong. It's much harder than I anticipated. I had no idea. No idea what I'd done."

He appeared so lost, hopeless even. Sage had never seen him like this. Hell, she'd never seen any Asiyan, especially one of the Paladin Band, wear his emotions so openly. Such vulnerability in the presence of a non-band member, and worse, an off-worlder, wasn't done. Even Lela, after all these years of friendship, still donned her mask when it suited her, when she felt most emotionally raw and fragile. Sage understood that but this with Ammon, she didn't. She had no answer, only questions.

Sage scooted to the edge of her chair, the pull to get up, walk around her desk and sit next to the Paladin strangely strong. She refrained, fighting the unexplainable urge to give comfort. Instead, she posed two questions. "What have you done, Commander? What did you think would be easy?"

In an indescribable flash, Ammon's eyes changed from a swirl of red-and-brown to only brown. For a split second, they were the light-brown of her own eyes, the color of home and family. Yet when Sage blinked, trying to refocus her disbelieving eyes, they were gone. She blinked again, only seeing the swirling mix of red-and-brown typical of many Asiyans. No light-brown, no home, no family, just two sad swirling specks peering dazedly at her.

"I died."

The voice was barely audible and, for a minute, Sage convinced herself Ammon had said something else. What that something else had been, she didn't know. But it had to be something else or Ammon was further down that crazy road than she'd concluded. Damn, seeing and listening to Ammon now, Sage had never been so grateful to be wrong or for Lela's stubbornness.

"Considering that you're sitting in my office, looking as healthy as me, I think it's safe to say that you aren't dead. I don't allow dead men or resurrected soldiers in this building."

Admittedly, she knew nothing of psychiatry and doubted her sarcastic words were the right approach in what was obviously a delicate mental health situation, but Ammon was spooking her out. To make matters worse, guilt was doing a number on Sage's conscience. She'd given Lela so much grief about letting go and finding love with someone else. She'd all but forced Ammon down her sister-in-law's unwilling throat. And now, there he was talking about having died, looking as morose and pathetic as any dejected lover or insane asylum candidate.

"Perhaps it was a bad idea turning to you, but I have nowhere else to go, no one else I can talk to, and no one else who will understand."

"I don't understand, Commander. I have no clue what you're talking about."

"I know I must sound like a maniac, but I'm not."

He stood and turned to face the wide window, shoulders slumped as if a terrible weight pulled them down.

"Asiyans believe," he started, his back to her, eyes fixed on the garden below her window, "that when they die their souls are reborn, eventually, into new Asiyans, a new generation, the future."

This Sage knew, but that knowledge didn't help her follow Ammon's train of thought.

"That's what happened with me. Well, sort of. For a time, just a little while, I was given a second chance, a new life, in a new body."

Ammon turned to her, and the light-brown eyes were back, bright and steady. This time, however, they didn't disappear when she blinked three successive times, forcing back the unbidden thought, the one that said the impossible was possible and standing in her office.

"I failed to go to the other side of the cosmos, Sage, the way I should have. I stayed and now, because of the Fates, I'm back to set things right between Lela and me."

"What are you saying?" Sage knew the truth. The Grace family eyes stared at her with intense, heartbreaking familiarity. Her throat became dry, and her mind whirled in rebuttal.

Ammon gently grasped her frigid hands. "I remember how you used to follow me everywhere I went, even slipstream skating with my friends. You were so afraid that first time, even though you tried hard not to show it. I was so proud of you that day. I should've told you that, instead of making fun of you for finishing last." He swiped a finger over her knuckles. "Always so brave, little Sage, much braver than I've ever been."

Stunned, she said nothing, not even when he raised her hands to his mouth and kissed her knuckles.

Long, stomach-churning, hearth-thudding moments stretched between them. It couldn't be true. It just couldn't.

"Zion…?" Sage whispered, her vocal chords constricting, her eyes trying to see past the physical and to the soul within.

Perhaps she was just as crazy as him for entertaining the idea. But she *was* entertaining it. Hell, Sage was doing more than that. It would explain Ammon's suddenly odd behavior, particularly the weird reaction he'd had to Lela the other night. Hell, at one point, Sage thought she would have to peel him off Lela, so fierce and long was his embrace. She hadn't understood his emotional, near desperate state then. But now, dammit, it all made a bizarre kind of sense.

"How can this be?" She shook her head, trying to make sense of the face that her deceased brother's eyes looked at her from another man's face. "It isn't… shouldn't be possible."

Yet those eyes. And what he'd said about their father and childhood. No one living knew those things, not even Lela.

He smiled at her, a weak but genuine lifting of his lips. Then he folded her in his arms, and she couldn't help but raise her wobbly arms and return the embrace.

"I wanted to do this the first time I saw you in Ammon's living room, looking so much like Mom and reminding me of home." Arms tightened before he kissed her cheek, then let Sage go.

Impossible. Yet… Tears threatened to fall, as did Sage, who fell back into her chair.

Wiping eyes gone misty, Ammon retook his seat in front of Sage's desk. Not Ammon, she reminded herself, but Zion. *My dead brother. Here. God, he's really here. How? Why?*

Wanting nothing more than a strong drink to clear her head and wash down the scientifically impossible phenomenon sitting across from her, Sage said simply, "Make me understand."

Sage listened to Zion's story, a tale straight from an old Earth supernatural drama. In the end, while her comprehension was only marginally better than when he'd begun, she couldn't deny all that he'd shared. The man across from her may not look like the Zion Grace she knew, but the words, the thoughts, and all too human behavior was all Zion.

Sage found herself hugging him again, no longer capable of keeping her tears at bay. She'd missed him. God, how she missed her brother.

After Nathan's death, she felt adrift, her heart a ravaged and neglected organ of pain, loneliness, and regret. All the fire she felt while serving as a sentinel no longer burned with the same zeal as when Nathan had served by her side. But Zion had given her life renewed purpose—a chance to serve the Asiyans, to build bridges between races, but most importantly, to care for and protect his family. Her charge, her honor, she thought, a second chance for her, a second chance for him.

"So what happens if you can't convince Lela to finish the other two nights of the Light of Nurzhan and to go through with the Unity of

Hearts?" she asked, their hands linked, neither willing to let go of the other.

More like the Unity of Bodies ritual, Sage thought, but kept the accurate but insensitive thought to herself. She'd never heard of a ritual whose sole purpose included the physical consummation of a romantic relationship. Then again, Asiyans had a ritual for when an Asiyan's hair reached their waist, a benchmark, in their culture, of puberty. So why not a sex ritual? There was more to the Unity of Hearts ritual than sex, Sage knew—sexual compatibility and emotional alignment was important to Asiyans. Still...

Zion shrugged, appearing small and fragile. "If I don't convince her to sever our connection, then my life energy will cease to exist. I've held on too strongly to my past life, and this is my last chance to make things right. For the both of us."

"The Fate of Purpose gave you this opportunity?"

"If one can consider being tasked with convincing my wife to forget about me and take another into her heart and bed is an opportunity then, yeah, I guess so."

Brittle, resentful words that tore at her heart to hear, but Sage knew exactly what Zion's death had done to Lela, her battle to keep going, to not give into the urge to follow him into her own premature death. The first year was the worst, Lela falling into an abyss so wide and dark that neither Sage nor Xavier thought Lela would ever find her way back to the light. Yet she had, bless her stubborn Asiyan soul, she had. And as much as Sage loved her brother, she refused to allow him or anyone else to set Lela back. Her sister-in-law couldn't handle losing Zion again.

"Do you plan on telling her?"

His eyes watered. Hope tinged with fear peered back at her.

"I want to tell her. I want to tell them both. I have so much explaining to do, and I can't do it if my wife and son believe I'm Ammon."

He released her hand and swiped at his stray tears.

"I really messed things up before I died. I never realized until today how royally I screwed up."

"I don't understand."

He sniffed, started to stand, then sank back into the chair as if he had no energy to spare.

"I overheard them talking. Xavier was so angry with me. Angry that I didn't call him home before I left on my fly-about. Angry his mother was by herself."

Sage knew, she being the one to inform her nephew of his father's passing. She was also in Lela's suite when Xavier arrived and went in search of his mother. He'd found her huddled on her bed, arms wrapped around knees pulled to her chest, shaking uncontrollably, and murmuring a prayer in her language. All the young man could think to do was cuddle up behind his traumatized mother and hold her, his own tears soaking her hair, an apology on his lips for not being there for her. Yeah, unpleasant times in the Grace household, ones she wouldn't allow to return.

"I know you want to make amends, Zion, but I suggest you think long and hard before you reveal your secret to either of them."

"I need to speak to her honestly, to explain. I don't think she and Ammon are close enough yet for her to continue with the courting rituals, least of all the Unity of Hearts."

There were so many things she could've said to him, truths he needed to hear but his pain was as evident as Lela's. Clearly, the past seven years, wherever he was, in whatever form, he'd suffered. He'd known his loss, and it was cavernous. Who was she to wag her finger, to pass judgment on her brother's last days? At the time, he did what he thought was right, no matter that she disagreed with him. The consequence of his shortsightedness was more than likely the reason for his return, the reason why his soul wasn't at peace.

Sage would keep her mouth shut, about his final days and her thoughts on the relationship between Lela and Ammon. Not the current, fledgling one, but the older one Sage was convinced occurred before

Lela met Zion. How much before and the extent of their relationship, she didn't know. But she was certain they were once romantically involved, Xavier having drawn the same conclusion. Zion wasn't ready for that truth, and she wouldn't be the one to drop that bomb on him.

"Zion," she said in her most soothing voice, "if you're here for a limited time, it probably wouldn't be the best move to let Lela and Xavier know. Their happiness at having you back will be short-lived."

"I know," he admitted, sounding so very tired and defeated. "But I did them a great dishonor, one I can't fix as Ammon. I need to make things right. I have to see her."

He jumped to his feet, a surge of reserved energy seeming to bolt through him, giving Zion power and purpose.

Sage leaped to her feet as well, rushing around her desk and taking hold of his arm before he reached her office door.

"Umm, Lela has to travel to D'ombor today. She's meeting with the leader of the Euridice Band." Sage made a show of looking at the chronometer on her desk before saying, "Her transport should be arriving any minute now."

"When will she return? D'ombor isn't exactly around the corner. And why is she going there instead of the leader coming here? She's the Regent, after all."

Sage plastered on a fake smile and nodded. Zion was right. No one expected, not even a Band leader, for the Regent to set aside time in her busy schedule to travel to their region of Asiya. Yet, Lela was more democratic in her approach to leadership than most planetary rulers.

"Lela rarely leaves the Hall of Concord, nowadays. But sometimes, like this meeting, she likes to take the opportunity to travel beyond these walls, seeing and allowing herself to be seen. It makes for great press, but it's hell on her High Stars. It's much easier to protect her here than on the road and in public."

Sage waited for Zion to respond, but he said nothing, so she kept going. "Lela will be gone a couple of days, maybe longer," she lied. She needed time, time to convince Zion to keep his mouth shut, time for him to see how selfish he was being. And, if need be, time to prepare Lela for the shock of her life.

Zion grunted, then sighed. "I really wanted to get this over with. I want to… to…"

The lost look reappeared and, for a moment, Sage felt guilty about lying to him. He was obviously still so in love with Lela and the irrational part of him thought they could simply pick up where they'd left off seven years ago. If her brother had returned as he'd been, given a true second chance at life, the reconciliation he desired would be possible. But the husband Lela knew hadn't returned, and the part of him that had resided in a man she was once romantically involved with. And even that state was temporary.

The whole thing was convoluted and giving her a damn headache.

"Zion," she said, gentling her grip on his arm, "Lela can't take losing you twice. Unless you can stay and be the husband she wants, then it would be best to say nothing. In the end, you'll just hurt her if you go away again. I'm sure you don't want that."

His head dropped, shoulders drooped. If it were possible, Sage would've sworn she heard his heart break. Then he shook his head and raised beseeching eyes to her.

"I want my family back. I want to be able to hold and kiss Lela and let her know how much I love her, how much I've missed her. Is that too much for a man to ask? Is it? Is it?" he repeated in a low imploring tone.

"No," she replied, her words just as low, heart even lower.

He kissed her cheek the way he did when she was sad or frightened and pretended to be neither. "I've missed you as well, sis, and you never were a good liar."

She released his arm, and he moved to the door. "I won't go to her today or even tomorrow. I'll also think about everything you said before I make a final decision."

He turned the knob, prepared to leave.

"But," Sage said, feeling she was missing something.

He turned, and gave a misplaced Zion Grace smile on Commander Ammon's face. "But she's my wife, and I want her back. I'll do anything, go through anyone, fight any battle, to make that happen. I'm home, and I plan to stay."

CHAPTER ELEVEN

Revelation

It had been seven days since Zion revealed himself to Sage. Yet he hadn't made good on his promise to share his secret with Lela. To make matters worse, Lela had done nothing to seek Ammon out, no less invite him to a second night of soul beholding.

Now, Zion found himself sulking, walking around Ammon's airy home trying to convince the Asiyan to share his memories of Lela. He'd been going at this since the Fate of Purpose first plopped him in the man's body. Ammon was indeed an open book, allowing Zion to seamlessly infiltrate his Paladin world without a raised brow from his band. But when it came to Lela, the book slammed shut with a resounding *thud*.

Zion and time weren't friends. He could no more stop the countdown than he could think of a sure-fire way to reclaim his wife with Ammon as his host body and only access to Lela. Then there was Xavier. How in the hell was he going to fix that problem? He'd left several data quartzes for him, the last one made the night before he left on his fly-about. Surely, the quartz would've explained everything to his son.

Zion scratched his face, thinking, while making his tenth trek around Ammon's living room, the wide, spotless windows letting in the rays from the alluring noon sun.

He thought back to the conversation he'd overheard between Lela and their son. Xavier hadn't spoken like a man who'd seen the data quartz. If that were the case, then, shit, Zion, could understand the younger man's anger and confusion.

Deep in thought, Zion nearly bumped into a ridiculously low and wide table situated in the middle of the room that, as far as Zion could figure, served no damn purpose but to annoy him and threaten Ammon's shins. Slipping around the glass table, he continued walking and thinking. *If Xavier hasn't seen the data quartz, where in the hell is it? I know I put it in the box with the other stuff I left for him.*

Tired of thinking and frustrated with his lack of progress on the Lela front, Zion plunked onto the nearest piece of furniture, a black upholstered reading chair with matching ottoman. The ottoman got the same treatment, Zion's booted feet coming up to rest upon the sturdy square.

He closed his eyes, and a vision of a very young Lela drifted into his mind. Zion added this to his growing list of problems he had with sharing Ammon's body. Ammon's long-ago images of Lela blurred with that of his own. In fact, when Zion slept his dreams weren't always generated by him. More often than not, he lived Ammon's dreams, and the Asiyan dreamed, nightly, of Lela. Yet his dreams revealed only bits and pieces of a past the two shared when Lela was but a young woman, untried and idealistic in a way so typical of youth. Even in his dream state, Ammon managed to filter what he wanted him to know about his and Lela's relationship, which made Zion even more curious.

Tired of waiting around and doing nothing, Zion jumped to his feet. He was wasting time he didn't have. He needed to see Lela, explain everything, see how she wanted to handle his return and what thoughts she had on smoothing things over with their son.

He took another step and stopped. A massive blue-and-gray ball of light materialized in front of him, blinding Zion with its sparkling rays. Shielding his eyes, Zion backed away from the ball, finding shelter behind the chair he just vacated.

The ball fluttered, turned completely white and then disappeared. Before him stood...

"Bartek, is that you? How is this possible? You're dead."

"So are you, but here we both are."

Zion stood from his crouched position, feeling like a fool for hiding from a ball of light containing his wife's long dead childhood friend. The man appeared as he had the last time Zion saw him—five feet and no more, battleship gray hair pinned high atop his head, black boots, pants, and tailcoat, purple shirt, and a pompous, resentful scowl.

He hadn't missed a thing about Bartek of the House of Okar, particularly the superior way he glared at Zion, as if he were a speck of annoying dirt under the Asiyan's fingernails.

"Is Purpose responsible for you being here?"

"They sent me to speak with you, Grace," Bartek said, with a too-familiar sneer. Yeah, he remembered that about the man as well. Members of the Verity Band, like Lela and Bartek, may have been responsible for upholding and promoting truth, in all its forms, but Bartek had been an envious, spiteful bastard in life. Now, gazing at him after death, Zion could see little had changed.

Despite the downward spiral their friendship had taken when Bartek opposed Lela's union with a human, she'd grieved his passing, as much as she had their tattered bond of friendship, when he was alive.

Zion had no idea why the Asiyan was there. He only hoped the Fates hadn't sent Bartek to deliver bad news—like his time with Lela would be cut short.

"I always wondered what made you so special," he said, instead of answering his question. Bartek glanced around the room, eyes settling on the window-wall and the impressive view of Ammon's acreage beyond.

"I thought time was on my side. I only needed to be patient, and she would one day see the truth."

Bartek's eyes refocused on him, and Zion tried to read the emotions there.

Time had never been on Zion's side—not now and not then. Bartek, the stubborn ass that he was, meant he'd thought Lela would grow to see that mating herself to a human had been a mistake. And, presumably, begin to see him as the man she should've chosen in the first place.

Neither of which would've happened, even if Bartek hadn't perished in a transport collision.

"Lela mourned your death. She honored you in her prayers and kept you in her heart." The Asiyan had no idea how much he'd meant to Lela, his pride and jealousy blinding him to the truth of her heart. She'd wanted to reconcile with him, but Bartek's unyielding stance against Zion and their marriage made it impossible.

His bigotry disappointed her, but his lack of faith and understanding brought silent pain.

Sadness. Bartek's brown swirl eyes, a shade darker than his skin and eyebrows, couldn't hide the emotion, not when Lela's name was mentioned. How could he still be in love with her after all these years? Then again, who was Zion to judge? His love for Lela hadn't wavered an ounce since his death.

"She deserved better. I was Verity. I would've made a far better mat—"

"For God's sake, Bartek, that was over thirty years ago. Lela never felt that way about you. I know you don't want to hear it, but we both know the truth. You were her friend, a good friend, but nothing more."

"Because of you."

This was a conversation long overdue, one Zion never wanted to have because it would've served no other purpose than as an outlet for his anger. Back then, he'd had to tread carefully, with Lela's political career and him as a foreign dignitary. There were bigger issues at stake than his pride and frustration. And Lela, on the cusp of Regency, needed allies, especially those from her band. What she hadn't needed was her husband ramming his fist down Bartek's big mouth, no matter how much the man may have deserved it.

"Not because of me." Zion allowed some of the anger he'd kept inside, for so many years, to slip free. First Bartek and then Ammon, not that Ammon had ever done anything to interfere with his marriage to Lela. Although Zion didn't like any man lusting after his wife, he could now admit that Ammon had respected Zion as a man and as a human.

More, he never belittled Lela for her choice of mate, and certainly not in front of her band, the way Bartek had done.

"It probably makes you feel better to blame me than to admit Lela never saw you as a romantic partner. She trusted you, relied on you as a friend and political ally, but she never loved you as a woman would love a man, the way you love her."

Bartek's fist balled and lips curled, his emotions pathetically easy to read. "How does it feel for you to be in that position now?"

What a petty dead man.

"Is that why you're here? Do you want to see my pain at having my wife not recognize me and treat me as if I'm nothing more to her than an old friend?"

Zion sat in the black chair, staring up at Bartek with unexpected weariness. The man's face was all hard angles of resentment, sorrow, and envy.

"I'm sorry for your pain, but I won't apologize for falling in love with and marrying Lela. If it makes you feel better, I understand how you felt back then more than I could ever before, to want someone so desperately and not have that sentiment returned. It's not a good feeling. Not a good feeling at all."

"But you've been given a second chance."

Not quite, but Zion nodded.

"Why? What's so special about you, Zion Grace?"

Now he comprehended. Zion stood again, closing the distance between himself and Bartek in four quick strides.

"Even in death, you haven't found contentment, come to terms with your fate."

"What do you mean?"

"I mean, you want this body, this opportunity."

Bartek looked away, and Zion knew he was right. How different and alike they were. Even in death, they both pined for the same woman.

"You've already had your time with Lela, you deserve no more."

Perhaps he was right, but it wasn't for Bartek to decide.

"She's my wife."

"Not anymore. You died and left Lela, while I stayed and watched over her."

"Is that why you're here instead of in the Realm of Thuraya?"

What in the hell was going on? None of this should be possible, yet there two dead men stood, arguing over something as old and as tired as the cosmos itself.

Bartek's eyes hardened to dark slits as he glared at Zion with open hostility.

"If you haven't gone to the other side, how is it your life energy is still intact, and you died before I did? Shouldn't you have dissolved or something, after all these years?"

"I can't explain it, Grace. The Fate of Truth sent me, and I'm here."

Zion didn't know what to make of that, but it didn't matter. Not really.

"Why are you here? I don't have time for your games."

Frost dripped from Bartek, his expression stony and lips thinned in disapproval. "You cannot tell her the truth."

"And why the hell not? Did Truth send you to tell me that? He could've spared me the light show and drama and come himself."

"For whatever reason, the Fates of Asiya have decided to give you a second chance with Lela's heart, but you must earn it."

"I've been trying to earn it, dammit, trying to save my immortal soul. It's not easy in the little time I've been given and in this body."

Zion thumped a fist against Ammon's chest, wanting to punch something, to smash any damn thing to bits. Anything, shit anything to ease the pain in his chest, the anxiety thrumming through his mind.

"It's not supposed to be easy, and Ammon is the perfect vessel for the task."

"Why? Tell me why Ammon was selected and not someone else." He pointed a trembling finger at Bartek. "You know, don't you?"

Bartek's gaze slid from Zion, scanning the living room as if he'd just arrived, taking it in with a longing he knew well. Ammon still lived, while Bartek and Zion shouldn't even exist, certainly not there.

When Bartek's eyes settled on Zion again, his lips parted, not in another sneer but on a soft confession of, "He loves her."

"I know that. Tell me what I don't know."

Bartek hesitated but kept his face turned to Zion. "Early in Lela's life," he began, Bartek's eyes piercing and clear, "he was the other half of her soul. Ammon came first."

No, no. Zion stumbled back, falling onto the ottoman.

Bartek smiled—ugly and with self-satisfaction. "Did you think she never loved anyone before you?"

This couldn't be true. Lela would've told him. And yeah, Lela had been Zion's second wife but Ammon her first love...? Shit, she should've told him.

Even as the thought came to his mind, Zion knew why she hadn't. Verity told the truth, mostly, but not when the truth served no greater purpose than to cause a person harm. No good, especially before Zion's death, would've come from Lela revealing her past relationship with Ammon.

Whatever feelings Lela may have felt for the Paladin, when she was a young woman, was no more by the time she met, fell in love with and married Zion. Her people didn't understand lies of omission the way humans did. Lela would've deemed what she had with Ammon as the past and irrelevant to her present life with Zion.

"So, why didn't they become mates?"

"I don't know. That was all he told me, all the Fate of Truth said I needed to know."

"So, there's more?"

"My mission was simple, Grace. You mustn't tell Lela the truth. You have to earn her affection in the time allotted or..."

"Or what? Purpose already told me what will happen if I fail to convince her to finish the Light of Nurzhan and perform the Unity of Hearts. What more is there? What else aren't you telling me?"

"I've said all I've come to say."

The blue-and-gray ball of light came again, spreading its rays throughout the room, Bartek's voice a hollow message in the distance. "They think you're special, have a destiny. If you love her, for once, proceed like an Asiyan and not a selfish human."

The light blazed brighter, burning Zion's eyes and then it was gone.

The room was cast in darkness, the sun having turned in for the night. Where had the day gone? His talk with Bartek felt like minutes, not hours.

He staggered to his feet, the pull of fatigue heavy and the weight of Lela's secret even heavier. Zion started to make his way to his bedroom, stopping in the hallway when he heard the doorbell. He swore. He probably missed a meeting while listening to Bartek's jealous rambling.

Walking in a fog of whirling thoughts, Zion mindlessly opened the door without first looking at the security cameras. Agitated, he swung the doors open.

"Your housekeeper said you've been locked in your living room all day. I know the life of the Paladin Band leader can be daunting, but I hope you're not too busy to have dinner with me."

"Lela…?"

Her shy smile sent a surge of warmth through Zion, right before unbidden images and memories flooded his mind—a man and a woman in a room, on a bed, bodies entwined, making love. Next came the voices, her voice, so clear and familiar. Lela was looking at him, speaking to him, her hands on his chest, his arms. But no, Zion knew this wasn't right. Lela and Zion weren't sharing the bed, smelling of their recent coupling. It was Ammon who'd just made love to Lela, and this was his goddamn memory.

First Bartek and now Ammon. He had no power, no control, forced to watch another man's intimate memories of Lela—Zion's waking nightmare.

"When is your battleship leaving?"

"Four hours."

"We don't have much time left then."

"No, the war is upon us, and I must lend my weapon to the cause. I will miss you, my love."

"I will miss you as well, Ammon, but it isn't too late to change your mind, to stay here with me."

"We've discussed this. My place is with my band. Your place is here. Just because you're Chief Magistrate of the Verity Band, I won't have you protecting me from my duty."

"I wouldn't think of it. I just... I don't want any harm to come to you."

"No Lumerian can harm me as long as I have your love. Do I, Lela?"

"Yes, I love you."

"Once this is over, I will return for you, and we will begin the courting rituals. Now, my love, I only need one hour to prepare. Let's not waste the other three talking."

The waking nightmare faded to black. Zion's head raged with sharp knife-like pain at the base of his skull. He took two steps back, felt his legs give. Lela reached for him, but it was too late.

Zion fell.

CHAPTER TWELVE

Barriers and Breakthroughs

Ammon felt weightless, as if he were being lifted on powerful wings, a graceful wind carrying him forward to a place he should know. Slowly and with much effort, he parted his eyelids, fading pain the reward. He blinked once, twice and then a third time.

He had to make sure. Opening his eyes wider, Ammon took in his surroundings without daring to move. It was dark, save for a glimmer of light off to his right somewhere. His body told him he reclined on a bed, the feel and smell letting him know he was in his bedroom.

But how? What happened?

A sliver of awareness prickled the base of his mind. A memory, many memories and one in particular.

Zion Grace.

Yes, he remembered it all, the invasion and his sense of powerlessness. For weeks, Zion Grace had occupied his body, controlling his movements and thoughts, living as him. Anger began to swell, but Ammon forced it away. Such raw emotions were futile. Besides, the ordeal wasn't over, the spirit of the dead man was still inside him.

Ammon gave a mental wince, but it was no longer from pain. He'd fought to assert his will, to reclaim what was his. Yet, Grace lingered, growing stronger each day he remained in Ammon's body. He was being taken over from the inside out and, to his dismay, there seemed very little he could do to control his fate.

However, there had been moments, a few timeless seconds in which he was the captain and Grace the troublesome stowaway. He was back and in control. But for how long?

"You're awake."

Ammon knew that voice, a melodic sweetness causing him to risk the pain he knew would come. He shifted, turning on his right side and taking in the petite form cast in shadow.

"Lela," he said, her name coming out as a contented sigh, followed by a raised hand. "Come closer, I can barely see you."

"Lights at forty-percent," she ordered before walking toward him and taking his offered hand. "How are you feeling?"

Lela's hand was soft and delicate in his own, his mind recalling the events of the last few weeks and how she'd slowly begun to open herself up to him. Then he had to fight a frown. It had been Grace to whom she'd bestowed all those smiles to, Grace who'd made her laugh, and Grace who'd used Ammon's body to reclaim Lela.

He must've been brooding for longer than he thought, Lela's gently probing voice coming again. "Are you all right? I was worried when you collapsed."

In spite of the concern in her eyes, Lela was as beautiful as ever.

"How did I get in here? You're definitely a force to be reckoned with, but I doubt even you can carry a man my size."

She squeezed his hand and then an emotion flickered in her eyes he couldn't decipher.

"The two High Stars Sage force upon me everywhere I go brought you in here. They each hoisted one of your arms over their shoulder, virtually dragging you into your bedroom and placing you on the bed."

Her free hand came to rest on his cheek as the same unnameable emotion glowed even more.

"I was quite worried about you, Ammon. You appear in perfect health, but—"

She cut herself off and removed her hand from his face. But he intercepted it before she could pull away from him fully. Ammon could name the emotion now—fear. Lela was afraid of... losing him? Could that be?

He trapped her hand within his, felt her tremble, and smiled. She was concerned about him. Apparently, very concerned. This unexpected development pleased him. Perhaps, Grace hadn't won after all. Maybe he still had a chance, if only he could rid himself of the unwanted soul occupying his body.

"I'm sorry if I worried you. I've been having the most annoying headaches for the last three months. They come and go, but I've never lost consciousness before." He paused, remembering the last time something like this happened. He'd awakened a prisoner in his body. But he couldn't exactly share that with her. No matter how he felt about the Fates using him, he would do nothing to complicate Lela's life. Besides, how could he possibly begin to explain such a disturbing set of events?

"Have you gone to see your personal physician?"

He grimaced. Shrugged.

"Paladin," she huffed. "Three months is a long time to experience headaches, and now you're blacking out."

With her unspoken scold and sighed judgment of the soldiers of his band, the fear he'd seen in her eyes returned, accompanied by a grave frown.

"Promise me you'll make an appointment with your doctor as soon as possible."

Another grimace.

"Promise me," she repeated, her frown turning fierce with determination. She wouldn't let this go.

Nodding, he conceded.

"Good. Now, are you hungry? I could make something for you."

She was smiling at him now, her hand still trapped, but she didn't seem to mind.

He shook his head.

"I would rather you stay for another night of soul beholding." It was a hopeful request, one he'd had a lot of time to think about while watching Grace play him as only a bumbling human could. Still, Ammon had to admit that Grace was nothing like the man he thought him to be.

While having a spiritual intruder literally forced down one's throat couldn't be classified as a lifestyle choice, Ammon had come to know all there was about Zion Grace. The man was as honorable and brave as any among the Paladin Band. His memories were open and fluid in Ammon's mind, Grace unable to keep a single thought from him. And the man loved Lela and Xavier with a ferocity Ammon couldn't help but envy.

Whether he wanted to or not, Ammon understood Grace's motivations. He would do no less if he were given the opportunity. Still, he was his competition, his enemy. Grace had no place on this physical plane of existence. Not any longer, and Ammon's body was not for sale.

Reluctantly, he released her hand and sat up. "Well, Lela, will you stay?"

"I've already stayed the night."

He gave her a quizzical look, and she laughed ever so enticingly.

"You've been asleep all night. The sun will rise in," she glanced at the chronometer on his nightstand, "about an hour or so."

So she'd stayed the night. But had she prayed for his soul? Had she glimpsed the most sacred part of Ammon? He was almost afraid to ask.

She laughed again, this time causing him to rise from the bed and take her by the waist. Her laughter ceased, and her eyes widened at their close proximity.

"Did you like what you beheld, Lela? Did my soul please you?" His voice was but a measured whisper, face turned down to her, body taut with desire.

She nodded slowly, eyes fixed on his. He couldn't look away and apparently, neither could she. "Your soul was… was…" She paused and closed her eyes. "It's hard for me to explain."

"Please try, I would like to know." He drew her closer, their bodies touching from knees to waist. "I need to know. I've waited so long."

Still, the words didn't come. He'd never known Lela of Asheema to be at a loss for words, yet there she stood in his arms, mouth opened but no words coming out.

"Perhaps we should talk first," he suggested, when the silence between them stretched, Lela unable to give voice to whatever thoughts swirled inside her.

Ammon backed up, took her hand and then made his way to a black chaise lounge sofa situated under his east bedroom window. He waited for Lela to sit before sitting next to her, her gaze curious, words still absent.

"I think I should say a few things to you first before you answer my question."

"We don't have to do this now, Ammon. It's very early and you should probably—"

"I didn't understand back then."

"Understand what?"

"You know what I'm talking about, the reason why the Verity Band ended the war."

Her face took on a stony expression at his words, the opening of a wound that had never healed properly now about to be placed under a microscope.

"I would rather not discuss that time in our lives. It was long ago. Why bring it up now?"

He no longer held her hand, but he could see how tensely they were linked in her lap.

"I owe you an apology."

She started to shake her head in protest, but he brought his hands to rest on either side of her neck, needing her to listen to him.

"You and your band stopped the Asiyan-Lumerian War. We were so close to absolute victory, yet you pushed and persuaded the other magistrates to call a halt to the war. It would have been a glorious victory,

Lela. The Paladins could taste the fruit of our labors, so close were we to bringing those murdering Lumerians to heel, to avenging the peace delegation and Regent Etemaad."

That thought used to bring a soldier's smile to his face, such was the power of his band, his people. But when the call for blood ended and the madness receded, the truth revealed itself—the acceptable death of trillions of innocent Lumerians for the actions of a few, for the life of one revered man. What kind of soldier could take pride in such a ruthless act of unjustifiable revenge?

"I know. It was madness, and we almost didn't wake up in time." Her voice was calm, regretful, but her pulse raced under his fingers, his persistent touch.

"You were the one who woke us from the nightmare we had been living. But I was too angry and consumed with vengeance to see my way out of the bleak tunnel. I didn't understand then, your call for peace, your weakness as a leader."

To her credit, Lela didn't flinch at the word *weakness*, no matter how erroneous his judgement had been back then, how unfair and heartless.

"And I resented you, as much as I wanted to slaughter every last Lumerian."

His voice dropped at the admission, shame flooding his heart. His words to her then were harsh, but he'd felt righteous. In his mind, Ammon had been the one betrayed. Betrayed by the woman he loved, the woman he intended to take as his mate.

A decade, Lela. Ten years of spilled Asiyan blood and you stop us a battle line from victory. Only a softhearted member of the Verity Band could make such a foolish decision. You don't deserve to be the Regent's heir. You've tainted the Hall of Concord, dishonored the Regent's memory, and consigned us all to a fate worse than death.

"You refused to see or speak to me after that day. I didn't know how to make you understand. We were killing ourselves. With each bloody confrontation, each Lumerian life taken, we were dying." She lifted a hand and settled it over her heart. "In here, Ammon. Our heart, our soul.

We were moving further and further away from the people the Fates of Asiya trusted to uphold their values. Peace, Ammon, we were supposed to be a people of peace—not war and certainly not vengeance."

She swallowed deeply before she next spoke, his hands still resting against her warm neck, pleased she hadn't shied away from the intimate touch.

"We forgot. I forgot. In my grief and heartache, I'd forgotten all that I'd learned at Regent Etemaad's knee and in the Hall of Concord."

"I know. For so long all I knew was revenge. I remember when I first learned of the attack. I'd never been so afraid in my life, waiting to hear if you survived or had been taken from me. When the news finally reached me that you were among the few survivors and the Regent murdered, I became enraged. I thought, by killing every last Lumerian, I'd never feel as afraid and helpless as I did in those hours after the attack."

"It's my fault." Her voice trembled, and tears fell. "I beheld your soul that night you came to me after the Regent's death. And what I saw was not your true soul but the soul I created with my vote for war. Your soul was small, coarse, and morose, nothing like the kind, gentle man I loved. I did that to you, to us all."

"You were one voice of many—Affiq, Paladin, Euridice, Devdas, Verity."

"I voted without thought."

"You voted from a soul drenched in senseless pain and death."

"Many died as a result."

"You saved even more. Don't you see, your vote was no more important than the other magistrates'. Four had already cast their vote for war before you made it unanimous. It was not our fate to decimate a people and destroy ourselves in the process. Purpose, Truth, Faith, our Fates. For ten years we lost them. But you helped bring the Fates back into our lives. You and your band found your way back to the light, then had the challenging task of waking the rest of Asiya from our collective nightmare. Paladins are supposed to be honorable warriors with a strict ethical code, protecting the innocent and laying waste to the guilty. But, somewhere in those ten years, we lost our way and our honor."

And his band hadn't cared, so entrenched in the war were they, unable to justify their cause against the thousands of Lumerians they'd killed. Yet they'd tried, excusing their war stance with righteous talk of "protecting the Homeworld from despots and disbelievers."

He wiped tears from Lela's cheeks, knowing she cried, in part, because of him and the pain and bloodshed she believed she brought to his life. He leaned in, lightly brushing his lips over hers. They were moist and salty from her tears, but also warm and soft.

"Did my soul please you this time, Lela?"

His heart thrummed a vicious, nervous beat, her lack of an immediate response doing nothing for his sanity. But when she finally spoke, it was with humbling certainty.

"Yes. More than I thought possible. Your soul is beautiful, radiant and at peace."

"You think you took that from me, but the truth is that you gave it to me. I doubt if my soul back then would've been as untarnished as you believe. I was always trying to live up to the man my father wanted me to be. He never understood and I was too afraid to make him understand. But you, Lela, you risked all for a truth that knows no bounds in a cosmos full of limits."

He pressed his lips to hers again, a gentle pressure but nothing more.

"Where do we go from here? Now that I know you beheld my soul all those years ago, that makes three nights, even though I haven't beheld yours."

Not that it mattered. Lela's soul shown in the eyes that met his, in her love for her people and family. A thought occurred to him. "Unless—"

"That night counts." A sheepish look crossed her face. "I shouldn't have begun the courting ritual without your permission. But that night was full of broken rules of propriety."

It had been at that, neither of them caring about norms and mores. Not when grief and lust were too tempting to ignore.

"Will you then consider moving on to the Unity of Hearts?"

He felt her stiffen and then relax.

"I must first complete the funeral rites before I make any decisions about my future. I can't consider moving on with you when I haven't laid Zion to rest, engaged in the Rite of Sephtis."

Yes, the eternal death ritual of their people. He'd assumed she'd completed it years ago. The fact that she hadn't probably also meant they'd failed to complete the Dissolution of Fidelity ritual before Grace's death. No wonder the human's soul wasn't at rest or Lela capable of gifting her heart to Ammon.

Lela was correct. He understood the ritual to come and why it was needed. It should've happened a long time ago, but clearly Lela hadn't been prepared to sever the last vestige of her marriage. Now she was, and he would support her in any way she would accept. But that didn't mean he was ready to send her home just yet. Zion Grace would have to wait.

"I'll wait until you're ready, if that's what you want. Is it, Lela?"

Her eyes bore into his as if she were searching for a sign that the precipice looming before her would hold them both.

A sigh touched his mouth a second before her tongue tentatively ran over his lower lip, the petite hands on his shoulders pulling him forward. Now, it was his turn to stiffen, and he did.

His face must've registered his shock, for she stared at him warily.

"You asked me to engage in the Unity of Hearts with you, Ammon, but you must understand something about me first. I may have an Asiyan soul, but I am no longer wholly Asiyan."

"I can see that."

"I don't think you do. I'm not the woman I was, and much of who I am now is very much human. I've had to come to terms with this truth. Thirty years of marriage to a human has a way of influencing one's actions and way of thinking."

"I'm not the man I used to be either, Lela. We've both changed in many ways, but in others, we haven't at all."

"I just… I need you to know what it is you're requesting. I want—"

"You won't shock me if that's what's worrying you."

"I think I already have."

Ammon's raspy laugh was his concession. "Well, I've actually never thought of using my tongue in that way. Is that how humans kiss? With their tongue?"

"Sometimes, but you didn't allow me to finish." Lela gave him a wickedly challenging smile.

"Oh, so you aim to send me running by showing me just how human you are. Thereby, proving to yourself and me that no one other than Grace could possibly accept you for who you are?"

The sparkle in her eyes dimmed with the truth of his words. Ammon didn't want to hurt her, but she must be made to understand.

"I accepted you for who you are, even when I didn't understand. Nothing you can do or show me will change that very real fact. I know you loved your mate, and I'm sure you love him still. But I also think you can love me again, if you would stop erecting barriers to the possibility. I can make you happy, and I think that frightens you."

"Why would it frighten me?"

A slow grin formed and his hands framed her face once more. "Show me how humans kiss with their tongue, Lela, and don't stop until I learn the lesson well."

With aching caution, Lela kissed him, and this time, he didn't recoil when her tongue grazed his lower lip. It slid from the left side of his mouth to the right, the texture smooth, inviting. She did it again and again, licking and nipping at his lower and upper lips, pulling them into her mouth and sucking.

He heard a deep-throated moan and realized, with manly shame, that it emanated from him. Ammon was wound as tight as a spring, all the blood draining from his mind to a much lower region of his body. Lela's lips and tongue were intoxicating, her slim form molding to his as he wrapped his arms hungrily around her, encouraging her exploration.

Then her tongue was in his mouth, and Ammon could do nothing but succumb to her expert probing. She tasted him in a way he didn't think possible, her tongue gliding over teeth, tongue, and gums. Lela urged him to explore her as well, pulling him into her mouth with determined gentleness, a sensual moan escaping from her when he explored her in return.

She tasted of magnolias and lost love, long winter naps and hazy summer days. And Ammon yearned for more of the lesson, more of her. But she released him with an abruptness that had Ammon groaning at the loss of contact. She stood, appearing as flustered and dazed as he felt.

He stood too.

"What's wrong?"

"Nothing, but I should be leaving. I have an eight o'clock meeting, and I must return home so I can shower and change."

He gave her a knowing, weak smile. One of these days she would kiss him and not feel guilty.

"Dinner?"

She shook her head. "I can't. Xavier will be back in two weeks, and I must have everything prepared for the ritual by the time he returns. I can't put this off any longer, for his sake as well as my own."

Which didn't mean they couldn't have dinner together. What it did mean was that, while preparing for her deceased mate's funeral, Lela would treat the ritual as if she were beginning her year of mourning. It was only right, he knew, for Lela to honor Grace's memory through seclusion and prayer.

She should've never come to him last night, in fact. But he comprehended why she had. When she couldn't reach him, as she'd said, she'd become worried and wanted to see for herself that he was unharmed. Her dinner invitation, last night, had been nothing more than an excuse to distract him from the true purpose of her visit.

She did care about him. But did she care enough?

"Is there anything I can do to help?"

She smiled at him, her eyes bright and free of tension.

"You can call your physician and schedule an emergency appointment."

"I meant—"

"I know what you meant. If you want to help me, then start taking better care of yourself. I don't want to lose you too."

She paused, and Ammon knew she hadn't intended on saying those words.

"You won't lose me," he reassured, taking her hand and escorting her out of his bedroom and to the front door, where he knew her High Stars and transport were waiting.

They walked in silence the entire way, Ammon sensing the first tendrils of a headache. He knew the signs well now, his helmsmenship almost at an end, the stowaway rising from his place of slumber. But he still had time.

Not yet, Grace, not yet.

Ammon opened the door for Lela, battling the raging storm rushing to the fore, threatening to swallow him whole. He wouldn't go, not without a fight.

"Will you come to the final day of the ritual?"

Unable to speak, he nodded.

"Good, then I'll see you then. Be well, Ammon."

"Be well, Lela." He couldn't let her go, not without— As she turned to leave, he spun her around and pulled Lela into a heated kiss. Not one to let knowledge go to waste, Ammon coaxed her lips with his tongue, as she'd done him, until she opened for him, granting Ammon the access he desired.

His head felt like exploding thunderclouds, but he ignored the pain, dousing it with the pleasure of Lela's mouth, lips, and tongue.

Finally, he let her go and nearly stumbled. From the blinding pain or overpowering euphoria of having Lela in his arms, he didn't know.

He waited for Lela to stroll down the walkway and enter the transport, a High Star helping her inside. Then she was gone, but the tingle on Ammon's lips where hers had been remained.

He slammed the door, sank to his knees and yelled his frustration to the Fates, who seemed to only care about answering the prayers of Zion Grace.

"This isn't fair."

"I know it isn't. I'm sorry."

"I want you to go away, to leave me alone."

"This wasn't my choice."

"No, but it's your wish."

"True. I want another chance with Lela."

"So do I."

CHAPTER THIRTEEN

Giving Up

"You have to find the data quartz for me. You're my only hope."

Sage regarded her brother, although he looked nothing like the man she'd known all of her life. No, she peered across her desk and into the strong face of Commander Ammon. But it was Zion who was speaking to her, making his request for the third time.

"How in the hell do you expect me to find one small data quartz after all these years? You don't even know what you did with it."

She uncrossed her arms and took a sip of her lukewarm coffee. It was bland and tasted of cooked dirt. Asiyans had no clue how to brew a good cup of joe. They tried their best to accommodate their human citizens. But God, it tasted like swill. Sage took a healthy gulp, needing the fortification to deal with her brother. If she could stomach the wretched drink, she could most definitely clamp her mouth around the asinine predicament she now found herself.

"It must be in Lela's suite of rooms somewhere. I remember recording it only two days before I…" He crossed his legs, uncrossed them and then crossed them again, all in less than thirty seconds, his angst evident and disturbing. "I recorded my last message to my son before I went on my fly-about."

Sage gave a small huff she hoped Zion wouldn't take the wrong way. This was day four of the Rite of Sephtis Lela planned for the resurrected man sitting before her. Fasting and prayer comprised the first three days. Lela and Xavier spending the majority of that time at Verity Temple.

In two days' time, the final rites would be performed, concluding the six-day ritual. Sage wasn't looking forward to that day. As it was, it was all she could do to watch the sorrowful faces of her best friend and nephew as they moved from one phase of the ritual to the next. While this ritual was seven years in the making, that fact did nothing to minimize the pain involved, including her own.

"Maybe Lela stumbled upon it and threw it away, not realizing what was on it," Zion suggested, his voice somber, his eyes even more so. He'd been in this state from the moment he'd entered her office. This surprised Sage. She was sure he'd be on cloud nine after learning, from Lela, of the recent night of soul beholding. Instead, he appeared as if he'd lost his proverbial best friend.

Sage shook her head. "No, Lela threw nothing of yours away. Hell, it took me almost a year to convince her it was time to pack your things away." She closed her eyes and took a deep breath. Those were difficult times back then, Lela holding fiercely onto any and everything that reminded her of Zion, refusing to relinquish the slightest physical reminder of him.

"So what did she do with my belongings?"

Sage smiled and shook her head. Damn, she had to be braindead not to think of it earlier.

"If that data quartz of yours still exists, then it's probably in storage. One weekend when Lela was off-planet, Xavier and I got the bright idea to box up your stuff from your bedroom, thinking it would spare Lela the pain of doing it herself."

Zion shifted in his chair, leaning forward, his face suddenly taut, eyes dark and dangerous.

"You two had no right to push her like that. If she wasn't ready to clear my things from our bedroom, you should've let her determine when the time was right." His lips snarled the words and Sage took another drink of her swill.

"Yeah, well, it wasn't doing her a damn bit of good having a bedroom full of clothing and shoes, and other things that reminded her of a life she would never have again. A husband who was dead. Three months of silent treatment bordered on the insane but we all got past it."

In truth, it was like radiation treatment—necessary to kill the cancerous cells but painful with tremendous side effects. Lela had gone ballistic when she'd returned home, and demanded everything be restored at once. It had taken all of Sage's and Xavier's resolve to refuse. Not only did they refuse to return the items, but they also kept the location of Zion's personal belongings a secret. That incensed her even more, making the next three months of their lives a nightmare, Lela shutting them out and herself in. Tough love, yeah, and it had hurt like hell.

Zion relaxed, his back returning to the chair, his eyes temporarily closing.

"What's going on with you? The last time I saw you, you were hellbent on telling Lela the truth. Honestly, I'm glad you didn't, but she seems to be slowly coming around. She wasn't as haggard when she came back from Ammon's house a few days ago as she'd been when she prayed for his soul the first time."

"It wasn't the first time," Zion said, his voice a resentful whisper. "She began the Light of Nurzhan ritual the night they became lovers."

Oh, shit.

Sage wondered if they'd been lovers back in the day, but damn. For Zion to know the truth, he must've—

Holy crap. It's one thing to know the man who deflowered your wife, but it's something different to see him do it as part of a cruel memory.

"Is that what's bothering you?" Sage suspected there was more to Zion's foul mood than jealousy. Decades in law enforcement had a way of helping one see beyond the obvious.

He shrugged, turning his face from her and to the open window. A small breeze must've taken pity on him, spreading its cooling fingers over Zion's overheated face.

"It hurts, but I have no right to my pain. I wasn't a virgin when she married me, and I knew she wasn't either. It didn't matter back then, why should it matter now?"

It shouldn't, but it obviously did.

"Are you upset that she never told you about him?"

Zion returned his gaze to Sage, dark eyes somber. "I never talked about my first wife with her, even though I knew she was curious. I just didn't want to go there, you know?"

Yeah, Sage did. Iman had died six months into her pregnancy, a deadly virus claiming both mother and daughter. She didn't think Zion would ever recover from losing his family, but time and distance from Earth had helped heal his wounds.

"By silent agreement, we decided to leave the past in the past." He shrugged, a nonchalant lifting of his shoulders incongruent with the pain etched around the edges of his eyes. "Why would I expect her to share an affair with me that was over well before she met me? Especially one that went against acceptable Asiyan behavior."

He shook his head as if trying to clear away an unwanted cobweb, his hand coming up to scratch at his hairless jaw. "She wasn't a virgin, but it was also clear that she didn't have much experience. That made it easy for me to forget that someone must've come before me, a male she held in such high regard that she risked her reputation and band sanctions to be with him."

She didn't know what to say. Lela never, as far as Sage knew, broke from Asiyan customs. And while her marriage to Zion may have been unusual at her political level, mating with an off-worlder wasn't prohibited on Asiya.

"I need you to find that data quartz for me. Xavier deserves to know the truth, to understand I didn't leave without giving him a second thought."

Sage pondered Zion's words and Xavier's anger over his father leaving without contacting him, without making sure he was home with Lela when Zion took his final flight. If she could help Xavier find peace after all these years, well, she'd shred every box in the storage room to locate the damn quartz. But there was one problem.

"Once we finally told Lela where we stored your things, she changed the passcode and didn't give it to Xavier or me."

"Hell."

"Exactly."

"So, how do you plan on getting the code? Or are you thinking about just breaking in?"

"I know you have a mountain of hair on top of your head now, Zion, that may be interfering with your brain, but I'm not going to break into Lela's storage room. She may have forgiven me for packing your things away without her permission, but I'll be damned if I violate her privacy like that again."

"So what are our options? I don't want her knowing the truth."

Since when?

"I'm going to tell her the truth." Sage pressed four keys on her video screen, then hit two more, canceling her afternoon meetings.

"I don't want her to know that I've returned, Sage, not now, not anymore. I just… I just want them to finally be able to lay me to rest and move on."

What in the hell was going on with him? Zion had done a 360 in less than two weeks. There had to be more to this than the data quartz.

"I simply meant that I'm going to tell her that I need to have a personal item of yours for the ritual, which is true, as far as it goes. The last day of the service involves giving away something of value to you that reminds you of your loved one."

Zion looked doubtful. "Why would something of yours be stored in a room with my things?"

"There isn't, but Lela doesn't know that. When I moved to Asiya, I used one of the vacant offices on the lower level of the Hall of Concord to store some of my crap. You know, the stuff you think you'll use but never do. Anyway, when Xavier and I decided to remove your things, we didn't want to move them far—"

"So you swapped my things for yours. Got it."

"Yeah, but Lela has never been inside to know otherwise."

"How do you know?"

"As hurt and angry as she was with Xavier and me for going behind her back, she knew we did the right thing. The pictures, the clothing, the bed, it was all too much for her to cope with."

He stood, the chair crashing to the floor, the sound not as loud as the tremor in Zion's voice. "You put our bed in storage. That was the first gift Lela gave me after learning humans annually celebrate their wedding day. She said since I'd given up so much to move to Asiya to be with her, the least she could do was spend the rest of her days sleeping on a human bed next to me."

He was seething, face no longer winter brown, but summer red. Lela had the same reaction, but without the froth at the mouth.

"No wonder she didn't speak to you or Xavier for three months. You had no right to strip everything from her out of some misguided notion of helping her." His words were ground out, hands balled into fists, legs shaking with the wrath of his anger.

Sage stood as well, but he didn't seem to notice. Zion's words tumbled out like water from a leaking faucet.

"Lela is strong in most ways, much stronger than I ever was. But in other ways, she's like a rare flower—beautiful to gaze upon but fragile. She feels deeply, much deeper than she leads on and she isn't impervious to pain. I know my dying left a huge void in her heart and soul. But we played the hand we were dealt, and when it was time for me to fold, I did, leaving her to play the next round without me."

His eyes bored into her, no warmth, kindness, or even brotherly love reflected back.

"I grieved for Iman almost to the point of denying myself happiness with Lela. After four years I still hadn't gotten past her death but do you know what kept me going?"

Sage knew it was a rhetorical question, so she kept quiet, not having heard Zion speak of his long deceased wife since marrying Lela.

"I had pictures, letters, data images, and videos of her. Whenever I thought I couldn't go on, when the pain burned me from the inside out, I would find my keepsake box hidden in my closet. Mom and Dad thought I was holding on too tight, that I should lock the keepsake box away and never open it again. But they didn't understand."

Zion's tone softened, but his body remained rigid, and Sage's guilt grew with each word he spoke.

"Iman's belongings supported me when I wanted nothing more than to crawl into a ball and never get up. But you," he pointed at Sage, "and Xavier took that from Lela thinking you knew what was best for her, thinking you knew better than her what she needed. Has it ever occurred to you that the reason she's found it so difficult to let me go is because you didn't allow her to do it in her own time? The more Mom and Dad pushed me to let Iman and the baby go, the tighter I held onto my memories of them, of her."

Overcome, Sage slumped against her desk. She'd been so positive they'd made the right decision, that they were sparing Lela the pain she seemed to be wallowing in. Now she didn't know. Hell, according to Zion, they'd only succeeded in bringing Lela more pain, and possibly, stalling her recovery. She didn't know what to say except, "I'll find the data quartz for you and give it to Xavier before the ritual concludes. That's the least I can do."

"Thank you, Sage. I didn't mean to snap at you. I've… well, I've had a lot on my mind, too much for a dead soul like me to handle."

Zion crossed the small divide that separated them. His features were infinitely tender and open, which frightened Sage because she didn't understand her brother's mood swing. It was Ammon's face, but something about it reminded her of the dying man who'd asked her to stay and take care of his family. The body, the voice was different, but the eyes were cryptically Zion's and Sage was afraid to guess why.

He wrapped Ammon's thick, muscular arms around her, pulling Sage from her chair and into a bear hug. "Thank you."

Why did his thanks sound terrifyingly like a goodbye?

Before she could interpret all that had been said between them, Zion released her, his face an emotional mask.

"Lela told me she invited you to the public farewell gathering after the concluding service."

Zion moved toward Sage's office door, without answering her. He opened it, then glanced at Sage over his shoulder. "I won't be able to make my funeral, sis. It's been wonderful seeing you again, but I don't think I have what it takes to convince Lela to complete the Unity of Hearts with Ammon. They have a history, closer than I would've ever imagined, but he's not the man for her."

"B-but," she stuttered, "you said you would cease to exist if you and Lela didn't complete all parts of the Light of Nurzhan and the Unity of Hearts ritual. You're halfway there, why give up now?"

"I have my reasons, and they're mine, so don't ask."

Dammit, she wanted to ask. Hell, she wanted to scream and shake him into rational thought. But he hadn't been rational since strolling into her office an hour ago.

"You can't leave Lela again, not when she's starting to open up, allowing herself to feel again."

"Trust me, it's for the best." His goodbye eyes found hers and Sage's throat tightened. This was it then? For whatever reason, Zion was throwing his second chance with Lela away, his soulful eyes dimming under the reality of his decision. "Find the data quartz and keep your promise. That's all I ask. That's all I'll ever ask of you again. Goodbye, Sage."

He left.

What in the hell was she going to do now? Sage reclaimed her chair, stunned. Like her brother earlier, she turned her face to the open window, the cool breeze washing over her. She felt nauseous, the bile of Zion's unfathomable decision slithering its way up her throat, the retching reflex strong. But she clamped her hand over her mouth, forcing it back down, along with her fears and tears.

Shaken yet determined, Sage got to her feet, grabbed her coffee cup and downed the grotesque brew in one long gulp. She had a promise to keep, and Sage would be damned if she screwed up this mission.

CHAPTER FOURTEEN

Rite of Sephtis

Xavier found an unoccupied prayer room within the temple. He entered, closed the heavy double glass doors behind him and then—for additional privacy—slid the thickly woven black draperies in front of the windows that bordered the doors. Once inside, he dimmed the lights and dropped his exhausted frame onto one of the three purple-and-white sofas, resting his head on a white pillow with thin purple stripes.

He closed his eyes and slowed the cadence of his breathing, contemplating putting himself into a meditative state. But the small, pointy object in his left pants pocket jabbed him physically and emotionally. Shifting, he removed the red quartz from his pocket, palming it in his large hand. It had been almost twenty-four hours since Aunt Sage had given him the data quartz, yet he still hadn't mustered the courage to play the sparkling device.

"Before your father died, he asked me to give you something. He wanted you to have it on the day of his funeral. But, as you know, he went on his fly-about and was never seen again. And your mother, well," Sage had shrugged, "couldn't bring herself to say her final farewells, have the funeral due my brother." She'd lifted and opened his palm, then pressed the quartz within. "Today is that day. This is yours, nephew. I hope it brings you peace."

He'd been off-world when his father had passed away. At the bull-headed age of nineteen, Xavier had joined the Asiyan Interdimensional Fleet, without his parents' knowledge. Eager to make a name for himself beyond being the biracial son of a renowned human arbitrator and the Regent of Asiya, Xavier left home in search of self. During his journey, his father had died, leaving Xavier's mother alone. Light years away, unable to return immediately, his mother had only Aunt Sage to hold her aloft.

His father, a strong man full of laughter and life, Xavier hadn't truly believed his time with them would be so short. Although he knew of the gift from the Fates of Asiya, a young man's brain could be quite proficient at deluding himself. So he'd run away from home on a fool's journey, seeking answers afar when they were found much closer to home. *Within myself.*

Xavier stared at the quartz and wondered how something so tiny and fragile could drown him emotionally. He had no idea what was on the quartz, and after seven years of lamenting—if not cursing his father—for not allowing him to be there in his final days, the answers may now rest in the palm of his trembling hand. Yet there he sat, afraid, much like the man-child he'd been when he'd finally learned of his father's death.

Xavier's dark eyes swept the room in search of—*ah, there.* On the mantel above the fireplace, a clear rectangular quartz reader. He stood, and walked to the fireplace, the reader glimmering like a beacon of hope. With care, he inserted the quartz, point down, into the reader before he reclaimed his seat, not too proud to admit that a deathbed message from his father might weaken his knees.

"Play message for Xavier Grace." He leaned forward on the sofa, elbows on his knees, ceremonial robe unzipped, and eyes shimmering when an image of his father appeared before him.

For a minute, all Xavier could do was stare at the tall, broad shouldered man whose form resembled his own. He wore a dark-blue suit, one of many Xavier grew up seeing him adorn. Blue, black, and gray, those were Zion Grace's colors of choice. Xavier smiled and wiped at a stray tear.

It had been too many years since he'd seen his father, grief preventing him from looking at old 3-D images. Yet there had been many pictures taken during his parents' marriage and Xavier's youth. Zion and Lela, despite their high status, managed their fair share of family vacations, even traveling to Earth when Xavier was old enough to make the long trip.

"Hello, son," the strange yet familiar voice came, pulling Xavier's attention back to the image hovering only fifteen feet away. The dimpled smile followed his father's greeting, the very smile that had tucked Xavier in at night when he was but a boy in need of a nightlight and his father's soft assurances that no ghost lived under his bed or in his closet.

Zion sighed and ran a nervous hand through his graying, cropped hair.

Unthinking, Xavier did the same.

"I thought… well, I hoped I had more time to do this properly. I wanted to see you one last time. I can't tell you how many times I started to contact your superior officer." One hand found his hair again while the other his pants pocket. A nervous habit of his father Xavier remembered well.

"I argued with myself over whether I should use my authority to break the rules for my son, to have your captain make that exception because of who your mother and I are and the power and privilege our positions yield. But that's not who we are, how we raised you."

A huff, a sigh, and then both hands found their way into his pockets.

"Honestly, Xavier, this seemed a lot simpler when it was just a good idea swirling in my head. I have no more time left, and it hurts like hell to know there's nothing I can do to comfort you during your time of need. I tried to make every moment with you count, unwilling to waste one precious second. We're both only sons. With that comes a very special bond."

As his father spoke, as the cadence of his voice swept over Xavier, soothing him the way it did when he used to awake screaming from a childhood nightmare, searching for safety he always found in his father's protective arms, he started to relax.

"I remember when I was about twelve or thirteen," Zion began, scratching his chin the way he tended to do when he was about to regale someone with one of his many Earth stories, "I had this great German Shepherd. He used to follow me everywhere—the park, slipstream speedway, even to school one time." His father chuckled at the childhood memory, a youthful sound incompatible with the prematurely aged man he'd become during the last year of his life.

It wasn't until Zion moved around an imposing marble desk and sat in a well-worn black, executive chair, did Xavier realize his father had recorded the message in his home office. The only room in the Regent's suite of rooms he'd loved nearly as much as the bedchamber he shared with his wife.

"Anyway, one day old Charlie just stopped running, jumping and playing. He would laze around the house barely able to eat or hold his weight. After a week of this, my old man, your granddad, took Charlie to the vet. The doctor diagnosed him with some kind of spinal disease." He shook his head and scratched his chin. "I can't remember the name of the illness, but it doesn't really matter. The vet said she could operate on my dog but that his chance for a full recovery was less than ten percent."

The clack of heels sounded in the hallway. The *click clack, click clack* grew louder the closer the woman got to the prayer room. Xavier stiffened, wondering if the time had come to begin the final rite. *Click clack, click clack.* The heels did not stop at his door. They continued past the room and down the hall.

"Old Charlie was in a lot of pain and the chance of full recovery was slim. Dad opted to put the poor dog out of his misery and allow the vet to put him to sleep. I remember begging and crying to ride with Dad to the vet. I had to see Charlie one last time before he was taken from me forever. Against his better judgment, your granddad agreed and allowed me to tag along. Even decades later, I can still see old Charlie's fading, weak eyes staring up at me as he took his last breaths of life. As much as I loved that dog, it's hard for me to think of him the way he'd been, before the illness, without seeing his dead, gray eyes."

Xavier slid from the sofa and onto the floor, the thick white carpet cradling his somber frame.

"You see, son, I don't want to be old Charlie to you and your mother. I want the both of you to have happy, fond memories of me, not a decrepit man wasting away, dying in bed or at my desk. I don't wish to be remembered like that. The way I remember my first and only dog. You deserve more. And while I have no more time to give you, I can give you that—my last gift. The only thing left I have to give you is my love, and that you've had since the day I learned I would be a father."

Weakly, Xavier stood and walked toward the image of his father. He reached out, his hand going through the optical illusion, touching air instead of warm, solid flesh.

"When you were eight, you wrote me a Father's Day poem. I carry it with me everywhere I go."

Zion's right hand disappeared into his jacket pocket. Seconds later, he lifted a folded sheet of crème colored paper. Unfurling it, he placed it on his desk. Staring at it for long seconds before raising his eyes, Zion grinned with pride.

"It's tattered and faded, and most of the words are so light I can barely make them out now. But that doesn't matter. I know each word by heart. This paper," he said, an index finger sliding over an edge, "is a constant reminder that while the cosmos took from me, it also gave me something so much more precious in return. It gave me you, and I'll carry this keepsake with me when I depart this physical place, hoping you'll understand and maybe even forgive me."

Zion refolded the paper, kissed it and returned it to the pocket of his suit jacket.

"While I'm no Robert Frost, Langston Hughes, or even a young Xavier Grace, I've written a little something for you. I hope it will comfort you the way your poem has guided and comforted me."

Zion cleared his throat, while Xavier felt a sudden lump form in his.

"They say that the cosmos is comprised of billions of stars. Those stars birthed even more stars. And those stars birthed galaxies, planets, suns, moons, oceans, and people. People, in their finite form but endless capacity to dream, birthed civilizations—claiming, building, and cultivating. From those cultivations came beauty and wonder, as well as the desire to know more and to be known. So they expanded their knowledge, exploring beyond conceived boundaries, navigating the dimensions of their mind to worlds vaster than the brain could ever imagine. Yet when the end comes, when people reflect upon all they've seen, all whom they've met, all they've accomplished, a simple truth emerges. Love is the birth of all. My heart to your soul. The beginning but never the end."

Blindly, Xavier reached for his father again, walking through the electrical display just as Zion whispered, "I love you, son, you're my greatest achievement. My hope. My pride. My faith. Be well, and I'll see you again where stars shine and love is the brightest one of them all."

*****

Xavier listened as his mother delivered the ritual prayer. Her face eerily calm, as it had been throughout the day, reminding Xavier of how she carried herself the first year of mourning. It was a shield then as much as it was today. But he didn't begrudge Lela her staunch stoicism. As a young man, he'd been too inexperienced to understand the necessity of such a safeguard for the heart.

In honor of Zion Grace and his religious beliefs, Lela recited the Lord's Prayer. A prayer his father had taught her many years ago. "Our Father, who art in heaven, hallowed be thy name. Thy Kingdom come, thy will be done, on earth as it is in heaven. Give us this day our daily bread. And forgive us our trespasses, as we forgive those who trespass against us. And lead us not into temptation, but deliver us from evil. For thine is the kingdom, the power and the glory, forever and ever. Amen."

Xavier reached for his mother, grasping her hand in his. The temple was now empty except for the two of them and Sage, who knelt on her own prayer rug on the other side of Lela. This part of the rite was for family only. The public recognition of his father's life and service would take place afterward, the ceremony streamed lived all over Asiya, as befitting a foreign dignitary and the mate of Regent Lela.

He spared a glance at his mother, her eggshell white robe matching that of his own, flowing down her arms, legs and over bare feet. Even in the flickering light of the white candles, he could make out taut skin over grieving features. Xavier raised her hand to his lips and placed a gentle kiss on her painted palm. A sun, moon, and star, symbols, she'd once told him, of all she held most dear.

"The moon is my faith, my light through the darkness life can often become. The sun is my purpose, the warmth that heats my heart and fuels my soul, born the day you cried your way into my world. And the single star, truth, helps me find my way home when I'm lost and lonely. Your father is the brightest star in my cosmos."

"I can recite one of the prayers, if you like, A'bra."

She inclined her head before sliding the oval crystal chest, lined in purple-and-black silk, in front of him. The name Zion Elijah Grace was emblazoned on the top of the box in gold letters, as well as the numbers 2298, the year of his death. Per Asiyan religious tradition, Lela had the small chest crafted to be used during the *Lathe*, the closing ritual in which mourners placed an item of sentimental value into the chest that represented their eternal bond to the deceased. Once all items had been safely enclosed, the chest was buried with the deceased. However, when a body could not be retrieved for proper burial, as was often the situation during times of war, or, in the case of High Arbitrator Zion Grace, vanished, the *lathe'la*, as the chest was known, was kept in a family vault. At the close of the ritual, per tradition, Xavier would make the five-mile trek to the Asheema family vault, on foot, thereby honoring his father's memory through the acceptance of his passing and the understanding that physical life was a journey, transitory but the soul lived on forever.

Xavier peered inside the chest. A silver framed photo of a toddler Zion, an infant Sage, and their parents, taken in front of the Grace family home, sparked memories of Earth and summer vacations. The decades' old picture was Aunt Sage's willing sacrifice to an older brother she'd followed to Asiya when Earth held little for her but loneliness and cold memories.

Still clutching his mother's hand, Xavier reached under his robe and into his pants pocket with his free hand, pulling out a plastic sleeve containing an antique card. The baseball card was from 1947 Earth and of the Dodger's Jackie Robinson, sliding into home plate. The day Xavier had come home—at the age of six—crying because some kids at school said he couldn't play with them because he wasn't a "real" Asiyan, his father had gone to his wall safe and dug out the priceless collectible.

"Jackie Robinson was the first African American baseball player to play in the Major Leagues during a time in Earth's history when people were treated cruelly and unfairly based on the color of their skin," his father told him. "Such prejudices were just as irrational and stupid then as they are today. But Jackie Robinson didn't let the bigoted views of narrow-minded people prevent him from being the best man and baseball player he could be, achieving what many thought he couldn't. Being different, son, doesn't make you inferior. Don't let anyone convince you otherwise. Be your own man. Light your own path."

With reverence, Xavier slipped the card inside the chest, next to the Grace family photo. Shutting his eyes, he began to pray. "'Two roads diverged in a yellow wood…"

When he finished, Zion turned to see his mother watching him, eyes unreadable. That wasn't the prayer she was expecting, the one that came next in the ritual. Technically, it wasn't a prayer at all. For a minute he thought she would be upset with him, his mother not one to appreciate the slightest deviation from religious tradition. But then she smiled, tears in her multicolored eyes. A kiss to his cheek followed. "'A Road Not Taken' by Robert Frost, Zion's favorite poem."

With care, Xavier lifted the chest and placed it in front of Lela. She stared at it for a long time, he nor Sage venturing to interrupt. Her hand began to tremble before she removed it from his. A twinge of hurtful rejection flashed through him before he quickly doused it. This was something she had to do on her own—a life battle that even a loving son couldn't protect her from.

With sullen movements, Lela removed first her engagement ring, then her wedding ring. Xavier gulped down his surprise. He wondered what his mother's sacrifice would be, but this, he never conceived. Hell, he'd never seen her without those twin gold-and-diamond bands. And there they were, in her shivering hands, awaiting their fate.

Suddenly, her perfect posture failed Lela. She slumped over the chest, hands on either side, head low with ivory locks covering her weeping face. Xavier made to comfort her, but a terse shake of the head from Sage stilled his movement, reminding him that this was his mother's battle to wage and win. So Xavier did nothing, hating to see how much Zion's death still ripped through his mother. Her tears could have been his own, so deeply did he feel his mother's grief.

But when she finally spoke, Lela's soft words broke through her body-wracking sobs. "May Mother Cosmos guide and protect you, ushering you home and into her bosom." She allowed one ring to slide from her hand and into the chest. But she wasn't yet done. There was a second part of the prayer to recite, giving voice to the dead and a message to the living. "Do not weep for me, my dear ones, for I am in a safe place, a happy place, a place where life begins and life ends. Do not look back on my existence with shed tears but forward and into the sunshine that was my time with you, my dear ones. Be not sad for me. Be not sad for yourself. Be not filled with pain and grief but with anticipation and joy that we will see each other again, reunited in soul, connected forever in heart."

The other ring dropped, and so did Lela Grace. Cradling herself in a ball, she cried and cried and cried. Unable to see his mother like that without offering comfort, Xavier laid down beside his mother. Wrapping his arms around her, he murmured the only thing he could think of to soothe her. "Ab'ba gave you thirty years, all that he had to give. If possible, he would've given you more... us more. It's all right to cry, A'bra. I got you. I will always have you."

CHAPTER FIFTEEN

Precipice

Lela's bedroom was dark, save for two white candles on each nightstand. The door, slightly ajar, admitted a beam of light from the hallway. A reminder that she wasn't alone in her suite. Thirty minutes ago, she'd left Xavier and Sage in the living room pretending to not watch her for the slightest hint of emotional instability.

Exiting the bathroom, she ignored the haggard image of the woman in the mirror. Lela didn't want to see the full-color details of her appearance. She knew what it would reveal—red, puffy eyes and dry skin. Since reaching the heartrending but no longer avoidable decision to arrange her husband's funeral, she'd lost weight she could ill afford to lose. Yet another reason why Lela cast her eyes from the mocking glass, and why Sage had filled Lela's dinner plate with a volcanic explosion of food. By the time she'd tired of her family's hooded, worried glances and urges to, "Eat as much as you can. It'll make you feel better," she was ready to sink into a black hole and disappear into blessed oblivion.

Lela eased onto her bed, wedging the fluffy, circular pillow under her throbbing head. Her green, sleeveless nightgown felt wonderfully soft against Lela's exhausted body. She was well and truly tired. Yet sleep wouldn't immediately come, nor had it since she'd made the dreaded choice everyone, except Lela, knew she must. Despite it all, her mind now told Lela her decision was a sound one, if not shamefully late in coming. But her heart... well, that delicate organ had yet to be convinced.

Crossing hands over her stomach, she entwined her fingers and rubbed them together. As always, Lela anticipated the familiar sensation of the smooth bands.

Nothing.

She caressed her short, thin fingers again.

Nothing.

She'd given them away—her precious rings, Zion's enduring symbols of his love and faith. They were gone, leaving her hands bare and soul bereft. A wave of morbid dawning threatened to consume her, as did the tears she couldn't seem to stop shedding.

Lela gasped. The violent gulping of air burned her lungs, thick and toxic. Her penance, her sacrifice, her soul that would never be whole again. One, two, three, ten, twenty desperate breaths and then a low shrill of pain held as a prisoner of war in her throat. She refused to submit, not now, not again. The Fates help her, if she broke down again, Lela wasn't sure she'd recover.

With resilience borne of years of being a diplomat and political leader, Lela forced herself to relax against the firm mattress. More importantly, she willed calm into her body while fighting the compulsion to bolt into the living room, rip open the chest and reclaim her rings before Xavier made the pilgrimage to the Asheema family vault. Her legs twitched reflexively, fingers balled into tight fists, and nails dug into innocent flesh. Mouth itched from dryness and head thumped an anxious, painful beat, compelling Lela to question whether she would survive what she'd done.

"It's for the best. You must let him go and learn to live again." Those had been her father's sentiments, echoing his own actions of two years ago when her mother had passed on. Lela had known the words to be true, which was why she'd made herself give away her most sacred reminders of Zion—her engagement and wedding rings. But truth was no balm from heartache, from fear, from unsympathetic loneliness.

Loneliness. Yes, Lela had been lonely… was lonely. The thought conjured an image of Ammon, who, to her surprise, hadn't attended the concluding ceremony. Ammon, the man her father had expected her to wed, angry when she'd gone against tradition and his wishes. But, like most loving fathers, he'd eventually come to accept her choice of mate once he'd taken the opportunity to get to know Zion beyond him being "the human who dares to despoil my daughter."

Despite his many fine qualities, Ammon wasn't Zion. *There was only one Zion Grace, and he left me.* Yes, he had. The unreasonable and selfish part of Lela hadn't forgiven her husband for doing so. For breaking her heart when he'd promised to keep it safe—always.

A soft knock came, drawing Lela away from thoughts of a deceased husband and a would-be suitor. Turning her head to the left and toward her bedroom door, she said nothing and the knock came again.

Peeking around the open door, Sage caught Lela's weary gaze. "I thought you would like to know that Xavier has left for the Asheema vault."

Lela smiled, as much as she was capable, considering the uneasy state of her heart.

Sage didn't move. She hovered, watching Lela for only the Fates knew what.

After a minute, Lela understood. Sage had assigned herself the task of checking on her grieving, pathetic sister-in-law before she left for her own suite. Xavier would likely do the same when he returned.

Lela closed her eyes, feeling Sage's concerned, brown orbs wash over her. The stubborn woman, Lela knew, wouldn't leave unless she was convinced Lela wouldn't melt into a shivering mass of tears as soon as she left her suite.

Overprotective. Overbearing. Loving.

"Come in, Sage."

"If you'd rather be alone, I can leave."

Lela would rather be left on her own. Yet, as she took in the melancholic image of her sister by marriage, sister of the heart, Lela understood it was Sage who needed the company. *I may have lost a husband in Zion, but Sage lost a brother.* "Join me." Lela scooted over in bed before raising an eyebrow to Sage.

Removing her shoes, Sage walked to the bed and climbed in. Unsurprisingly, Sage began to squirm, searching for a comfortable spot on a mattress not intended for the soft curves of a human's physique. Lela recalled Zion's first experience on an Asiyan bed, as well as the many nights afterward when he'd conditioned his body to the firm, unyielding mattress.

Once he had, their lovemaking had been… With a jerky shake of her head, Lela revolted against the sensual memory. By the Fates, she wondered when she would be able to think of Zion and their many wonderful years together without feeling like a butcher of dreams was gouging her heart out with a dull blade.

"I don't know how—" Sage started before clamping her lips together in a tight, thin line.

"Zion did it," Lela finished for her. "It's all right. I won't erupt into a fit of hysterics whenever someone mentions his name. This week has been trying, I admit, but it'll get better. Things will be back to normal soon enough, and then you can stop treating me as if I'm a potsherd—fragile and in need of careful handling." Lela's much smaller hand reached out and found Sage's, giving it a quick, reassuring squeeze before letting go. "I know I haven't been myself lately, but I won't break. I accept Zion's death."

"Do you?" The tone bespoke of a woman with doubts, which, in all fairness, Sage had every right to her disbelieving stance. Asiyans were known for their cool heads but hot hearts. Her people forgot nothing, forgave even less, and loved eternally.

"I accepted his death a long time ago. What choice did I have?"

"That's good to hear," Sage said, with the same unconvinced tone. "Now if only you would also accept that you are an attractive woman in the prime of her life. As an Asiyan, you have many decades ahead of you. Why should you spend them alone?"

A familiar argument Lela chose to ignore. If Sage thought to draw her into yet another lecture about "moving on" and "letting go," she would unearth only disappointment. When Sage said nothing more, Lela breathed easier for a full minute. Then her fatigue-clouded mind cleared, and she caught her miscalculation. If she didn't act quickly, Sage would capitalize. Because, by the Fates, the woman was as tenacious as her brother. No way, this side of the cosmos, did Lela intend to discuss Ammon and Unity of Hearts.

Again.

Sage opened her mouth to speak, but Lela interjected with a swiftness that bordered on rudeness. "Since you think your friendship entitles you to poke and prod in my life, then you shouldn't mind what I've done."

Sage moved again, still unsatisfied and clearly uncomfortable. With a grunt of frustration, Sage gave up and shifted onto her side, elbow on the mattress, head propped on her hand. "What are you talking about?"

"Two weeks ago, I had an interesting conversation with one of the ambassadors."

Lela waited for the expected question, and Sage didn't disappoint.

"Which ambassador?"

Her face revealed nothing when she answered. "The Earth Ambassador—Mr. Bayden Vance. He's a fascinating man," Lela added, enjoying Sage's attempt to mask her shocked and worried expression. Zion called it a "poker face." And while Lela never acquired an interest in human card games, she understood his point well enough. Clearly, Sage had not mastered this "poker face."

"As Regent of Asiya, it's your responsibility to speak with the ambassadors. Why would I care if you met with him or whether he's a fascinating man or not?"

"Of course, you're correct. It is my responsibility to have a good working relationship with all of the ambassadors, but," she paused for effect, drawing Sage in, making her work for her false calm, "our conversation had less to do with business and more to do with the two of you."

"T-the two of us?" she sputtered. Sage sat up, eyes big and bold and so much like Zion's.

Lela smiled, not the least bit ashamed for deliberately unsettling her best friend.

"Ambassador Vance seems to be quite enamored with you, even asked if I had any advice on how to best handle a 'woman of Sage Grace's intellect and beauty'."

"He did not say that. God, please tell me Bayden didn't ask you something so inappropriate."

Sage's weak attempt at nonchalance melted away when their eyes met and held.

"Why did you not tell me about the two of you?"

"Why did you go see him?"

"I wanted to 'clear the air,' as the human saying goes, make sure we understood each other."

"What in the hell does that mean?"

"You're my best friend and sister. I'm the Regent." Lela shrugged. "You've secretly dated a man for almost a year."

And I never noticed. What kind of friend am I? How could I have been so blind?

"You've known for a long time, haven't you?"

A nod.

"Why didn't you mention it before?"

"You know why."

"Because you didn't feel it was your place and you respect my decisions, even if you disagree."

"Yes."

Sage cast Lela a cool look. "Is that your way of saying if I continue nagging you about your relationship with Ammon you'll suddenly feel inclined to have sisterly conversations about Bayden?"

There was no relationship with Ammon, despite the sweet kisses they'd shared.

Lela returned the cool look but softened it with a shallow smile. "We could stay up late drinking amber wine while you explain why you turned down his proposal of marriage."

"Goddammit, I can't believe he told you that, too. I told him—"

Lela's laughter stopped Sage's tirade and earned her a mutinous glare.

"You devious little— You had no idea about the proposal. I just gave that right to you, didn't I? And here I thought we were friends."

Sage looked so put out, Lela couldn't stop laughing. And, before she knew it, Sage had joined in, laugh tears rolling down their cheeks— caged birds unexpectedly set free.

"Okay, okay, I get it." Sage wiped her eyes with the back of a hand, smudging her mascara. "Let me out of your Asiyan spider's web, and I'll promise to give advice only when asked and to let you do things in your own time. No more mother-henning." She put her first three fingers up. "Scout's honor."

If "Scout's honor" meant Sage would no longer interfere in her romantic life, such that it was, then Lela had made her point.

"Aren't we a pair?" Sage relaxed back on what used to be Zion's side of the bed.

"A pair of what?" she almost asked, before thinking better of it. Being married to Zion, she'd learned that sometimes it was better not to know. Human sayings were tedious at worse, strange at best.

Sage laced her fingers together and rested them on her stomach. "Maybe I'll just take a little nap while I wait for Xavier to get back."

"You could wait in the living room or return to your own suite where you have a nice, soft, human mattress you can sink into. I told you, I'll be fine."

Sage didn't move, although she appeared none too comfortable. "I'm already here. Besides, has it occurred to you that perhaps I actually enjoy your company, no matter how mean you've been to me the past five minutes?"

"You're a strong woman. I'm sure I put nary a dent in your Grace armor." Lela reached for the folded white blanket at the end of the bed. Unfurling it, she covered them to the waist. "However, I find that I'm glad for the company, even if it means the sharing of my bed."

Sage chuckled low. "Yeah, I think we're a little too old for a slumber party."

"An overnight party in which guests, usually girls, wear night-clothes, socialize, and spend the night at a friend's home. Asiyan's don't have slumber parties."

"Okay, then consider this your first one. Although," Sage said, pulling the blanket to her shoulders and huddling deep, "I think we'll be asleep before the fun starts."

"I'm sure you're right."

They fell silent for several minutes. Even though it was just Sage, it felt strange to share a bed with someone other than Zion.

"What are you going to do about Ammon?"

"I don't know. What do you plan on doing about Ambassador Vance?"

"I have no idea."

"You're right, we are indeed a pair. A pair of women too afraid to let go of the past and step into the future with men who dare to love us in spite of ourselves."

*****

Zion sat on the gray-and-white marble bench in Ammon's plush garden. Yellow, white, and red flowers whose petals were as strong and vibrant as the floral aroma that surrounded him, played with his senses and memories of old. His wife adored flowers, and he'd made it his mission to buy them for her as often as possible. Anniversaries, birthdays, holidays, hell, Zion would use any excuse to indulge his desire to spoil his wife. She'd never understood his need to purchase her trinkets of his affection, although she appreciated every gift he'd given her—a smile, a kiss, a blush of sensual satisfaction.

"Lela." He whispered her name, a sacred prayer on his lips. It had been three weeks since she'd spent the night with Ammon. He could still taste her lips, the kiss that was meant for another. Yet, she hadn't returned to the house, hadn't even called in the week following the funeral. But that was for the best, he reasoned, ignoring the critical gaze of his unwanted visitor.

"I thought you came out here so we could talk and not draw attention to yourself. But you haven't uttered one word."

"Ammon's staff already thinks he's losing it, why add to the rumor mill." Zion leaned over to smell one of the flowers. He didn't know the name of the red bloom, although it reminded him of camellias, with its oval-shaped dark-green leaves and multiple layers of rich velvety petals.

"I must be the only guy in the cosmos who requires this much attention. First Purpose drops me off in this body. I'll call her the ghost of Christmas present. Then Bartek poofs into the living room full of blistering jealousy that had yet to abate. I assume he was my ghost of Christmas past. And now you."

"I know this Earth lore." A nod and then a smile. "I guess that makes me the ghost of Christmas future."

"I guess it does, though I can't quite see you in a red suit and a belly full of jelly."

The Fate of Faith gave him a squelching look, and Zion shrugged.

Gray-and-purple locks ran from head to toe, thick and coarse and humming with magic. The same height as Ammon and as dark as chocolate mousse, a deep red flower that smelled of vanilla and hot chocolate, the Fate's feet were bare, and he wore the lavender ceremonial robe of the Regent of Asiya.

"Why did you come as Regent Etemaad?"

"I thought you would be more comfortable with this form. I could always—"

Zion raised his hand. "Please spare me the afterlife theatrics. I'm not in the mood."

"So I see. Then I'll get to the point of my visit."

"Please do."

"You don't have much time left, Zion, and you seem to be making no effort to win Lela."

"She's unwinnable and," —he swatted a bug away from his face— "I'm willing to lose. In fact, I give up."

"Give up?"

Zion ignored the Fate's surprised and disapproving tone. How dare he and the other Fates toy with his afterlife? Coming to Zion as Lela's beloved Regent Etemaad, the man whose murder brought Lela and Ammon together in a way that gave Zion migraines, couldn't be anything other than purposeful.

And Bartek, Zion snorted. That had to be the Fate of Truth at work. Seeing the Fate of Faith there, as Regent Etemaad, brought Zion's uncomfortable and confusing conversation with Bartek into a depressing kind of clarity. Truth, a liar revealing hard to accept truths.

Until recently, he hadn't thought the Fates of Asiya cruel. He'd never pretended to understand beings like them, yet he always thought them loving and caring creatures. They had, after all, saved and extended his life, which made these current events all the more disturbing and painful.

"Yes, I give up. Now zap me out of this body, or whatever in the hell you and the other Fates did to get me in here."

"If you give up now, you won't be able to return."

"I don't care."

"Do you also not care about your life essence? You cannot go back to that previous existence. You must truly let your family go before you can go to the other side. If you do not, you will be lost forever, Lela unable to meet you when her time comes. Are you willing to take that risk?"

Zion had considered all of his options, weighing each one against his heart and his love for his wife. "I understand the consequences, and I'm willing to accept them. Can we go now?"

He made to stand, but the Fate stilled him, placing a gentle hand on his sleeve. Zion sat and stared at the Fate who appeared exactly like the man he'd seen in paintings, books, and sculptures.

Regent Etemaad was revered on Asiya, almost as much as the Fates themselves. He was their beloved son, slain because he dared to stand on the side of peace and nonviolence. Until sharing a mind with Ammon, Zion had no clue as to the emotional and psychological toll his assassination, and the subsequent war, had taken on the Asiyans, including Lela.

"It was a long time ago, Zion. Don't let it ruin Lela's future."

"What do you mean?"

"Ammon and Lela. That was a very long time ago, and it had nothing to do with you. Don't allow jealousy to interfere with what needs to be done now."

Zion shook his head and gave a low, growl of a laugh. "This isn't about jealousy, although it does make sense why Ammon was selected. I now know they shared something very special. Lela thumbed her nose at the courting rituals and gave herself to Ammon because she loved him. But with me… well, she made me perform each and every godawful ritual, holding off on the Unity of Hearts until our wedding night." His words had turned uncharacteristically bitter, the truth of the double-standard hitting him like a plasma blast to the solar plexus. Why had Lela denied him when she'd given herself so freely to Ammon?

"The situation was very different with them. You've been linked to Ammon's mind long enough to know that. She was young, inexperienced and in love for the first time. She'd also just lost her mentor and father figure."

"I guess you think you have all the answers, huh?"

The Fate shook his head. "Not all, but I know Lela. One misstep on her part, back then, would've damaged her political career and position in her band. Power and politics can be brutal and ugly, Zion, even when no bloodshed is involved. Lela makes few mistakes, but when she does, she learns from them."

"Are you saying Lela viewed her relationship with Ammon as a mistake?"

Faith shook his head again. "No, but she would have preferred to handle it differently, especially the ending. She wasn't meant to be with him then, and Lela knew it. She's always known, even when she didn't understand."

Whether the Fate was fudging the truth to get him to feel better about seeing his wife making love to another man never entered Zion's mind. Despite everything, Zion felt no deception coming from the being. And yes, there were more than a few kernels of jealousy inside him ready to pop. But that wasn't the reason why he was giving up. He could handle a few uncomfortable memories if Zion thought he had a true chance with Lela. But he didn't.

"Even if it means the death of my soul, the diffusion of my essence to the proverbial winds, I won't continue this charade any longer. I won't convince Lela to reignite an affair of the heart with Ammon. He's not the man for her, and you damn well know it. It's cruel, and I'll no longer be a part of this farce. I'll die, cease to exist in any form before I help Ammon draw Lela in any more than she already is."

The Fate of Faith stood, his eyes hardening at Zion's outburst. "You don't understand what you're doing." His voice matched his eyes.

"No, I know exactly what I'm doing." Zion rose to meet the Fate's intractable gaze. "For God's sake, Ammon is dying. Why in the hell would the three of you encourage a relationship between Lela and a man dying of a brain tumor?"

CHAPTER SIXTEEN

The Proposition

"The brain is a highly specialized organ. Everything we do, from our words, to our actions are controlled by our brain. Even our emotions, our feelings, are controlled by the brain, not the heart, the way many people believe. The organ is so complex that some theorists believe we will never be able to fully understand it. We do, however, know that each part of the brain has a specific, important function, often a profoundly important function, and each part contributes to the healthy functioning of our body."

Zion stood in Dr. Paloon's office like one of the Queen's Guards from old, standing in front of Buckingham Palace rigid and unmoving—face blank. A sentry in black-and-purple, reminding one more of a statue than a living, breathing person with a mind, a heart, a life. But Zion's last hope of a life, even the strange one he'd been living for the past month had just slipped through his fingers, like snow brought inside a warm home—never meant to last under such conditions.

"While rare among our people, Commander Ammon, brain tumors are known to come in four basic types with some variation within each type. At this point, you have a grade three tumor, called astrocytoma. An astrocytoma is a glioma that develops from star-shaped glial cells—astrocytes— that support nerve cells."

Dr. Paloon placed his aging hands on his desk, pushed himself upward and stood with weakly disguised effort. His white robe hung tightly on his stout, frail form, the wide sleeves swinging as he made his way around his too-wide glass desk and toward his stunned patient.

"Is there someone I can call?" His age-spotted hand came up to rest on Zion's solid shoulder, his apologetic white, brown, and beige swirl eyes belying the business-like strength of his voice. "Your aide? A member of your band?"

His reply came out as a hiss of brutal reality. "No, no one. No one at all."

Zion stumbled back to the marble bench smartly placed in the center of Ammon's personal garden, a stone path leading from it to the back of the Paladin's solitary home. Indeed, Ammon's family home resided on acres of sprawling green land, enough to accommodate a brood of children, in-laws, and the stray, unwanted family member. But he was its sole occupant, the last of his immediate blood family. No heir. No wife. Who would mourn Ammon when the time came? Who would care?

His band?

Lela?

"Zion," the Fate said, "you don't understand."

No, he didn't understand. Wasted, pointless effort, that's all this had been. He wouldn't do it. He couldn't do it.

"I don't know what game you're playing at, but I want none of it. I don't have to understand a damn thing and I sure as hell won't be part of any plan that will cause Lela more pain."

And she would be in pain, grieve Ammon's loss. If not for Lela's concern and the promise she'd gotten from Ammon, he would've never gone to the goddamn doctor, would've never known the awful truth that would be the Paladin's unfair fate.

Purpose, truth, faith. What a joke. And it appeared to be on him.

Zion pushed to his feet, crossed in front of Faith, and found the stone path, its bright colors and intricate shapes neatly forming a winding road between manicured bushes that were no more than five feet in height and double that in width. Hands clasped behind his back, Zion strolled in silence, taking the path further away from the house and toward the sound of running water.

A minute later, the Fate, wearing the face of Regent Etemaad, stood beside him, hands in his robe's pockets. Zion knew the Fate wouldn't go away until he listened to whatever point he wanted to share with him.

"Speak your piece and then take me from this place."

The men continued to follow the path, the surrounding shrubbery fading into green specks the closer they got to the sound of water, the sun overhead causing beads of sweat to form on their foreheads.

Faith placed a hand on Zion's forearm, and both stopped, looking ahead instead of at each other.

"You must continue. You've made great progress with Lela these past few weeks. Progress Ammon couldn't have made on his own. Asiyans view the cosmos with infinite patience, and Ammon is no different, thinking, in time, Lela would seek him out. But you know better. You know how deep such wounds go and how hard it is to let go of the past in order to form new bonds, build a different future for yourself."

Zion did know, recalling the image of Iman's and his daughter's tombstone. He pushed the unbidden memory away, annoyed at the Fate's simplification of his predicament. The Fate of Faith totally missed the nuance in the comparison. But what did Zion expect from an immortal being? What did any of the Fates know about the human heart? Apparently, very little.

"When I finally let go of Iman and embraced my feelings for Lela, I didn't know I wouldn't have a lifetime to give her."

"Would that have changed anything?"

Zion pulled his arm from the Fate's and resumed walking, his pace brisker than before, Faith, despite his shorter legs, keeping up with him.

"Lela knew what you and the other Fates did for me when I asked her to be my wife." She'd called it a "miracle." And it had been. He'd been blessed then. He didn't feel blessed now.

"Did you honestly think she would turn down your proposal?"

Zion stopped at the clearing. A waterfall with crystalline liquid flowed down a high, flat cliff and into the lake below.

"Yes, I knew she loved me and, no, I didn't really think she would spurn my proposal in spite of my limited lifespan. Lela's not like that. But I now wonder, perhaps Bartek was right. Maybe I should've stepped aside and allowed her to find and fall in love with someone else, an Asiyan who had more time to give her."

Zion made his way closer to the lake, the soft currents rolling from north to south. Colorful fish luxuriated in the translucent water, life so simple for them that Zion felt an irrational pang of envy.

That was the first time Zion admitted that aloud, although not the first time the thought had crossed his mind. It wasn't until the twenty-fifth-year mark that he began to feel death calling him, when the truth of his expiration was no longer some far off inevitability that he could pretend was nothing more than a malicious dream promulgated by Morpheus.

"Is that how you truly feel? Do you think Lela would've been better off without you, without Xavier born of your truth and her faith?"

They found a gazebo near the lake and sat, the weave of the thick vines making for a sturdy spot from which to view the water and surrounding landscape. Zion found himself staring across the lake and at the towering mountain in the distance.

His heart told him she wouldn't have been better without him. And he damn sure knew he would've been miserable without her. Yet, he'd watched her watch him, her eyes growing sadder as he began to fade right before her helpless eyes. If he pushed this relationship with Ammon, encouraged her to give love another chance, she would have to go through that all over again, forced to watch Ammon succumb to a rare and fatal brain tumor.

"I won't put her through that again. At least I had decades to give her. Ammon doesn't even have that. Six months. Nine. Not enough time, not nearly enough."

"True," Faith conceded, toying with the sleeve of his ceremonial robe, "but there are things worse than death."

"Such as?"

"Such as spending decades lonely and in isolation."

Zion twisted to better see the Fate. "What are you talking about?"

For a moment, for the briefest of seconds, the illusion that was Regent Etemaad wavered in its corporeal form, a shimmer of blue energy a nimbus around his body. Then it winked out, bringing with it a deep sigh from a man who was no man at all.

"Lela is very special to the cosmos, to Asiya, and to me." Faith raised his hands, staring at the appendages with a look Zion couldn't decipher. With a shake of his head, Faith dropped his hands. "You have no idea how special she is. She's meant to be so much than she is now. Lela will be given more time, decades, to learn and grow and prepare herself for what is to come. And we don't wish her to spend all those years alone."

Riddles. The Fate spoke in riddles. Zion knew what made Lela special to him, Xavier, and Sage, but what made her so special to the Fates?

"You and Ammon are required. Without you then and Ammon now, Lela cannot, will not, fulfill her destiny, her ultimate purpose in life. She needs him."

Fulfill her destiny? He didn't get it. But Zion did comprehend one thing. And nothing the Fate had said changed the horrible truth.

"Ammon can't do a damn thing to help Lela. He probably won't last the year. Why set her up for more pain, more heartache? I may not like it, but she obviously cares for him. He's not a bad guy, and if it weren't for the war, they would've become mates. I'm no fool. I saw his memories, the time they spent together. She was happy with him, loved him. They could've made it work, but Lela put her guilt and political duties above her personal needs and Ammon allowed pride and anger to cloud his judgment."

Zion thumped his fingers on the back of the bench, the wood carved smooth, triangular patterns embedded deep within, the raised grooves pleasant to the touch.

"Unlike humans, Asiyans mate for life. It's extremely rare for an Asiyan to take another, but it isn't unheard of. While humans, as you know, may wed multiple times during their short lives."

Zion felt himself tense. He didn't like talking about Iman, which he'd been forced to do since returning home.

"You gained something of value, Zion, with each marriage. Both of your wives were pivotal in helping create the man you would become—a wife of truth and a wife of faith. They gave you purpose, supported your dreams."

While he didn't agree with Faith's interpretation of his wives and marriages, he had to admit the notion wasn't easy to dismiss. But what did this have to do with anything? With Lela?

Faith stood, moved to the edge of the gazebo and then turned to face Zion.

"Your first wife, Iman Grace, what did you learn from being married to her?"

Zion leaned back against the bench, stretching Ammon's stocky legs in front of him, crossing them at the ankles. He considered the Fate, then just gave into his persistent gaze.

"I guess, I learned that it was important to work hard, study hard, and fight harder. She pushed me at every turn, always trying to be the best, be number one. Iman was a natural leader, thinking there was no battle she couldn't win."

Yet there were some battles that weren't winnable. It had taken Iman months to admit, what the doctor and Zion had known since the beginning. There was nothing anyone could do to save her, to save their unborn child. The opening of planetary borders brought knowledge, skills, and technology the likes of which humans had never known. But with the good came the bad—crime, overpopulation, pollution, and new diseases.

"She was a soldier with the heart of a doctor. She protected and she cared, and she refused to fall apart when she could no longer deny the truth." Zion swiped at a rebellious tear, angry with Faith for bringing up Iman and angry at himself for being so damn weak. "She was so afraid of falling apart, of losing what was left of her survivor's instinct. She did it for me, and she did it for our baby."

Abortion. The doctor recommended aborting the fetus, but Iman wouldn't hear it, no matter that the procedure would've likely added a few months to her life. But she'd wanted their daughter, wanted to leave a part of herself behind, wanted to replace her spot in Zion's heart with that of their child. So she'd fought until she couldn't fight anymore. Until the virus and the toll of the pregnancy on her weakening body claimed her life.

So yeah, Zion had learned much from his first wife.

Faith nodded and smiled thinly. His sage expression was both annoying and soothing

"And—"

"What did I learn by being married to Lela?" Zion interrupted, not needing the Fate to state the last sentence as if he were incapable of following the flow of a simple conversation. Although, this conversation could've been a lot simpler if Faith had just accepted the fact that Zion had no intention of palming a dying Ammon off on an unsuspecting Lela.

Another nod and an even thinner smile. Faith moved to the other side of the gazebo, reaching out to finger a bloom from a nearby tree, his gaze fixed on the sky.

"She was always meant to be Regent, to rule this planet and care for its people. We placed her soul in a new body, then watched her grow. So many times, so many times. But this time, this time was the last. She is ready."

The Fate of Faith lowered his head, and Zion swore he swayed with the light breeze.

Ready? Ready for what?

The Fate twisted to face Zion, his eyes an unnatural, otherworldly shade of gray. "What about Lela?"

What hadn't he learned from her would've garnered a much shorter list. But Faith didn't want a list, and Zion was tired of talking in circles. This was the last question he would answer.

"While Lela may have been raised and trained to be a politician, she's not simply of the Verity Band. Lela is more than any one band. Life experiences have made her all five—seeker of truth and knowledge, defender of peace and justice, holder of faith and God. Everything I did before, including marrying and loving Iman, prepared me for Lela, for our life together."

The thin smile widened, and the nod was firmer. Faith came to stand before Zion.

"Lela could never love a man who is singular in his thinking. She fell in love with Ammon because he was a fierce Paladin with the soul of a Verity. If she doesn't open herself up to Ammon now, Zion, she'll never know romantic love again. Lela will spend the rest of her days alone. In time, after Xavier finds his mate, she'll gradually remove herself from Asiyan society."

"You've seen this future?" Zion asked, rising to his feet and causing Faith to take several steps back.

"Yes. Lela is needed in ways you can't begin to comprehend. Her destiny is in jeopardy."

Zion rubbed his fingers over his temples, moving them in a circular motion he hoped would stave off the headache he felt hovering behind his eyes.

"If Lela can bring herself to engage in the Unity of Hearts with Ammon, if she opens herself up to that level of emotional and physical intimacy, she'll understand that you didn't take that part of her with you."

"What you're saying doesn't make sense. She'll open herself up to a man who will die on her, leaving her alone the way I did."

"Yes, but she would've proven something to herself that she doesn't even know needs proving."

"And what in the hell is that?" Zion snapped, dropping his hands, the temple massage wasted effort.

"That there is life after Zion Grace. Seven years later and she still doesn't believe that to be the case. Xavier and the Regency are the only things that have kept her from total seclusion. But Xavier will soon have his own family and Lela won't be Regent forever."

The headache was back and with a vengeance, forcing Zion to take refuge on the wooden bench once more. God, could this get any worse? Was there no way out of this mess? A happy ending for any of them? For Lela? Especially for Lela.

Zion slumped against the back of the bench and Fate looked on in concern. "Is there anything I can do for you?"

Taking deep gulps of fresh air, Zion tried to clear his mind and slow his racing heart. "What you're telling me is that if I don't help Ammon, Lela will turn into a recluse. Thereby, denying herself any chance of happiness and a yet undisclosed destiny. On the other hand, if I help Ammon, she'll open her heart to love again, but he'll die before they have a chance at happiness. Yet, she'll remain a strong, needed presence in Asiyan society because she would've proven to herself that grief doesn't have to be eternal and debilitating."

"Now you understand."

"Actually, I don't," Zion said, his voice surprisingly strong considering the dull ache in his occipital lobe, the region where Dr. Paloon said the tumor was located. "It sounds like Lela will be hurt either way. Sure, the second option leaves Asiya in a good position, but what about Lela? Will Ammon's death convince her that she could love a third?"

No answer.

Yeah, that's what Zion thought. Asiyans mate for life, second marriages rare, just like Faith said an hour ago. Lela would do her duty for her Homeworld, for her son, but not for herself. It wasn't fair. Dammit, it just wasn't fair.

"Then heal Ammon."

"We can't."

"Why the hell not? That would solve everything. You healed me. Gave me thirty years. Do the same for him."

"We can't."

Zion glared at Faith, and the Fate returned his gaze with a look of sympathy tinged with what Zion thought to be calculation.

"Can't or won't?"

No change in the Fate's expression, nothing to give away his inner thoughts because Faith damn sure didn't seem inclined to answer his question.

"This is total bullshit. All of it, and you damn well know it."

For a second, Faith's eyes shifted down, and Zion knew, in that moment, that the Fate's played the long game. If given more time, perhaps he could figure out their ultimate plan. But he had no more time, and neither did Ammon.

"Is there a third option, Faith?" The question was asked in desperation. The thought of going through the Unity of Hearts with Lela, seeing the hope for renewed love in her eyes while knowing the same eyes would be shedding tears for Ammon in the near future, was morbidly better than envisioning her locked away in a temple somewhere for God knows how long, wasting away and pining for a husband who left her all too soon.

"Please tell me there's another choice." He was begging now, pride be damned. "I'll do anything, give anything."

More silence, enough to hang a man with, the noose sliding over Zion's neck, Fate of Faith the hangman. Or perhaps his deliverer…?

Eyes lifted, shrewd and all too human. "There is one way, but it has never been done before. The cosmos doesn't take kindly to such interference—balance and all that."

Zion sat straight up, not knowing whether to take that held breath or collapse from the stress of the wretched day.

"Anything?" Faith asked. "You'll do anything, Zion, to see Lela happy?"

"Yes!" Empathic. He was prepared to give up his life essence for Lela, have it scattered to the four corners of the cosmos if it would spare her any more pain. "Just tell me the damn option.

"The cosmos requires balance. Without it, anarchy ensues. There is one way," he said, raising an index finger, "for you to remain here, bond with Lela, and prevent her unhappy fate."

"Why in the hell didn't you tell me this earlier?" He started to jump to his feet, then felt a wave of cranial pain grip him. Deciding that anger, a headache, and standing wasn't a good combination, Zion remained seated, giving Faith his best sardonic glare.

"This isn't an option I'm offering willingly. As it is, I'll have to confer with Purpose and Truth."

Tired beyond measure and not bothering to swallow the pill of a lie the Fate just spouted, Zion rolled his eyes. "Tell me what I need to do." The Fates spoke as one. He knew that, even though he sometimes forgot, easy to do when they came to him one at a time.

"Ammon is the only one who Lela will consider loving, but he's dying. Except for the tumor, Ammon is in perfect health. You, on the other hand, have no body but a vibrant life essence, the same life essence that was taken from you when you died on that wretched road. By merging with Ammon, you could... well, for lack of a better word, *cure* him, staving off his illness with your additional life energy."

That sounded way too good to be true. There had to be a catch.

"What aren't you telling me?"

Faith rejoined him on the bench. "If you merge with Ammon, it won't be as it is now. You will be giving him your life essence. You won't be in control the way you have been. He'll have your memories, but your conscience will cease to exist. All that you were or are will be inside of him, but Zion Grace will be no more. He will have Lela, and you will have nothing." The Fate gave him a pointed look. "Are you prepared to give her up to another man, a man who you know, with time, she'll grow to love, take to her bed, and make her his mate? You see, Zion," Faith said, his brows knitting together, "it's much easier to allow Ammon to die, to accept the ending of your own life, even an electrical one, than it is to let go, to give up your own dream in exchange for the happiness of another, even when that other is Lela. Can you do that for her? Are you strong enough, unselfish enough to release her to love Ammon?"

Selfish? Had he been the selfish one? Was his refusal to let her go the reason why she couldn't let him go, move on with her life? Dear God, he hoped that wasn't true. But the way Faith stared at him, his immortal gray eyes boring into Zion, looking through him, it must be.

It did hurt seeing Lela fight the attraction she had for Ammon. No matter how much he tried to convince himself that Lela was only responding to Ammon because she sensed Zion inside of the Paladin, he could no longer lie to himself. Whatever bond they shared as young adults was slowing reforming, twining its way around Lela's heart. Eventually, she would embrace it, the same way he did when he finally accepted Iman's death, no longer viewing Lela through a widower's grieving eyes, but the eyes of a man very much in love and poised to strike a new path.

"That's the least I can do for her." Zion heard his voice and the lack of conviction. He was no good at this. This hurt like a firebrand to the heart. He would die for Lela, but was he willing to live for her? He was. Without a doubt, he was.

"I'm willing. I love her, more than I hate the thought of Lela falling in love and finding joy with another man. But that doesn't sound like a balance to me. Is there more to this, or do you like referring to the cosmos as if it's some sentient being who will strike me down for mucking things up with my little mortal problems?"

Zion could've sworn the edges of Faith's mouth wrinkled in what could've been a burgeoning smile.

"You're correct, of course. There is a part of this proposition that Ammon must agree—a sacrifice for all parties involved."

Zion wondered what in the hell Ammon would have to agree to that would rival what he was getting in return. A long life with Lela and a clean bill of health, what in the hell could Ammon offer to top that?

"In exchange for your life essence, Ammon will spend his afterlife without Lela"

Zion blinked in confusion, bringing a hand up and to his eyes. He wiped away the perspiration and scratched his forehead.

"I don't get it."

"Upon death, Lela's soul will join with your soul. When Ammon dies, your soul will part from him and wait for Lela's to join you in the Realm of Thuraya."

"Wait. What?"

Faith slowed the cadence of his speech, as if Zion's lack of comprehension had something to do with how fast the words came out of his mouth. If Zion weren't so lightheaded, he would tell the immortal pain in the ass exactly where he could stuff his slow talking.

"Lela pledged her soul to you when you mated. On the rare occasion an Asiyan has taken a second mate, the soul-binding portion of the ceremony isn't duplicated, even when the Dissolution of Fidelity ritual has been performed. That is the reason for all of the courting rituals, Zion. Asiyans need to know that the mate they have chosen is the one they truly want to spend their physical and spiritual life with. For Asiyans, there is no 'till death do us part.' Death is simply an interruption, not an end."

"Are you saying that no matter how many years Lela is with Ammon she will still want to spend eternity with me?"

"She chose you as much as you chose her. Lela could've explored any latent feelings she had for Ammon any time after she met you. She also didn't have to bind her soul to yours, but she did. Those were all her choices, and they had value to her. In time, Lela will come to care for Ammon as a lover and mate, but that won't change the choice she made on your wedding day. For the merging to occur, Ammon must understand this and accept it. He will have her love, her body, part of her heart, but never Lela's soul. That, Zion Grace, will always belong to you."

With those haunting words, the Fate of Faith stood, and placed his hands on Zion's tense shoulders. "Talk it over with Ammon. Remember, you must both agree."

Zion nodded numbly, opened his mouth to ask a question and then closed it.

The Fate was gone, leaving behind a cool breeze and a dazed Zion.

CHAPTER SEVENTEEN

Coming to Terms

Zion felt like an idiot sitting on the floor in the middle of Ammon's living room talking to himself. It had been hours since Faith dropped his little bombshell and vanished like a shadow during an eclipse. And Zion was pretty sure during those hours a lot of pacing, swearing, and smashing of fine crystals had taken place. He'd blacked out, coming to in an upturned living room, not knowing whether he or Ammon had wrecked the once immaculate place. Now, among broken china and glass, strewn papers, cushions, and books, Zion sat, trying to coax Ammon out of his resentful, stubborn shell.

It was one of those humorless moments, Zion thought, when he cleared a path on the messy floor, located a discarded throw pillow and sat. A moment in which he realized, as he attempted to meditate, that he was trying to speak to the very man whose body he'd inhabited for nearly two months. He actually found himself laughing at the harshness of it all. Six weeks and it had never occurred to him to attempt this before. Six goddamn weeks. No wonder the man was silent, refusing Zion's pleas. But this was about more than Zion and Ammon. It was about Lela's future, and Zion needed Faith's plan to work. Meaning, Ammon had to stop being a prideful Asiyan and start talking to him.

"Neither one of us have time for this pissing contest, Ammon." Zion leaned his back against the sofa, legs stretched in front of him. "The Fate of Purpose told me I had two months for this mission. I didn't understand the rush, but I do now. She meant *you* only had two months. I've been here for nearly seven weeks. You're dying, Ammon, and I don't want to find out what happens by week eight if we haven't struck a deal."

Not that he thought Ammon's body would keel over and die by week eight. Dr. Paloon assured him he had time to "get his affairs in order." So what was the deal with the two-month time limit? As Zion waited for Ammon to answer, he spent it thinking. And the only explanation that made any sense to him was that the Fates either knew or had a pretty good idea when Ammon would find out he was dying. And Ammon, they feared, would abandon his pursuit of Lela, failing to get close enough to Lela to complete the Light of Nurzhan and Unity of Hearts rituals before he died.

Enter gullible, desperate Zion Grace, the Fates' pawn in a life and death cosmic game he had no name for. But it didn't matter, neither their motivations nor their secrets. Truth was truth. Zion was dead. Ammon was dying. And Lela, if a compromise couldn't be struck, would live the rest of her long life alone and heartbroken.

So Zion waited. Fifteen more minutes went by before he felt, rather than heard, words sliding along the stem of his brain.

"Why must humans talk so much?"

Finally. Zion wanted to breathe with relief but knew it was far too soon.

"We need to speak."

"Yes, but thinking usually precedes talking or even doing. Have you ever done either before moving forward with a plan? Or do you simply hope that good intentions will lead to a satisfactory conclusion?"

Another insult. Zion ignored that as well.

"Actually," Zion said calmly, swallowing his annoyance, "I've given it considerable thought. And I've concluded that it's a shitty plan that I'm willing to submit to."

Zion thought he sensed a tremor that felt like it could've been a laugh.

"Humans and your colorful language. I too think it's a... shitty plan, but I'm not yet ready to make a decision."

Not ready? How much time did this guy think he had? If he died, they both would, and so would Lela's chance at any type of happiness.

"You heard what the doctor told me. And I also know you've been having headaches for a while now, refusing to seek medical attention, thinking you could tough it out like any good Paladin soldier. Well, I hate to tell you this, my friend, in a few months you'll be just as dead as me—a soul without a body, yearning for a woman just beyond your reach."

The tickle of laughter was gone, replaced by a small fury that sent a wave of pain through Zion's head.

"We're not friends," the strong pulse came. *"You're nothing more than a leech of the worse order. You've taken from me, used my body, my life, my history with Lela to get close to her, to sip from that boarded-up well one last time. You don't deserve her."*

Annoyed calm be damned. "And you do?" Zion snapped. "You, the one who ripped through Lela's heart like a war cruiser through enemy territory. And for what? Because she helped end a war that had taken so many Asiyan lives, a war that almost decimated an entire people? Did you not know or trust her enough to think that she must've had a very good reason for what she did? Did you not love her enough to forgive?"

Another bolt of pain rocked Zion, then another, and another until he was splayed on the carpeted floor, clutching his head in his hands.

"You arrogant, self-serving human. You acted like a little boy, slinking away instead of staying by her side until the end. So afraid to die, afraid to embrace death with your chin held high and your heart free of regrets. But no, you ran away, taking Lela's comfort, security, and love with you. Don't you dare lecture me. You have no moral standing here."

"You're right." The pain in his head began to recede yet Ammon had opened up a scabbed-over wound. "It was selfish of me. A fly-about," he laughed, bitter and self-deprecating. "No one goes on fly-abouts anymore, especially on their deathbed. A part of me knew I wouldn't make it. But a larger part hoped the Fates would grant me a little more time."

It had been so long since he'd seen Earth, Zion surprised how desperately, during the last few weeks of his life, he needed to see that little blue planet one last time. It was the place of his birth. Why shouldn't it also be the place of his death? His parents were buried there, as were Iman and their daughter.

So no, Zion hadn't been thinking of Lela when he decided on his fly-about. Well, not only of her, anyway. As he'd confessed to Xavier, he didn't want his family's last image of him to be that of a silent, unmoving body—a shell and no more.

"I didn't want to die, although I pretended I was okay with it. I was ashamed of myself. I'd been given so much—three decades, a loving wife, and the best son any man could ever want. Yet, in the end, I wanted more. More time. And I couldn't handle the way Lela had come to look at me, watch me with growing sadness and worry. She saw everything I tried to hide, yet she said nothing. But it was all there. Her fear. Her silent helplessness. So I went away, thinking I was strong, thinking it would be better for her if she didn't have to see me die, didn't have to bury her husband and father of her child."

"You were wrong."

"Yes." More than he knew, more than he could've imagined.

"So was I. I too regret the past. Honor and pride in a man know no boundaries of race and space. And I am well acquainted with anger. For too long it consumed me, drove me nearly mad, even after the war ended."

"She would've been there for you, if you had allowed her."

"Yes, I know that now."

"But I'm glad you didn't." Zion ventured to pull himself to a seated position, sliding to the sofa and using it to hoist himself up until he lay lengthwise. "I'm selfish and honest enough to admit that if you'd been a little less Paladin and more Verity in your stance, Lela would've never traveled so much as a peacekeeper, making allies of different races, including humans. Even if she had, she would've been committed to you, viewing me as a political ally and nothing more."

There was no response from Ammon for a long time. Zion knew he was thinking, trudging through memories and emotions, weighing his options. But options were limited to two—life or death. A simple yet complicated choice.

"I unknowingly gave her to you once, now you ask me to give her to you again."

"It seems like I'm the one giving her to you." Zion winced, hating the way that sounded. Lela wasn't an object to be exchanged or bartered like a fine piece of glasswork. She was a person with a mind of her own. And that very acute mind might very well decide against a union with Ammon. One thing was for damn sure, Lela would be appalled, if not insulted, by this entire conversation, the deal they would make before the night was over. Ultimately, no matter what he and Ammon decided, Lela's decision was all that counted.

"My life energy in exchange for your dying one," Zion said. "I don't know how much that amounts to, but I'll bet it's a damn sight more than thirty years."

The words tasted like frothy, bitter coffee, but Zion accepted the rancid flavor, willing to swallow anything to spare Lela more pain and loneliness.

"But you'll have her for eternity. She bonded herself to you. Asiyans don't take such declarations lightly. There is, of course, a ritual to dissolve the bond, but I have no doubt Lela would ever engage in the ritual, even if she desires to become my mate."

Another long silence from Ammon and Zion knew the man was tasting his own bitter brew, deciding if the flavor was too foul to swallow or if he was better off spitting it in Zion's face.

"I've heard humans refer to Asiyans as 'hardheaded.' I had no idea what they meant, but after getting to know the humans who joined the Paladin Band, I realized they meant we could be a stubborn, willful

race of people. While I think the odd term can most assuredly apply to races other than Asiyans, on occasion, it has been true of me."

Zion wanted to laugh then cry. Ammon sounded so much like Lela. He could understand her, by being Asiyan, in a way Zion never had. Even after three decades of marriage, language and other cultural differences still managed to weave their way into misunderstandings, and yes, even arguments.

"I don't want to be stubborn anymore," Ammon conceded. *"And, like you, Grace, I can selfishly and honestly admit that I love Lela enough to use your life essence to have a chance with her, knowing how much it will hurt when she refuses to recite those binding words with me."*

Another lengthy pause, the silence thrumming uncomfortably along Zion's heart.

Was it done? Had they struck that most sacrilegious of deals, come to terms with the insane, the unthinkable?

"What do we do now, Grace?"

Zion sat up and then stood. "I don't know." He didn't want to think about what he'd… they'd just done. He simply wanted it over and done with before someone smacked some sense into him. Sage popped into his mind, and Zion couldn't help but smile, knowing his sister was the perfect person for the job.

But then there was no more time for pondering or second thoughts. Three blinding flashes of light appeared out of the darkness like Haley's Comet streaking across a quiet, morbid sky. And then they were there—Purpose, Truth, Faith. The Fates of Asiya were before him, just as they'd appeared to Zion so many years before, granting him his deepest desire, an unasked-for prayer.

The light hovered about their angelic, unreal forms, their flesh nearly translucent, causing Zion to feel as if he were in the presence of Gods. No Bartek, no Regent Etemaad, nothing so mundane as those deceased men.

Zion's eyes began to water, overcome by the magic and divinity of it all.

In unison, they reached for him. Faith's and Truth's hands fell to his shoulders, while Purpose's found his cheek, a gentle caress from the female Fate. Fathomless eyes sparkled with something akin to relief, satisfaction, pride maybe. Then they spoke, not with lips or tongues, but their joined minds. The words were undecipherable, but the warmth and their love unmistakable.

Then he was falling, falling, falling.

*****

Lela looked around the spacious room and nodded her head in approval. Seated in their finest suits and uniforms were row after row of smiling happy faces—Humans, Asiyans, Amakas, and more. Disparate races intermingled as equals and friends, having come together to celebrate this most blessed of unions.

Lela's watery eyes settled on Sage—her best friend. She'd never seen Sage so beautiful, so happy, so at peace. In fact, Lela smiled broadly, she'd never seen Sage in a dress before. And there she stood, in a room full of friends and dignitaries, in a flowing white wedding dress designed by Lela herself.

"I now pronounce you man and wife," the gray-haired Reverend Hein said, his satisfied smile almost as bright as the one on Sage's new husband's face. "You may kiss the bride."

Bayden Vance didn't need to be told more than once. His lips descended on Sage's, his arms pulling her close, the cheers of the crowd encouraging the ambassador to claim his new wife with much ardor. Xavier was among the loud wedding goers, his exuberant whistles and clapping causing Lela to scoot a little away from him. Only to find herself wedged up against her father, the Asiyan, surprisingly, just as loud as his grandson.

Hasani of Asheema, Lela's father, displayed none of this enthusiasm at Lela and Zion's union ceremony, which made him no less joyful for the couple. Asiyans, as a people, weren't nearly as openly emotional as humans. Yet, on this day, surrounded by so many humans, the Asiyans in attendance, including Hasani, discarded conservative Asiyan decorum for unguarded ebullience.

Hasani could love Sage no more if she'd come from his genetic loins, Bayden subjected to intense fatherly scrutiny once news of Sage's engagement reached the older man.

The crowd stood. The humans and a few High Stars tossed rice as the bride and groom made their way from the altar and down the aisle. The pool of people followed, their cheers dying in intensity and volume until Lela could barely hear them at all.

"Are you coming, A'bra?"

Lela turned to her son, so handsome in his formal captain's uniform. His eyes sparkled with a level of excitement and happiness she hadn't seen in far too long. Something had changed in Xavier since his father's funeral, something profound and freeing. She hadn't asked him the details, the reason behind his exceptional mood.

The particulars didn't matter. All that mattered, all that ever mattered to Lela, was her son's happiness. He'd finally come to terms with Zion's passing and choices on his final days. The how and why were immaterial. Lela was just pleased to see the return of her lighthearted, good-natured son.

"In a minute. Why don't you walk with your grandfather? I'm sure he's interested in hearing about your most recent mission."

Both men beamed.

"I heard you traveled to the Nala System." Hasani slapped Xavier on his back, the much shorter man smiling with so much pride Lela couldn't help but watch the two make their way down the aisle, talking and laughing.

Smiling, Lela retook her seat. She gazed at the stained glass windows, the image of the cosmos encircled in the locked hands of the Fates of Asiya. One word was written under each Fate.

Purpose.

Truth.

Faith.

Three Fates.

Five bands. Affiq: knowledge and understanding. Paladin: honorable warrior. Verity: truth. Euridice: justice. Devdas: servant of god.

One people. One Mother Cosmos.

She closed her eyes, taking in the calm of the chapel and the contentment of the silence.

In spite of Sage's reticence, she had finally accepted Bayden's offer of marriage. It had taken a bit of persuading on his part, and intrusive goads on Xavier's, but, in the end, Sage conceded, no longer able to deny her love for the man or her lonely state. Nathan was gone, but Sage remained, and a heart couldn't stay locked forever.

"Young Grace has accomplished much at such a tender age. Even I hadn't ascended to the rank of captain before my thirtieth year."

Lela smiled and opened her eyes. "That's only because you were jaded and disagreeable."

"Perhaps."

Ammon claimed the space next to her, his smiling eyes filling Lela with unexpected warmth. It had been ten months since the third night of the Light of Nurzhan, neither having ventured to contact the other. Lela, for her part, needed time after Zion's funeral. The thought of continuing the courting rituals with Ammon had been too much for her to cope with.

But there he sat, not in his usual Paladin uniform, but in a well-fitted black tailcoat with a purple shirt, the fine material emphasizing every line of his toned musculature. Ammon was definitely healthier than the last time Lela had seen him. Even his eyes were brighter, different from before. She didn't know quite what it was about him, but Ammon radiated... something. Lela couldn't explain it. But the word *more* kept coming to mind, the longer she gazed upon him.

"I wanted to thank you," Ammon said, those bright, different eyes holding her own, her body having the strangest reaction to his nearness.

Lela shook herself, forcing her mind to focus on his words. "Your recommendation made all the difference."

"I only spoke the truth, when asked."

"Yes, but you were asked, for a recommendation, twice before. Why me?"

"You were the ideal choice." She glanced back at the image of the cosmos on the windows. Purpose. Truth. Faith. Lela turned back to Ammon. "You were ready."

"Was I not ready to be Chief Magistrate of the Paladin Band those other two times?" It was a genuine question, not born of ego or spiteful accusation. This Lela knew with certainty.

"No, you were not." Lela touched his hand, placing hers overtop of the one resting on his knee. "On three occasions members of the Council of Magistrates came to me, seeking my advice as to who should replace your brother."

Selecting a Chief Magistrate was a decision best left to each band. But when a band couldn't agree, the Regent was often consulted. Such was the case with the Paladin Band. After Ammon's father had retired, his brother secured the nomination, holding onto a fragile alliance within the band his entire tenure. Yet, when he died, a decade ago, no clear nominee emerged, leaving the Council without a member and the Paladin Band no representative in Asiyan government.

"Ten years, Lela."

"I had no honest recommendation to make. The Council needed a voice that could speak and listen in many tongues, not just one. And the Paladin's required a strong yet open-minded leader."

"And you believe I'm the one, the Paladin leader our government needs?"

Ammon's other hand came to rest above Lela's, the heat of him holding her hand causing her heart to race and flutter.

"I always thought you would make an excellent Chief Magistrate. But you wanted it for the wrong reasons. Pleasing a short-sighted parent was never a good motivator."

"What made you change your mind?"

The grip on her hand tightened, followed by a softly stroking thumb. Lela swallowed, wondering what it was they were talking about and how Ammon had this effect on her. She gave herself a mental shove, and continued.

"I've watched you over the years, especially since becoming the leader of your band. You've brought them out of the darkness and showed them the light and benefit of interracial cooperation. It has made leading a planet, with scores of off-worlders, infinitely easier and more productive. They no longer hold onto the fears and concerns from the war, no longer angry and cautious of anyone not Asiyan. Their new outlook has impacted the entire planet, and it was all due to your refined and patient leadership."

Ammon gave a bemused laugh. "I think, my dear Lela, you give me too much credit. I simply, after too many years, began to follow your lead. I listened to your words, observed your selfless actions, and found wisdom in them—truth."

"Can a female not give a male a compliment without having him turn it around on her?"

"Can a male not give a female thanks without her turning it around on him?"

Lela gave a shallow bow of her head, acknowledging his point.

Ammon stood and reached his hand down to Lela. She took it, allowing him to assist her to her feet. "May I escort you to the reception, Regent Lela of the House of Asheema?" Ammon asked, with what Lela couldn't help but view as a very un-Asiyan-like flirtatious tone.

She looked up at him, and his eyes held the same flirtatious sparkle as his voice. Lela smiled demurely. "It would be my pleasure, Chief Magistrate Ammon."

Ammon gave her his arm and Lela accepted, linking her own through his and walking down the aisle, refusing to acknowledge how they appeared. Luckily, only the two of them remained in the Hall of Concord's chapel, no one present to see how they looked together.

"I've missed you," Ammon whispered in her ear when they reached the doors to the banquet room.

"I've missed you as well."

"I heard the Botanical Gardens have a new exhibit. Are you interested in taking a stroll with me around the new Water Garden?"

Two High Stars on guard opened the heavy glass doors for them, Lela nodding her appreciation. They entered, arm-in-arm, to music and the astounding sight of Sage and her new husband regaling the crowd with a lively dance. Her sister-in-law's wedding dress was hiked up past her knees, allowing Sage plenty of enthusiastic movement.

Lela laughed and turned to Ammon who, to her surprise, was staring down at her with a smile that didn't belong on his face. She almost stumbled back, but his hands were there, holding her steady against him.

Lela reached up and touched his cheek. She smoothed her slim, trembling fingers over his bright, different eyes and down to his oddly familiar smiling mouth. She brought her other hand up to his chest, Lela's eyes entranced by Ammon's, and with great difficulty, Lela parted her mouth to speak.

But the only words she managed to say were, "It's not possible."

CHAPTER EIGHTEEN

A Paladin's Fate

"So, who's the man who keeps darting looks your way?"

Ambassador Bayden Vance, a full foot taller than Lela, nodded over her shoulder. She didn't bother to turn in the direction his eyes had settled, for she knew to whom Sage's new husband referred.

An instrumental piece—violin—played in the background. Its slow, melodic cadence compelled the guests to shift from the up-tempo jazz swing, of a moment ago, to a languid sway. Lela had one hand lightly gripping Vance's palm, while the other rested on his strong shoulder.

He smiled down at her, the dimple in his right cheek pronounced and, according to Sage, one of Bayden's most "adorable" features. Asiyans didn't have dimples, and Lela had no opinion as to whether the natural indentation in his flesh made him more attractive than any other male. Yet, the fact that Sage had made the comment at all, spoke to her absolute besottedness with the man.

The dance was his idea, which she'd accepted with growing affection for her brother-in-law. Unbeknownst to him, Bayden had gifted Lela with a timely escape, a desperate flight from both Ammon and her disturbing thoughts. Had she only imagined the Grace eyes and Zion's boyish grin? On Ammon's face?

Impossible.

Right?

"That would be Chief Magistrate Ammon. He's a—"

"Oh, so that's him."

Lela looked up at Bayden, and he down at her, his downturned eyes shining with barely suppressed humor.

Oh, he and Sage would make an interesting mated pair indeed. With Sage's conservative, tough outer layer and her soft, playful inner layer, to Bayden's spirited intelligence, quick deductions, and endless streams of mirth.

"I kind of figured it was when the two of you strolled—arm-in-arm—into the reception together. And if I wasn't certain then, the way the man has been stalking you with his eyes for the last half hour, and you pretending not to notice, I would be positive by now."

Of course, he would've noticed. Even if Ammon wasn't so obvious. With Bayden's military background, she expected nothing less of him.

"Sage?" she asked him, knowing her sister-in-law had likely filled him in on some of the details between Ammon and herself. Not that Lela worried that Sage would've divulged the more personal aspects of her relationship with Ammon. Their friendship and sisterhood left no room for such betrayals of trust.

"You got it."

"How do you think I convinced her to wear a dress to her wedding?"

The quietly hypnotic violin solo transitioned into an even mellower flute duet. More people crowded onto the dance floor, the leisurely thrumming of the human music not so different from Asiyan musical taste.

"A compromise?"

Lela shook her head. "Blackmail. Sage said she would wear her High Star's formal uniform to the wedding if I didn't allow her to invite Ammon… with boots," Lela added in disgust. "You would've been appalled to see your bride traipse down the aisle as if she were preparing for a military incursion. Besides, it's just not done."

Bayden laughed, his tone rich and high. A second later, Lela was also laughing.

"She would've, too, if for no other reason than to annoy you and to let me know that she's too old and stubborn to change. Accept her or reverse course."

He was right. Sage was definitely set in her ways. But she was also warm-hearted beyond measure, which her new husband well knew.

Lela cast Bayden a warm smile, looking forward to him being a member of her family. While she knew him well professionally, as she did all the ambassadors, she was only now beginning to know the man that had stolen her friend's heart.

"It turned out to be a white dress in exchange for an invitation." A dainty shrug. "It's her wedding and reception, Sage had a right to invite whomever she wanted. I had no claim over such a decision."

"Except that Sage and the magistrate aren't exactly friends, and she would've had no legitimate reason to invite the newest member of the Council of Magistrates to her wedding and reception."

Bayden glanced over her shoulder again. "He's still watching you."

"I know."

The tall man moved them around the dance floor, his strides amazingly graceful for a man of his large size—six foot three and two hundred twenty pounds. When they finally stopped, they were on the other side of the room.

Bayden laughed, then spun Lela so that she faced the opposite direction. And there was Ammon—watching, waiting.

"He's relentless. I didn't know if that would work, but the Paladin has it bad, Lela. You've got yourself an old fashioned stalker." It was meant as a joke, but Lela knew something the human ambassador did not.

"He's chasing me," Lela whispered to herself, dropping her eyes to avoid Ammon's.

"It wasn't my intention to upset you. I only meant your magistrate is clearly taken with you, just like Sage said he was. But if he's making you uncomfortable, I'll go have a nice, long talk with him."

Under the fog that had clouded her mind once Lela realized what Ammon was doing, she recognized the thinly veiled threat in Bayden's words. His protective tone was one she'd never heard from him before.

"That won't be necessary. I started this. I ran, now he's chasing me."

"Chasing you?"

Lela nodded and then sighed. "It's a Paladin Band courting ritual."

Humor skated the edges of his mouth and eyes, before he leaned down and whispered in her ear. "You call stalking a woman around a dance floor a courting ritual? Is he a lion in heat or doesn't he know what century this is? Modern women may still like the strong, silent type but that's taking the cliché a bit far."

If they were both human and this Earth, Bayden would be correct.

"You don't understand. It's an ancient ritual that harkens back to the first Fates of Asiya but..." Lela trailed off. There was no point in explaining the Gahiji to him. It wasn't as if she was an expert on Paladin Band rituals, nor would Bayden find the concept of a submission ritual palatable to his overprotective male taste. But it wasn't the type of submission he would think of it as, and Lela would have to make her explanation quick before the former military general took matters into his own hands. In the end, it simply wasn't worth the stress headache.

The music stopped, and people began to make their way back to their tables, waiters already bringing out the first of three courses of meals.

Sage came to claim her new husband, an enchanting and undeniably happy grin on her face. Bayden extended his arm, and Sage clasped her hand on the inside of his elbow, giving Lela a warm smile before they made their way to the head table where they would be served. Bayden gave her one last scrutinizing glance over his shoulder.

She waved in a way that conveyed the message that she was fine and Ammon of no threat.

Apparently satisfied, he allowed his wife to lead them through a throng of people, the calming music echoing his concerned retreat.

Lela walked in the opposite direction of everyone else. She passed the threshold of the banquet room, made her way down a well-lit corridor and turned right, then took a lift up two levels. Once off the lift, she walked down the hallway and toward her office suite. She spoke to the guards on duty, letting them know to expect a visitor and to let him pass when he arrived.

*****

"Lights at fifty percent," Lela said, when she entered her office. She'd considered raising the lights to full capacity, when she heard soft footfalls behind her, but fear prevented her from doing so. Did she really want to see Ammon's face, brought into stark relief by bright lights? Was she ready to believe the inconceivable, the impossible?

"Have I told you today how beautiful you look in your ceremonial gown? I've always thought you looked especially regal when you wore that particular shade of purple."

Was he flirting with her? Asiyans did not flirt. And had he actually complimented her on her clothing? They didn't do that either.

She turned to face him. "Are you feeling unwell, Ammon?" Perhaps he wasn't as healed from those headaches as he appeared. Maybe she should increase the lighting, check for herself. "Lights at—"

"We need to talk, Lela."

"—eighty percent," she finished. "About what?" It was a futile, worthless question meant to stall.

Gracefully, he edged closer to her. One step forward.

Two steps back.

Forward.

Back.

Forward.

Back. To her dismay, Lela's desk put a halt to her not so subtle retreat. Cautiously but persistently, Ammon placed one large hand, then the other, on each side of Lela's face. She gulped, seeing a flicker of masculine awareness in his eyes.

Before she could protest, question, or move, Ammon slanted his mouth across hers, kissing Lela with soft, sweet but demanding lips. His right hand slid to the nape of her neck, pulling her even closer, his muscular chest rubbing against her ever-tightening nipples.

Lela was torn between pushing him away and giving in to the slow ache starting to build in her loins. She hadn't felt this way in so long. Didn't think she would ever experience such carnal desire again. Yet each time she did, Ammon slowly but surely coaxing Lela out of her shell, overwhelming guilt wracked her. This sensation, this slow burn of arousal, hadn't been felt by Lela since the last time she and Zion made love.

How could Ammon make her feel like this? How could he ignite a long dead flame? A flame that once burned only for her beloved mate, was now set anew by the man claiming her mouth with hungry possession.

Confused, Lela struggled, hands sliding between their bodies and shoving with force. Nothing happened. Ammon only repositioned his arms, wrapping them tighter around her waist, his mouth and tongue gliding to her pulsing throat and sucking.

Just the right spot, with just the right amount of teeth and tongue. He shouldn't know this about her, but he did.

His breath caressed her warm neck. His whispered plea stroked her much lower. "Submit."

"I—I can't." The words were a struggle, and so was the ability to stand upright. Her knees, she knew, would give way soon, so light-headed and boneless was she.

Ammon's lips roamed up her neck, to her cheek and around to her ear. His tongue darted out, its point circling the shell of her ear and then dipping inside just long enough to bring an unbidden moan from Lela. She felt him smile against her ear, and she clenched her fists, angry for giving in that little bit.

"Submit," he said again, then twirled his tongue around her lobe, his mouth incredibly hot, wet and torturously erotic.

She shook her head and pushed at his brawny chest again. Nothing. The man was as heavy and solid as a war cruiser. Unless Lela wanted to fight him for her freedom or scream for help from her High Stars, she was trapped. In more ways than one.

Frustrated and aroused more than she was willing to admit—to him or to herself—Lela switched strategies.

"This isn't the proper execution of the Gahiji."

"Much you know," he said with a mocking laugh. "You're Verity, not Paladin." He raised his head from her ear, eyes twinkling with more than mischief. But that tiny distraction proved to be enough for Lela to breathe and think clearly without the thumping of her heart in her ears.

"There is no 'proper execution' in the way that you mean, Lela." He smiled at her, then brushed his lips across hers with sensual confidence. "There are no ceremonial clothing, lighting of candles, or prayers to the Fates. Only the hunt." A languid tongue rimmed her slightly parted lips. "Only the chase."

Lela was stunned, and it was all the distraction Ammon needed. His tongue deftly breached her lips, sliding inside with nary a defense from her. And, *ohhhhh*, where had he learned to tongue kiss like that? He drove deep, exploring with carnal tenderness and ripping another submissive moan from her. If she could curse him, or her weak body, Lela would have, in all the languages she knew. But she could do neither, her tongue engaged in a duel she was unwilling to lose.

She would not submit.

After long, glorious seconds, Ammon ended the kiss, his breaths coming in short gasps.

So were hers.

"Submit."

"No." Her voice was low and defiant. But Ammon's eyes were just as resolute, maybe more so.

"I want you and," he said with a pompous smile, "you want me. You're just too afraid to admit it, too afraid to lose yourself to love again."

"I'm not afraid of losing myself to love," she countered quickly, too swiftly to convince herself or Ammon of the veracity of her declaration. "The Gahiji is a Paladin Band ritual, and, as you so clearly stated, I'm Verity Band. Since it's the female who initiates all courting rituals, regardless of the band, I do not have to abide by the ritual of another band to which I am not bound."

There, he couldn't argue against that.

Lela shoved against his infuriatingly solid chest, expecting him to release her. Ammon was a man of honor, upholding the norms and mores of their people. And she'd just given him a logical argument. He should have released her. But he didn't, his massive arms still snaked around her waist, an overconfident smile still plastered on his dangerously handsome face. If she weren't mistaken, it might have even grown wider, more of his white teeth showing.

"Very good, Lela. I've always admired your tactical mind. It's an asset to our people, and why the planet has flourished under your leadership."

Ammon's arrogant compliment unnerved Lela, and she knew she'd erred in some important way. But she didn't know how.

"What you've said is true—"

"Great, then you can let me go."

"—except in this case," he said, ignoring her interruption.

Lela gave Ammon a puzzled glare, and he ignored that as well.

"A female may initiate a courting ritual from another band, if it is her desire to accommodate the Asiyan male in question. This practice, as you know, only arises when the couple is from different bands. Such compromises are not uncommon. More importantly, it shows that the couple is already committed to bridging the differences that may divide them if they continue with the union."

Lela did know this. In fact, she'd engaged in numerous foreign mating customs when she decided to join with Zion, and he'd done the same. It simply made sense, but it didn't here. So far, the one ritual she and Ammon had engaged had been from her band.

"There you are mistaken, Ammon. I did not initiate the Gahiji with you."

He gave her that same annoying smile. The one that said she was a fowl in an invisible cage.

"You began the ritual the morning after the third night of the Light of Nurzhan."

Lela thought back to that day, the conversation they'd had and the revelation of Ammon's forgiveness. She didn't remember anything she could've done that would lead him to believe she wanted to engage in the Gahiji ritual. They kissed, and she went home.

Wait. She'd kissed him. Realization dawned like a shooting star. Lela had done more than that. She'd challenged Ammon, taunted him with her adopted human practices. She'd questioned whether he was capable of accepting a mate who wasn't entirely Asiyan in thought and actions. And she had done more.

"The tongue kiss?"

Ammon nodded. "You offered a challenge, dared me to accept and I did."

He hugged her impossibly tight, every part of them touching except their faces. Sensual heat swam through Lela, Ammon's body exquisite in its raw temptation.

"I submitted to you." Ammon's voice came out low and husky in the otherwise silent office. No one else, save for a handful of guards, were on this level of the building this time of the evening. No one else around to witness Lela's looming defeat. "You wanted me to and I did. I accepted what you offered. Are you now saying the kiss meant nothing to you?"

It was a perfectly worded tactic, one that would either dishonor her, if she lied, or rip away another layer of protection for her heart. There weren't many layers left, if any at all.

"I meant it," Lela conceded. "I needed to know if you could accept me as the woman I am today, not the woman-child I was when we first fell in love."

"That was important to you?"

"Yes."

"Why?"

Lela closed her eyes and tried to dislodge the lump in her throat, slow her pounding heart. When she reopened them, she felt no calmer for the seconds she'd taken between his question and her response. "Your opinion matters to me." Her gaze held his when she admitted, "More than it should." Lela shook her head, forcing the words and truth out her mouth. "You stir me in a way that only Zion ever has. I didn't think it was possible for me to feel that way with anyone else."

"And it frightened you?"

"Yes. I vowed to always love him," Lela admitted, feeling that old familiar twinge of guilt churning in the pit of her stomach. She pushed it away, refusing to submit to that as well.

"Yet you care for me."

It was a statement, not a question, but Lela replied with a soft, "Yes."

Ammon's lips grazed her cheek, his right hand coming up to twine in her thick ivory hair. "Is there no room in your heart for me, Lela? I think there is, but you have to be willing to submit."

"You want me to submit to you?" she asked, inhaling with a sharp gasp when Ammon's left hand started the most enticing massage across her lower back and hip.

"You misunderstand, my love. I don't expect you to submit to me but to yourself."

She didn't understand, and her gaze must've registered as much, prompting Ammon to mutter, "Verity Band." The smile that followed let her know that he was, uncharacteristically, playing with her in the way of courting couples. "Do you know the best kind of victory, Lela?"

"One that doesn't involve humiliation and bloodshed."

Another, "Verity Band," crossed his lips, Lela too entranced by the feel of Ammon's hands on her to defend herself and her band at the teasing insult.

"That is a good response and one I would expect from you. But you're overlooking the best and most rewarding answer. You see, Lela, there are many types of victories, and just as many ways to make a man or woman submit. But the best victory, the most sacred form of submission, is the one engaged in willingly."

Ammon's roving hands stopped, his eyes and tone turning serious. "The kiss wasn't the true challenge, Lela, only the vehicle. After a long war with the Lumerians, Asiyans trusted few off-worlders, especially those we didn't have a relationship with before the war, like humans. Yet Grace married you and relocated here knowing that he may not be accepted fully by Asiyans. That he could, quite possibly, be shunned by the more xenophobic groups among us. He had and raised a child with you, secure in his humanity and your union that such a biracial offspring would be surrounded by love, not narrow-minded prejudice."

His thumb stroked her cheek, coming away wet with tears she hadn't known she'd shed. "You were unconsciously asking whether I was willing and able to accept that you would always love Zion Grace because he is the other half of your soul. You wanted to know if I could submit to the fact that you could grow to love me, be devoted to only me, and be happy with me as your mate, but never give that most sacred part of yourself. The part you've already gifted to another."

Lela closed her eyes, unable to look into Ammon's a moment longer. He had read her heart, even when she did all in her power to keep it from him. A part of her felt ashamed. Ashamed she couldn't give Ammon what he wanted, what he deserved.

Lela couldn't. And that was the true reason she hadn't contacted him after Zion's funeral. Why should Ammon settle for a woman who would never love him completely, the way he deserved to be loved? And what type of person would she be if she allowed him to make such a sacrifice?

More tears fell and those soft lips of his touched hers again.

"I've submitted to myself, accepted this fate. You, Lela of Asheema, are my one true love. Will you submit with me? Accept our shared fate and admit that I am your love until death takes your soul and rejoins it with Grace's."

More tears and a firmer, more demanding kiss, Lela's answer caught in her throat and on quivering lips. The last barrier of protection crumbled, a quiet destruction of all that kept Lela inside and Ammon's love and promises of a bright future outside.

"I submit, to myself, to you, to our future."

He was kissing her again, burning a path of uncontrollable desire down her mouth, to her breasts and nipples, and much lower.

"Ammon," Lela moaned, her head thrown back, accepting the passion she long denied herself. Accepting him. Accepting her life without Zion Grace, knowing she would see him again.

"I love you."

Her heart burst with joy.

Lela eased out of the passionate embrace, found Ammon's handsome face with her hands, and offered her final submission. "I love you, Ammon."

She did. Not with a young woman's innocence, or a widow's lonesomeness, but with an experienced woman's cautious hope.

Love. Yes, a shy emotion that, once cultivated, would grow and flourish.

His entire face lit up, unsuppressed elation encircling them both.

Ammon ran a teasing hand over Lela's shoulder and down her front, stopping over a breast, cupping, massaging. She gulped, and her eyes fluttered close. It had been too long. Then there was more kissing, Ammon pressing his aroused body into Lela's, and Lela nearly atop her desk in what she imagined was a very undignified position for the Regent of Asiya.

"Lela, where are you?" Sage's raspy, annoyed voice came over the intercom in Lela's office.

At her abrupt voice in the quiet room, Ammon and Lela jumped apart, as if Sage had just walked in on them and they adolescents caught doing something wholly inappropriate.

"Clearly you know where I am, Sage," Lela replied, a false calm smothering her overheated reaction to Ammon's mouth and hands.

"I meant, why are you in your office instead of at the reception? We're about to cut the cake and that son of yours keeps trying to put candles on it, saying he needs to know my exact age just in case that many candles set off the sprinklers."

Ammon laughed, and Lela shushed him.

"And," Sage said, Lela hearing the rustle of fabric, "this damn dress is about to undergo a major alteration. I swear, if you don't get back here and quick, the bottom half of this thing won't make it through what's left of the reception."

Lela smiled at Ammon and knew it was time for them to leave the privacy of her office. There would be more time for exploration later. They had waited this long, there really was no rush, except, of course, for the fact that every inch of her tingled with reawakened sensual need. How did Ammon know her body so well?

The few times they were together, many decades ago now, couldn't have been enough for him to play her body as if she were his personal instrument. Even then, as a young woman new to physical intimacy, Lela hadn't yet discovered all her body craved—and how. Yet Ammon...

"I'll be right there, Sage, and don't destroy Xavier or your wedding dress while I'm en route."

"I make no promise on the nephew front." More rustling and then loud swearing. "Bayden, why are you adding more candles to what's supposed to be our wedding cake? I swear I'm going to—"

The connection ended.

"I think I better get back." Lela reached her hand to Ammon. He took it, lacing his fingers through hers.

"If we go in like this, everyone will know." Ammon gestured to their entwined hands.

"Yes, well, I think the only person who is surprised by this development is me."

"I think you're right."

Ammon gave her one last kiss—a deep, knee-weakening one—before they left Lela's office.

CHAPTER NINETEEN

Confession

They were all stunned. Shocked. And Ammon was the cause. Xavier seemed torn between wrapping his robust arms around Ammon in a debilitating hug or using his very long and strong fingers to throttle him for ruining what should have been a simple family dinner welcoming Sage home from her honeymoon.

Ambassador Vance, for his part, was a very wise man indeed. He kept all thoughts to himself, continued to eat, while his wife roared, swore, and paced her displeasure from one end of the dining room to the other.

"What in the hell were you thinking, Ammon?" Spinning to face him, Sage answered herself. "You weren't thinking. You can't just drop a bomb like that and think we'll all smile, nod, and say, 'That's great, welcome to the family, say hello to Zion for us, now pass the chicken, please.' "

And then there was Lela. Ammon glanced in the direction Lela had gone—presumably to her bedroom. The urge to run after her raged deep within. The protective soldier in Ammon compelled him to his feet when Lela ran from the room. But a growled warning of, "Don't follow," from Xavier halted his movement. The "or else," was implied in the angry and, yes, hurt look the young man leveled on him.

So he returned to the table, and there he sat with a nervously eating Ambassador Vance, an entranced Xavier, and a crazed female who cursed the likes he'd never heard before—male or female, human or Asiyan.

Ammon had never felt so uncomfortable, but he hadn't told the truth to make himself feel relaxed, good, or even happy. He was already happy, had been in that ecstatic, blissful state the last month—ever since the day of Sage's wedding, when Lela submitted.

I love you.

Those beautiful, long-awaited words reverberated in his pain-free head. For once, she'd kissed him. *Him.* And there was no guilt, no shame, no regret he could detect in her eyes.

I love you.

A month. A month of quiet talks and long walks. A month of brief, stolen lunches and extended, glorious dinners. A month of sweet hugs and kisses and burning, suppressed passion. A month of happiness. A month of lies.

I love you.

Not a lie exactly, but not the truth either. Telling Lela was never part of the pact between Zion and Ammon, but the more time he spent with Lela, courting her the way he always dreamed, the more the desire for her to know the truth weighed on him. Until today, when he'd decided finally to lay down his burden.

If this fragile, new relationship with Lela was going to be built on a foundation of marble, instead of marsh, they all had to know the truth. They all had to accept. There was no shame in what he had done. And there was no man who loved his family more than Zion Grace. They'd needed to know that as well.

If the truth ended in the dissolution of Ammon and Lela's courting, then so be it. She had a right to know, full disclosure necessary and so utterly dangerous.

But Ammon was never one to run from himself or inevitability. And it was inevitable, this metaphysical, spiritual truth that swung like a pendulum between them all. One swing to the right and Lela looked into his eyes seeing Ammon. Two swings to the left and she glimpsed Grace. An inevitable, wholly improbable truth that Lela couldn't or wouldn't entertain. But it was there between them, in her curiously probing eyes.

I love you.

And he loved her. So much, in fact, he would risk it all. Tempt fate and the cosmos itself by giving Lela the ultimate gift—truth, verity.

"You're driving us all crazy, Sage, with that pacing." Ambassador Vance reached for his wife, arm outstretched, smile thin but loving. "Please sit. Your anger and worry aren't helping an already tense situation."

The ambassador held her stern, agitated gaze, and slowly, almost imperceptibly, those hostile eyes of hers softened. Sage placed her hand in that of her husband's and allowed herself to be pulled gently to him before reclaiming her chair.

Amazing.

Apparently, Xavier thought so as well, a muffled "Snake charmer," coming from his end of the dining room table.

And there they all sat, stilled tongues and squared shoulders, cool, appraising eyes locked onto Ammon. Great. Wonderful. Now, if only Lela would return, her gorgeous eyes would make it a consensus, bringing the ratio to four against one.

Ammon shrugged inwardly. Manageable odds, he thought.

Silence—long and nearly soul crushing.

Ammon felt as if they were all waiting for something. For him? What else did they expect him to say? Except for revealing that Sage knew more than she'd led on, he'd told them everything. Sage could make her own confession, although, Ammon was pretty sure Lela and Xavier would put all the pieces together.

Xavier stood and walked to stand beside Ammon. The young man towered over him, his eyes searching Ammon's face and causing a part of his soul to twist in fatherly recognition.

It took all of Ammon's self-control not to stand and meet the silent challenge, Xavier's standing form a position of power to Ammon's seated one. But Ammon didn't move. In spite of his posture and menacing visage, Xavier wasn't truly challenging him. Many a battle had been lost and wars waged over perceived insult and pride.

Ammon refused to be a casualty. Nor would he allow Xavier to fall prey to his own conflicted emotions. So he submitted, accepting the silent interrogation, their eyes locked—not in a battle of wills, but in a battle for understanding, for truth.

And at the end of that long, dark and lonely tunnel, Xavier slowly emerged, his right hand creeping to his side and finding Ammon's hand. Xavier's hand was warm and sweaty, his long, thin fingers wrapping around Ammon's and squeezing.

"Thank you." The words came out in a whispered sob. But it was the unspoken ones that ripped through Ammon's body, tearing at his heart with the force of a late-in-season winter storm—fierce, wild, and unexpected.

Thank you, Ab'ba, for coming back, for loving me, for being selfless. And thank you, Ammon.

He heard them all and Ammon stood, pushing the chair back. He and Xavier faced each other, tears in their eyes, understanding conquered, truth achieved.

Then Ammon was being hugged. And all those years of loneliness, a man without a mate, a child, a family of his own, was poured into him. An empty shell filled with an invisible but substantive glow of life— Xavier's life, forgiveness, and acceptance.

When young Grace released him, Ammon knew the power of a son's love. In that moment, he truly knew Zion Grace, the human soul that fueled his Asiyan body.

"Thank you," the young man said after releasing Ammon. Xavier took a step back and looked over his right shoulder at his aunt. "Thanks for helping Ab'ba get his data quartz to me. That message meant the world to me, Aunt Sage."

Xavier faced her fully, placed his balled right hand over his heart, then lowered his eyes and bowed deeply at the waist. A Paladin gesture of upmost respect for a superior officer, not often, if ever, given outside of the Paladin Hall. Sage stood and mimicked her nephew, her bow not as deep as Xavier's but just as sincere, just as deeply felt.

Xavier returned his attention to Ammon, his face serious but warm. "You'll find A'bra on the balcony. It's her favorite place when she wants a bit of solitude to think and admire the beauty that is our planet's capital."

Ammon hazarded a look at Sage, who was paying them absolutely no attention, her husband having captured both her attention and her lips. Ammon shook his head, the image of a hostile, belligerent Sage much easier to swallow than the weak-kneed, in love newlywed before him.

"Get a room you two," Xavier said laughing, then held his stomach and made a retching noise. "I'll never be able to keep my dinner down if you keep doing that. Ewww."

The joking Xavier moved away from Ammon, his voice becoming more animated as Sage responded to his taunting.

"You were gone a month. That should've been more than enough time to dot every I and cross each T. Although," he said, retaking his seat at the head of the table, the one his father used to occupy, "sex isn't spelled with either of those letters."

"Well, if I have it correctly, Xavier," Sage said, her voice tart, "you and your girlfriend are only up to courting ritual three, which means you aren't *up* to much of anything at all. No dotting of I's or crossing of T's."

Sage's rich laughter and Xavier's chafed snort had reached Ammon before he opened the balcony doors.

Ammon didn't hear the rest, the glass doors serving as the perfect sound nullifier.

The sun was just beginning to set, but the waning day was still relatively warm, the first glimpse of spring. The official day was only a week away, and Ammon wondered if the fresh season would herald new blooms or old rain showers.

Ammon sighed, tucked his hands into the pockets of his black tail-coat, and sat on the empty bench.

In front of him Lela stood, her hands on the railing, back to Ammon. There was nothing more for him to say. He'd said it all in her office a month ago and in her dining room today. A male could only do so much.

"Our people," Lela began, her voice low, back still to Ammon, "believe in the cyclical nature of life. We believe the cosmos puts every soul where it needs to be, even when the soul in question doesn't understand. We believe that all life is sacred, but no one soul is more important than any other. We are equals, equally chosen, equally destined, equally loved—the part no greater than the whole."

Her blue-and-white evening dress swayed with her movement when she turned to face him. Her eyes held unshed tears. "I—I don't understand, Ammon."

She didn't, but he did. Lela wouldn't. Selfless people never comprehended such things, too busy giving, never wanting or asking for anything in return. He and Grace, however, weren't so high-minded, and neither was most of the cosmos.

Ammon stood and went to her, opening his arms, and Lela—thank the Fates—filled them without hesitation. Ammon exhaled, holding Lela close, breathing in her sweet ginger scent, her long hair warming his face.

"Oh, Lela, you have no idea how much you are loved."

She shook her head, a brief sob breaking free. "No one should be loved that much. The cosmos is not at my beck and call—such exceptions should never be made."

Ammon hugged her tighter and placed a soothing kiss on her cheek. The woman was a stubborn saint who truly didn't understand her vital place in the cosmos. He wondered if she'd even grasped the magnitude of how much her decisions—even the ones she regretted—had irrevocably changed life on Asiya, for the better. How much her strength and determination had impacted his life and the lives of everyone she'd ever come into contact with—up to and including the three Fates of Asiya.

Of course, she didn't, for if she had, Lela wouldn't be sobbing in his arms, denying the truth. She was special. And all the men in her life had known it—her father, Regent Etemaad, Bartek, Zion, Xavier, and him. They saw, they knew, they believed—in her.

She would never see, though. Ammon knew that with certainty. But she would accept, he knew that as well. Lela was far too pragmatic not to.

Finally, she straightened and wiped the tears away with the handkerchief he'd given her, looking embarrassed at her break in decorum. She'd get over that as well, Ammon thought. In time, Lela would accept that there was no emotion she couldn't share freely with him.

"Do you think they've had dinner without us?" she asked, smiling at Ammon with those dazzling eyes of hers, the ones that invariably made his heart pump that much faster.

"Ambassador Vance is probably on his third course, but I'm sure they won't mind foregoing dessert until we've eaten."

Ammon turned toward the balcony doors, offering Lela his arm. She happily took it, giving him a different kind of smile this time. He paused and stared down at her, a quizzical look forming on his face. Lela laughed, and his heart contracted at that, too. Was there anything this woman could do that wouldn't result in some part of his body standing up and paying attention? Probably not.

"What is that look all about?"

"I was just thinking about dessert," Lela answered with a coy smile. "And rituals," she added, pulling him to the closed doors.

"Rituals?"

He opened the doors for her, and they entered, Ammon sliding and locking the doors behind them. The sound of laughter and talking was just as enthusiastically wonderful as it'd been earlier.

"Which ritual?" He grabbed Lela before she got too far away from him. There was no way he was going to allow her to get away with that little tease and leave him hanging for the breadth of an entire meal. She was up to something, and he wanted to know what. And—the Fates help him—she was giving him that same smile again, the one that was doing amazing things to his body. The one that made him want to do wonderful things to her body.

"I hear," she said, placing her hands on his chest and leaning in, "the Paladin Band has an interesting variation on the Unity of Hearts ritual." Lela kissed his chin, cheek and then his quivering lips. "I think I would very much like to find out for myself. A research project, if you will."

Ammon returned the kiss, breathing in her sensuality, wishing suddenly they were alone in the suite, but not caring who could walk in on them. The living room, where they were now, was empty and dark, but across the hall was the dining room where three laughing people could interrupt any minute, or not at all.

He prayed for no interruptions, prayed even harder that his time away, cloistered with the Council of Magistrates, at their annual retreat, wouldn't put too much of a hindrance on the courting rituals. Because, if he interpreted Lela's words correctly, she'd just suggested the Unity of Hearts, the courting ritual that ended, if both parties so desired, in the physical consummation of their relationship.

And, yes, Ammon so desired.

More, the Unity of Hearts concluded the courting phase of a pair's journey toward marriage. But they hadn't progressed through all the courting rituals. There were still more to go. Had Lela decided the other courting rituals were immaterial, considering all they'd been through, the melding of his body with Grace's soul and her submission to herself? Her words and, yes, the way she was kissing him, suggested as much. Did he dare to hope? He was, and he did.

"When?" Ammon breathlessly asked. But he kissed Lela again before she could answer, pulling her to the sofa and onto his lap.

She laughed when they landed inelegantly, her arms coming up around his neck to steady herself.

"I have to first formulate my hypothesis before I undertake the experiment."

"Experiment?" The woman was maddeningly playful when she was happy. Lela hadn't been truly happy in far too long, and Ammon vowed to do all he could to keep her that way. But this teasing of hers, well, he knew a little something about torture techniques.

"Yes, a comparison."

"Ah, a then and now type of experiment."

"Exactly," Lela responded, then she gasped and moaned.

"I see that's still one of your..." Ammon touched Lela there again, making her squirm and moan into his mouth when he kissed her.

"That's not fair," she finally got out, glancing about the room to make sure they were still alone and that no one had heard her low cries of pleasure. "Every woman is sensitive there, Ammon, that proves nothing."

"What about here? And here? And, yes, Lela, here?"

Ammon covered each would-be scream with his mouth, denying Lela that release, but giving her another.

"Oh God," she whispered, slumping weakly in his arms when he'd finished with her.

"We can conduct the experiment even better—and longer—when we're naked and alone."

"Unity of Hearts?" Lela asked, her breathing deliciously labored.

Ammon kissed her soft, wet lips but she pushed away from him and jumped to her feet before he could do more.

"Now that we've had dessert," —Lela walked away from him, her coy smile back— "I think we should rejoin the others and have dinner."

Ammon took five steading breaths and willed his body to calm before venturing to stand. Lela was going to drive him crazy, and he couldn't wait for her to take him as her mate.

"When, Lela?"

"Soon," was her echoing reply.

*****

"Come to bed, love." Lela moved over and patted the empty space beside her. They'd only been married four months, most of which Ammon spent with the other magistrates at the Hall of Order in the southern region of the planet. Literally, half a planet from the Hall of Concord and Lela.

She'd taken that time to move into Ammon's home, an unprecedented act for a Regent of Asiya, who always resided in the Regent wing in the Hall of Concord. The High Star headquarters were located there, as were the ambassadorial offices. And while Sage respected Lela's decision, she didn't like the "unnecessary risk" she thought she was taking by leaving the safety of the secure compound.

Ammon's home, however, was in a secluded location of the capital, with miles of land between his property and that of his closest neighbor, making Lela's security easier to manage. Still, Lela comprehended her friend's concern and how seriously she took her job as High Star Chief of Regent Security. And Sage, quite reasonably, recognized why Lela couldn't live with Ammon in the same dwelling she'd shared with Zion.

As attractive as ever, made even more so by the eager, boyish grin on his face, Ammon joined her in bed, appreciative eyes taking in her flowing hair, bare arms and shoulders, and thin, knee-length nightgown that left very little to the imagination.

No, she could not have brought Ammon into her and Zion's suite, in spite of him holding the soul of her first husband. To be honest, Lela had found that fact to be more than a little disturbing. But once she calmed from the shock of the revelation, needing air and space to think about the odd turn her life had taken, she'd realized that it was Zion who'd taught her that it was all right for her to move on with her life.

He'd come to her almost two years ago in the guise of Ammon, still clinging to her and their former life together as much as she clung to memories and life with him. In the weeks that followed, he'd reminded her how good it felt to laugh, to enjoy one's friends and family, to treasure oneself and not take anything or anyone for granted.

Zion had gifted her with a new outlook on life even when she fought against the revealed perspective. He'd brought closure and contentment to their son, renewing Xavier's faith in his father's love and giving him the courage to start a life with Nailah.

Lela moved close to Ammon, taking his cold hands in her own, and kissing each palm. Despite his persistence to get Lela in this very spot—his home and his bed—Ammon was nervous about this new arrangement, which made him infinitely appealing.

And Zion had given Lela Ammon. He'd sanctioned their union, freeing Lela of any lingering guilt about her feelings for the Paladin. She loved Zion even more for his overwhelming gesture of love. How could she not, he was—after all—her soulmate.

But there was Ammon now, and Lela loved him as well—deeply and passionately.

"I've missed you." His smile widened, and eyes dropped to her mouth, then lower.

"Not as much as I've missed you."

He ran his hands through her hair, massaging her scalp in a way that was new to him but old and familiar to Lela—Ammon but also Zion.

"I assume you're completely moved in."

Lela nodded, her eyes closed, the pleasurable vibrations making speech difficult. Ammon knew this, and he had no shame in showing Lela—repeatedly—how well he did on their then and now experiment.

"Another science project?" he asked, bringing their mouths together. He tasted delicious, his lips smothering her own, tongue gliding easily and possessively in her mouth. Ammon's hands slipped down her back, cupping her backside and pulling her atop him.

Lela's head began to spin, a not so slow burn coursing its way from the pit of her stomach to the demanding ache between her legs, which she opened, straddling Ammon.

At the feel of the position and Lela's lower body suddenly flush against his arousal, Ammon's eyes flew open. Lela smiled at his satisfied expression. And she was even more pleased when his large hands found her hips and began a scintillating back and forth glide.

She leaned over and kissed him, her lips lingering on his neck, then his chest and finally his muscled, quivering stomach. And if she went lower—the way Lela wanted to—this reunion joining would be over all too soon. Oral pleasure would have to wait. She would get to it, but she had other things on her mind.

"A demonstration," she said, "not another science project. I already know the result, even if you do not."

He'd accepted the actions that made Lela different from any other Asiyan female—although she had not yet shown him all the inventive and breath-stealing ways humans engaged in lovemaking. Tonight, well, tonight he would learn, as she once had.

Ammon watched as Lela slid to his thighs and opened his night robe before removing it from his body. He sat up, one strong arm holding him upright, while the other managed to help Lela off with her own sleep garment. Then they were both naked, Lela's eyes feasting on the hard, powerful body under her own.

To her growing astonishment—if not embarrassment—Lela was captivated by the way her small, soft frame responded to Ammon's. One touch—sometimes even a look—and she found herself taut with desire, like she was now. Her need to join with him on the most physical, sensual level proved overpowering and immediate.

Lela pushed Ammon onto his back and crawled up his body—a stealth cruiser stalking its prey. But Ammon was no defenseless Paladin, their mutual submission a foregone conclusion. She joined them, their bodies melding together as one, as their hearts already had.

Lost and found heart.

Lost and found love.

CHAPTER TWENTY

Now I Lay Me Down to Sleep

Lela of the House of Asheema was tired, so completely exhausted and weak. She had been for a very long time. Too many years to count. In fact, she'd given up chronicling the endless cycles of her life. One cycle bled into another into another and yet another until the rising of the sun and the setting of the moon were nearly interchangeable in her mind.

Rich ivory hair had given way to thin, limp onyx. Smooth, flawless skin softened, wrinkled, and spotted. Strong, flexible bones became stubborn, stiff, and achy. And while the body slowly, steadily, unrepentantly succumbed to the ravages of time, Lela's mind remained as keen as ever.

I wish I could forget.

But she'd forgotten nothing over her long life. A curse most days, others, an old woman's blessing.

She tried to shift on the bed. Nothing. Lela commanded her body to move, to make herself comfortable. Nothing.

Her body. Her traitorous body. Lela began to laugh, startling the young nurse tending her.

Lela never laughed, couldn't remember the last time she'd done so. Had any cause to do so. But she laughed now, like a lunatic.

Her body. It had betrayed her, enduring when others had wilted away.

Her laughter was surprisingly loud, uproariously bitter, sending the concerned nurse from the room, probably in search of Lela's physician.

Her body.

Strength. Traitor.

Longevity. Traitor

But it was finally listening to her, finally ready to rest. Finally heeding her prayers.

And what did Lela of the House of Asheema, disciple of Regent Etemaad, Chief Magistrate of the Verity Band, Regent of Asiya, mother of Xavier Grace, and wife to Arbitrator Zion Grace and Chief Magistrate Ammon of the Paladin Band pray for?

Peace.

Forgiveness.

Death.

Elusive wants. Shadowed needs.

But death was no longer so far out of reach. She could feel it magnificently slithering its way from her immobile legs to her arthritic hips and back.

Her mind would be the last to go, the one that was neither devoutly Asiyan nor strangely human. The one that made her remember, the dreams, the nightmares.

The cost of living too long, seeing too much.

Feeling. Yes, feeling too much. Losing even more.

A curse. A burden.

Time began to slow, and the air filled with the sweet smell of anticipation, the floral scent of long denied relief.

Lela heard but no longer saw.

Footsteps.

Worried, hushed voices.

Machines.

Beep. Beep. Beep.

Beep. Beep.

Beep.

Silence.

Weightlessness.

Freedom.

Death.

CHAPTER TWENTY-ONE

I Pray to Lord My Soul to Keep

How could a soul weep? Feel pain? Know sorrow?

Lela had no answers, only sensations. And her soul did indeed rage with emotions she'd only ever experienced when it was tethered to her vessel of a body. The body that had outlived, outpaced, and outmaneuvered all understanding of Asiyan mortality.

Unnatural. Yes, it was unnatural to live so long.

Her soul floated in the dark void that was her new existence, her new home. For so long, she'd wanted this cessation of life, a sin to wish for death, a greater sin to court death to the point of suicide. She hadn't gone that far, would never. But living, some days proved nearly intolerable. Lela laughed, a harsh, bitter sound that echoed in the starless, sunless abyss. It ricocheted off invisible walls of space, sending it back to her even more mirthless than when it escaped a throat that only existed in her mind.

We are the cosmos, living, breathing manifestations of energy, light, and life. When we die, when we breathe our last, blackness of space awaits our arrival. Stars we will become. Souls we are. Complete we will be, in a glorious place that birthed us all.

Lela's words to Zion when she'd attempted to explain Asiyan's belief in the cycle of life and death to a man who only knew the concept of Heaven and Hell.

Home, back to the Realm of Thuraya. That was an Asiyan's Heaven.

Yet there was another place one's soul could travel upon death, one rarely spoken of by any band. The knowledge wasn't hidden or discourse forbidden, but a possibility few wanted to entertain. A hereafter no one prayed for, a curse an Asiyan wouldn't make even against their most vile enemy.

Yet Lela's soul had traversed the cosmos, moving at quicksilver speed, a blind person guided by internal sight.

Now she was there, a place where no hope dwelled and only ghosts were allowed.

Ghosts of the mind.

Ghosts of the heart.

Ghosts of the soul.

*****

Zion's star dimmed, the normal luminosity lost to the growing bleakness of his soul.

Where is she? Why hasn't she returned to me?

Yeah, he'd been asking himself the same questions since he'd sensed Lela's death. That had been three months ago. Zion was uncertain how this death, hereafter, and mated souls thing worked, but he was pretty sure once both parties were dead that they—somehow—reunited.

The stars surrounding Zion twinkled, the cosmos alive with reborn life. An existence unlike anything he could have ever imagined as a child. Sure, every culture had their beliefs about what happened after death. For him, Heaven was normally somewhere in the mix. But he was never quite certain of that fact. But the idea appealed to him. Almost as much as the idea of a burning, eternal Hell didn't. No way did he want to end up in a place like that. Those Sunday morning guilt sermons he and Sage sat through were enough to make a wild, rebellious teen rethink certain choices.

Well, he was there. Had been since Ammon's tumor came out of remission with a vengeance. No one had expected that. But his deterioration had been quick. He didn't suffer long or linger. A matter of weeks and it was done—Zion separating from the man upon his death. Two souls finally parted, both unwilling to leave Lela alone, but knowing neither could stay.

That had been twelve years ago.

And Zion had waited. Learned much of what the Asiyans thought about life after death to be eerily accurate. He had indeed been cast back to the cosmos, a star with thoughts and feelings still intact.

"We are eternally bound. Our souls are now one," she'd told him the night of their wedding when she'd performed Lerato, the soul binding ritual. Zion could never quite reconcile Lela's religious belief with that of his own, when he was alive. Yet now he was part of the conscious dimension that was the cosmos, unbelievably able to "mentally link" with others who had come before and after him. Family. Friends.

Spiritual reunions made possible by a wonderful, indescribable design. The Realm of Thuraya—unfathomable to the disbelieving mind, but simple in its straightforward singularity.

Lela, she was the most important spiritual link Zion wanted to make. But that long-awaited connection seemed to be blocked, making Zion think about old-fashioned human telephones. Zion was calling, but Lela wasn't answering, her "phone" disconnected, shut off, out of order. Or whatever the hell 21st-century humans called it. The bottom line—Lela's star, her soul had made no effort to connect with his.

Frustrated, Zion searched for the one star in the cosmos he thought could help him. He'd done it before—against his better judgment—and Zion hoped she could be of assistance again.

After what felt like an eternity of impatiently waiting for the link to connect, Zion felt the familiar tingle that always streaked through him when a link was formed, each star growing brighter with the connection.

Zion wanted to say, "It's about damn time," but that was no way to address a being who, more than likely, had the answers he sought. Instead, Zion swallowed the anxiety tearing away at him, striving for calm when all he wanted to do was roar. "Where in the hell is she?"

Okay, that didn't exactly come out right. In fact, it came out all wrong. Zion knew better, but dammit, he needed answers. He needed Lela.

But the voice that reached out to him, stroking him like a wayward child, was soft and gentle. "Far away from here, Zion, I'm afraid."

"But I thought—"

Zion gasped as the link morphed into a visual connection, the non-reality roiling past him like a cruiser at warp speed. This, Zion hadn't quite gotten used to, the swift optical illusion jarring.

There she was. The Fate who, quite literally, had held his fate in her hands. Unlike Faith and Truth, the Fate of Purpose had only ever come to Zion in one form. It wasn't her true form, he suspected, although he had no idea what her true form to be. But she resembled an Asiyan female, if that female shimmered like gossamer dipped in gold flecks of magic.

Of the three, Zion had always trusted Purpose the most. He had no idea why, the other Fates no less kind, annoying, or mystical to him than the being before him. Yet there was just something about Purpose that set him at ease when he was in her presence. Not that he was particularly at ease now, but there was an unstated warmth to Purpose that pulled Zion in, no matter how angry or confused he felt.

He paused, looked up at the Willow Tower, an imposing edifice built into a mountain on the planet of Ranbir. It had been there, where he'd first met Lela, a petite woman with a heart, intellect, and fortitude larger than the mountain itself. Down the road from the immense structure, a mile or more, was where his life ended then converged with that of the Fates' magic—their gift. This illusion was no coincidence. For whatever reason, the Fate of Purpose had created this image for him. Zion wasn't up for the psychological manipulation, so he did his best to ignore the emotions the unwanted landscape evoked.

"I want her here as well, Zion." Purpose turned away from Willow Tower, her eyes stark and disturbingly haunted. "She's gone to a place where neither one of us can reach her."

Purpose's voice had gone utterly soft—sad even. When the Fates had come to him, on this road of blood and hope, Zion had noticed one thing. Whenever they spoke of Lela, there was so much tenderness in their voice, particularly Purpose's. Like there was now. But also concern, perhaps even a fair amount of fear.

"I thought all souls came here. That's what Lela told me. That's what Faith assured me would happen when I made that damn pact with Ammon."

A look of guilt crossed Purpose's pretty, angelic face, and Zion's non-existent stomach began to knot. "What aren't you telling me? Where's Lela?"

"You look like you did when you addressed the Verity Band, declaring your fidelity to Lela and challenging anyone, with the strength of your passion and love for Lela, to dare oppose the union."

He'd done exactly that, tired of Bartek and others like him looking down their noses at Zion because he was from another planet, viewing him with unjustified suspicion and disdain. Discrimination, he despised all forms it took—on Earth, Asiya, and every planet he'd ever visited.

Shameful. For all that races could now traverse the cosmos, their knowledge of science and technology both amazing and frightening, they hadn't evolved beyond cultural disputes steeped in ideas of superiority.

Purpose created the form Zion currently took—healthy and hale and thirty-five-years-old. His black suit perfectly cut to fit a form Zion had long since forgotten could be so strong, tall, and formidable. That was how he'd felt when the President of the United Republic of the Western Hemisphere appointed a peace negotiator from New York as Earth's representative on the newly-formed Confederation of Worlds. He'd also been afraid back then. To be honest, he simply didn't want to mess up, proving doubters right that he was "too young and inexperienced" for the important post. Well, he'd gotten himself killed, which was the height of failure. But, thanks to the second chance he'd been given, he'd also flown higher than he ever could've imagined—would've ever thought possible without Lela by his side.

"You created this," Zion pointed to himself. "Why?"

"It's how I see you, where it all began for you and Lela." Purpose floated closer to Zion, the space between her brows pinching. "She's in trouble, and I don't know how to help her."

"What kind of trouble?"

The Fate's body shimmered, even more, her magic sparking around the edges of her diaphanous form.

"There is one other place a soul may find itself after death." Purpose raised a single finger when Zion made to interrupt. As far as he knew, there was no other place for a soul to travel.

"Asiyans rarely speak of the between cosmos."

"The what?"

"Between the living world and the Realm of Thuraya is a slither of existence Asiyans have come to call the Realm of Drogo or the between cosmos."

"Lela never—"

"Spoke of it?"

Zion nodded.

"Few do, even among the Verity Band. But Lela, like all Asiyans, know of its existence."

"Are you saying Lela is there?" This made no sense to Zion. Why in the world would Lela's soul go there instead of here?

"I'm saying Lela was prepared to die but not quite ready to live."

"I have no idea what that means. I don't know why you Fates never speak plainly? I want to know why my wife is in some in between cosmos. She always told me we would meet again where the stars gathered and lit the way for the next generation. I'm here. Why in the hell isn't she? She died months ago. I felt it. Hell, if I were a betting man, I'd say you felt it too."

Because, yes, there was a connection between the Fates and his wife they had kept from him and Lela. And he damn sure wanted to know what in the hell it was. But the Fates couldn't be bullied, bribed, or tricked into divulging something they didn't wish to share. But there was something, something of importance, Zion concluded.

"I feel them all." A long pause, then a truth that rocked Zion to his core. "All that have my blood, even the smallest amount. Their births. Their joy. Their heartaches. Their deaths. All of them. Lela most of all."

What in the hell? Lela was descendant from the Fate of Purpose? Wait, then that would mean the mystical being before him had once been mortal…? Flesh and blood like Lela, Zion, and everyone else?

Zion stumbled and dropped to the road, mouth agape, eyes staring at the Fate, who—damn her—shed her mystical form right before his blurry eyes.

Bare feet planted on the ground and as corporeal as one could get in this strange reality, stood an Asiyan female who looked far too much like Lela for Zion to not think them relatives. High cheek bones, ivory coils down to her heels, Picasso marble eyes with more tan than in Lela's, but the facial features were undeniably Asheema. She could pass as Lela's aunt, so closely did Purpose resemble Lela's mother.

Zion couldn't figure if Purpose's truth brought clarity or simply more questions. As he stared at the silent woman, Zion concluded it was both. The genetic link explained why Purpose had taken such an interest in Lela's happiness, he guessed. But it didn't come close to explaining why Lela seemed to have been singled out from all the other descendants Purpose alluded to. Now that he was thinking, Zion's mind beginning to clear, he wondered if the other two Fates had also been mortal once. And, if they had, had they known each other in life? More, how had they become the Fates of Asiya?

Too much. Too damn much to think about. He'd called Purpose to help him get Lela back, not to open up Pandora's Box of immortal secrets and lies.

"She lived a long time, Zion."

He glared at the Fate, disliking how easily she wore a face too similar to his wife's and the soft eyes that held no guilt for her huge lie of omission. And, he knew, with the stoic way she watched him, there would be no more truths forthcoming.

Dragging himself off the ground, Zion stood to his full height of six feet, which still left him feeling small in Purpose's mystical presence.

"I know." Ironic, he'd died prematurely and his Lela…

"I don't think you truly do. Long life isn't always a blessing. In Lela's case, I'm afraid she came to view it as a curse, which wasn't our intention." Guilt. A flicker. A second, but there. "A punishment, she thought of it. A sign of our disapproval."

Punishment? Disapproval?

He frowned. Lela was the best of people—Verity through and through. She led and ruled by her ideals, using the power of Asiya and the strength of her allies to promote peace and build bridges that divided people.

Zion didn't get it. What was he missing?

"Have you forgiven her for finding love and happiness with Ammon?" The question was asked with no malice, but Zion felt as if the Fate had dropped a battlecarrier on him.

"W-what?"

"You said you wanted Lela to find peace, happiness. Was that a lie? Or did you feel so guilty about leaving Lela alone that you felt you had to atone?"

Zion's eyes narrowed, then his image shifted, adding a few pounds and gray hair at the temples. This was how he saw himself. Not the naïve, young man who'd left Earth on a goodwill mission having no clue as to the depth of the waters he was about to wade into—warfare and bloodshed hard lessons to learn, to survive. No, he wasn't the man the Fate of Purpose tried to paint him as. No more. Never again.

Purpose gave an unimpressed shake of the head, a glimmer of amusement lurking behind her penetrating gaze. "How you appear matters not, Zion." She touched one finger to the area over his heart, then his head. "It's what's in there that matters most. She cannot come to you the way you are now."

Zion's head reeled. How had Purpose switched this around on him? He shook his head, bogged down by the possibility that there was more than a shred of truth to the Fate's words.

"I-I knew she would grow to love Ammon. I" —he sucked in a fortifying breath— "just didn't realize how much Lela would love him." Zion conjured a chair and sat.

Gazing into the face of Lela's ancestor, Zion knew she'd known all along, not just that Lela would love Ammon but how deeply her love for him would run.

"You said I would have no consciousness once I merged with Ammon. That he would be dominant to my submissive."

No, Faith had made those claims to Zion, not Purpose. They'd come to him as one when he was bleeding out and dying, healed him as one, spoke as one. Three but also one. Soul bound, he now wondered, just as he was to Lela and she to him. Could it be true? It would explain, in part, their odd connection to each other and, in a way, to Lela.

"Faith said the merging of two souls in one body was unprecedented. We weren't certain what would happen." The Fate had the audacity to shrug slim shoulders when she conceded, "You were a willing test subject. For all intents and purposes, it was a successful experiment. Besides," Purpose crossed her arms over her chest, "you were the one who asked for another option."

He had, but surely the Fates had to have known what he would do once Ammon's condition became known to him. Surely they couldn't have thought Zion would want to promulgate that level of fraud against Lela, setting her up for heartache when Ammon died. So yeah, he'd begged for an option. And lo and behold, Faith pulled one out of his magician's hate, all the while ignoring the easiest solution to the problem—curing Ammon.

"There were times," Zion admitted, wishing he could erase the intimate images, "when Ammon was totally relaxed, content. Sometimes I could see through his eyes. A second or two, if I was lucky. Minutes, if I wasn't."

"Zion, he made her happy."

Compassion rimmed words that rang hollow to his ears. He knew just how happy Ammon had made Lela. He didn't need the reminder.

"We all wanted that for Lela. She wanted it for herself, but didn't know how to do so without betraying her feelings for you."

He jumped to his feet, sending the chair crashing to the ground. "Well," Zion snarled, a sudden burst of anger lacing his tone, "she sure as hell got over that, didn't she?"

Purpose sighed and backed away. "With that attitude, you'll never be able to link with Lela, help her find her way from the Realm of Drogo."

Zion balled fists that wanted to lash out at the whole damn cosmos. "If she wanted to be with me then she would be here." His voice sounded certain, but nothing else about him was.

"You know nothing. And unless you get a handle on your conflicted feelings, Lela will be lost to us forever."

"I have a handle on my emotions, goddammit." He began to pace, slamming his fist into a door of the Willow Tower each time he passed the structure. "Can't you see, I'm boiling over with checked emotion? I'm oozing it from every dead cell of this fake body."

Zion ranted louder the longer Purpose ignored him, eyeing him with infinite patience if not finite empathy. Zion felt like an ass when he'd finished his temper tantrum, picking up the chair and dropping his frustrated load.

"She's lost," Purpose said, as if Zion hadn't just had a mental breakdown. "Emotionally lost," she clarified. "Lela knows exactly where she is and why she's there. What she probably doesn't know is how to move past that realm, or whether she is deserving to do so. We know she is, of course, but she must believe it as well."

The Fate of Purpose conjured her own chair, placing it in front of Zion and sitting, her elegant purple gown tucked neatly around her. "Even if she solves the mystery that is herself and reaches out to you, she'll meet the wall you've built around your soul."

"I haven't—"

"No more self-deception, Zion. This is Lela's afterlife we're talking about. We could lose her forever because of her guilt and your jealousy."

Jealousy? Was he jealous? Of her love for Ammon? Of the intimacy they'd shared over their decades' long union? Of the woman-lost way she looked at Ammon when he laid in his deathbed? The very way Zion never wanted her to see him—weak and lost.

"I want her to want me."

"She does."

"How can she?"

"She does."

"Lela and Ammon were married much longer than the thirty years I gave her. I can't compete with that."

"You don't have to. You never did."

Zion gripped the arms of the chair, hearing Lela's honey rich laughter whenever Ammon would swing her around in his arms, her bountiful hair tickling her husband's face and causing them both to bubble over with joy.

Had Zion ever made her laugh like that? He hoped so, but he honestly couldn't remember. It had been so long since they'd last been together. How could she still view him as her soulmate? Still want him for eternity?

Purpose touched Zion's trembling arm, pulling him back from the cliff he was about to plunge himself over.

"She committed herself to you. If you doubt her choice, so will she. If Lela thinks there's nothing for her here but pain and regret, she'll succumb to the hopelessness of the realm. And when that happens, her soul will be forever lost."

Forever lost. No.

"What can I do?"

"Be patient. Lela was always good at fighting her own demons. I have faith in her. But when she's ready to come home, you have to be ready for her. If you aren't..."

Purpose didn't have to finish. Zion knew. He would lose her, forever this time. But what Zion didn't know was what to do with his jealousy, his fear.

He wanted Lela, as much as he ever had. The Fate assured him she wanted him just as desperately. But did Lela only feel that way because she'd pledged herself to him when they took vows?

If at all possible, Lela never broke her word. Never. Not in all the years he'd known her, even when following through was clearly a pain in her very proper Asiyan behind. Was he simply a follow through? A promise she didn't want to break because it went against Asiyan norms of proper behavior?

Shit, he hoped not. But, damn, it had been a marriage and several decades ago. Even an honorable woman like Lela couldn't be expected to hold a promise that long.

Above all else, Lela was as upright as they came. And Zion didn't want her coming to him out of honor. He wanted more—so very much more.

But did she? Or had Ammon, over their long marriage together, displaced Zion in her heart?

If so, what would eternity be without her? God, he didn't want to find out.

CHAPTER TWENTY-TWO

Triumvirate

Darkness surrounded them, held them, molding them in a bond more loyal than friendship, deeper than love, brighter than a stellar explosion. And so the three radiant stars, fixed at three different points in the cosmos, beamed for the planets below, a triangular guide for those souls ready to join the Realm of Thuraya.

Not that all believed or even knew of such a place. Beliefs were as diverse and plentiful as fish in the oceans. Yet mortals learned, becoming swift believers, the transition into the afterlife, the immersion back into the cosmos, an amazing molder of minds.

Yet they'd failed to guide one home. In all their long years, a lamb had gotten away from the ever-watchful sheepherders. Wandering off, following the wolf's trail into danger, to a place where only solitude dwelled and lost souls fell for perpetuity.

This was not acceptable, an error that must be set right. And set right soon, or the lone, vulnerable lamb would be no more, forever changed by the bleakness of the heart, the delusion of the mind, and the melancholia of the soul.

Light years away, but of a linked mind, Purpose joined with Faith and Purpose to plot someone else's troth.

She's still in that wretched place.

We know. The two thoughts merged, answering in the singular, understanding in the plural.

What do you suggest we do?

Purpose was afraid for Lela's soul and the future of mortals if she could not be brought home to fulfill her ultimate destiny—just as Purpose had done.

If we leave them to their own devices, I fear time will become our enemy.

The Fate of Truth, always the first to speak the obvious. Oh, how she loved him and the eternal bond they shared, made that much stronger once they shed their mortal bodies and joined Thuraya in celestial bliss.

It's already our enemy, one that cannot be slowed, halted, or defeated.

True, but like a tide, it's inevitable and predictable. It will come when it comes.

Yet another truth from her beloved.

So, we can either meekly await its arrival, permitting it to wash us away in its filth and silt or...

Or step aside and deny the beast its meal.

Ah, the Fate of Faith—an optimist even in the gloomiest of times. She loved him as well, adored him in fact—his wisdom, his patience, his fortitude.

So I ask again. What are we to do? Purpose.

Set candles of light before them. Faith.

Ah, I see—a path.

Yes, one for them and them alone. Faith.

Which candles?

Many stars around them shimmered and turned in their direction, as if requesting to be one of the candles of light.

An electrical smile reached from Purpose to the other Fates, then out to the hundreds of stars, a silent "Thank you," sent.

We have many from which to choose. But there is only one correct selection and one opportunity to get this right. If we don't... Truth.

Yes, we know. We'll get it right. We won't fail them. Purpose.

But what if they fail themselves by taking the wrong path?

Faith was not blind to the truth of the grim possibility of failure.

All we can do is set the candles before them. They have to be the ones to walk the path, to make the journey of fear and doubt. Truth.

They have to be strong. Purpose.

Yes.

They have to be willing. Purpose.

Yes.

They have to love themselves. But love each other more. Truth.

Yes.

So we are in agreement. But we have yet to select. Two candles for Zion Grace. Purpose.

Yes, two candles, but complimentary flames.

Faith understood. He always did—even as a man with hopes and dreams far too large to be achieved in a single lifetime. But, as a Fate, he'd accomplished so much more than what a mere mortal could ever envision.

Coping and dying? Are we in agreement? Purpose.

Yes.

Good, now for Lela.

Three candles for Lela of the House of Asheema. Of course, Truth held the mirror to Lela's heart. *Friendship, family, forgiveness.*

In that order? Perhaps—

We have to do this right. We cannot rush her by going to the flame of forgiveness first. For within that one candle of light is the echo of another. Truth.

Guilt.

Yes, guilt. We must tread lightly, although time is but a nightmare away.

Of course, you are right. I just—

We all love her, Purpose, want her safely with us, as one of us. Truth.

I know, but I've waited so long, could do nothing more over the years than watch and wait and pray. Purpose.

Then pray some more, my love, and we will join you. Faith.

They prayed, united as one, Lela and Zion their souls of focus.

The prayer that began with three blinking stars, gleaming as single entities, cascaded on bands of light and energy, others quickly joining, adding their own unique essence, until Mother Cosmos from three divergent but bonded points was awash in light.

Energy. Prayer. Hope.

For them. For love. For life.

CHAPTER TWENTY-THREE

Coping and Dying

Zion died a long time ago. He wished he could remember how many years, the exact date of his death—his crossing from man to mist to myth. But his soul, well, his soul refused to recall the precise moment when his light flickered and extinguished like so many before him. No, Zion didn't truly want to remember his death, for to remember meant he had to feel. If he felt, then he would hurt. And if he allowed the pain to come, to crash over him, a tiny pebble in an unforgiving wind, he would simply crumble.

There were no winds in the cosmos, just silence and time. So much time and endless solitude, despite being surrounded by thousands of stars. Yet loneliness had become a constant companion—his afterlife incomplete without her.

Lela. The name vibrated around him, an echo from long ago.

Lela. The name burrowed inside him. Raw. Sweet. Bitter.

Lela. The name singed the star, compelling his soul to remember, to never forget, to never give up hope.

And Zion had given up hope. Lela's soul was out there somewhere. A place where Zion couldn't follow. No chance of rescue. No help. Just her. Alone.

Like him.

Perhaps that was the fate he deserved, to exist with only half a soul.

The moment the depressing thought formed, Zion felt the electrical pull—soft and coaxing. Zion knew it well, but he wasn't in the mood. Not now, not for her.

The tug grew stronger. Their bond gave her a direct link to him. But he could ignore it. He had in the past.

Stronger. Harder. Determined. She never requested his presence with such urgency before. And their link, nor her, was so strong as to compel him to do her bidding. Yet today, the force on Zion was strangely penetrating, unusually powerful, and annoyingly persistent.

Giving in, Zion went, his star not happy with the intrusion. Wallowing in Lela's abandonment and his loss was an act best done alone.

But he went, led like a trained dog that wanted nothing more than to bite the hand of the smiling kid holding his leash.

Just when Zion could take it no more, his surroundings brightened before him. Darkness and solitude gave way to artificial light, blue-and-yellow painted walls, and a brunette.

"Hello, Zion."

He brought his hands up, then looked down at his legs. He had a body. Zion felt strong, young, invincible—the way he did as a man of his twenties. He didn't bother with searching the room for a mirror or something to show him the image she'd created. She settled on the representation of him she most liked, last remembered. He could alter himself if he wanted. He'd done so before. But really, what was the point? If she preferred to see him this way, then so be it. He wouldn't be there long.

"Hello, Iman."

She smiled at him, and she too appeared much younger. Like she did when they'd first met—a couple of college kids just beginning life, having no idea where it all would take them.

Dark shoulder-length hair framed a beautiful face that gazed at Zion with affection and concern. Light-brown eyes held his, their shade a touch lighter than the complexion of her skin—winter brown with highlights of summer sunshine. Slender and graceful, like that of a ballerina, her nearly six-foot height intimated many men, especially when she wore three-inch heels without an ounce of concern for their fragile ego.

Lovely. Iman Grace had been such a lovely woman in life—body and character.

Zion glanced around. It was Iman's first apartment after college graduation. He'd spent many a day and night in the overpriced, under-sized flat. He'd always liked the place, it smelled of daisies, chocolate chip cookies—his favorite—and the future.

But this was an illusion, a trip down memory lane Zion had no interest of taking.

He squared his shoulders. "Why have you brought me here?"

She smiled. The same sweet, shy smile she gave him whenever he asked her out on a date.

The tender, familiar gesture pulled at his heart, made him see her as the girl she had been, the woman she would grow into, and not as a deathbed patient.

Zion shook his head. No, he remembered that all too well.

"Just tell me."

Iman moved closer, her flower print dress reminding Zion of spring-time and renewed life. What a joke. She'd succumbed to the virus in the spring, just when nature awoke from its winter slumber, bringing col-ors, light, and longer days. Yet she'd wilted, spring flowers and sunshine casting her death in a morbid glow of mockery. No renewed life, just an unforgivable death—a husband's wreath of guilt.

Smiling, Iman reached out, her soft fingers finding his. She twined them, her delicate hand so familiar and soft.

Zion wanted to rip his hand away from her. To turn from the love and trust her eyes revealed. He didn't deserve her love or want her trust.

"I was taught," she began, her voice a soothing caress, "like you, that upon death the soul would travel to one of two places—Heaven or Hell." Yeah, Sunday morning service had pounded that bit of faith into him as well. "I never imagined any other afterlife."

Neither had he, although they both studied other cultures. A person didn't have to travel beyond Earth to discover various ideas about life after death.

Iman laughed. "In the end, I guess it doesn't really matter what one believes during life, death is the great teacher of all things cosmic and eternal."

True.

Iman released his hand and stepped away from him. She moved to the three-sectional sofa, sat, and nodded for him to join her.

With reluctance, he did, leaving one cushion space between them.

"I don't remember my death."

He knew. She'd told him before. Why was she telling him again?

"I remember the pain and then the cold numbness that would set in after each injection." She looked down, her hands gripping the folds of her dress. "The baby. I remember our baby, wanting her so much, wanting her to live, even if I died."

He didn't want to hear this. But it was her right, her life, her death.

She'd died because no cure yet existed for the virus she'd contracted. She'd died because people like Zion argued against harsh, discriminatory immigration laws. He'd helped negotiate interplanetary immigration policies, laws granting off-worlders immigrant and nonimmigrant visas—increasing communication, collaboration, and travel between Earth and other planets.

It had been a good idea, a politically and financially smart move for Earth. But a good idea, even one that benefits many, didn't mean it couldn't also be one fraught with consequences—even planned-for ones. But how could a planet vaccinate their population against unknown diseases?

"I know, I'm sorry." *Sorrier than you will ever know.*

Her slim fingers reached for him again, forcing Zion to unfurl the fists he didn't know he'd formed.

"After I died, I had a lot of time to think." Iman chuckled, her eyes twinkling. "In death, I guess we do all the thinking we should've done while we were alive. Then, we have the erroneous belief that we don't have enough time to talk, to think, to do. Here" —she gestured to the room, but Zion knew she meant the cosmos— "we have endless time to ponder our mistakes. To even make new ones."

Zion could see some truth in her words, but they mostly rang hollow. He wished she would just get to the point so he could leave. Really, what good would rehashing old wounds do? Some things were just better left dead and buried.

Like his bond to Lela.

Iman tightened her grip on his hand. She wanted his full attention, which he gave, despite his agitation.

"What is this all about?" He knew he sounded weary, in spite of the impossibility of true fatigue.

"This is about you." She gave him a pointed look. "And Lela."

Zion did pull away from her touch then and stood.

Iman remained where she was, her eyes sympathetic.

"You need to get past this, or you'll lose her forever."

Yeah, that's what Purpose said. But it wasn't him. It was Lela. She was the one who hadn't joined him in the Realm of Thuraya. She was the one who married and loved another while claiming to still mourn him. She was the one who—

"There's nothing for me to get past. I'm perfectly fine. Been fine. Will always be fine."

Pathetic liar. You haven't been fine for longer than you want to admit.

"It's not your fault."

Zion stopped his pacing and whirled to face his first wife.

"What wasn't?"

She stood, but didn't advance, giving him the space he needed.

"My death, Zion. It wasn't your fault."

Yeah, right. The woman was delusional. Of course it was his fault.

"I fought for the immigration policy."

She shook her head, straight, dark hair falling into resolute eyes.

He stepped toward her. "My holier-than-thou high moral ground killed you. I thought the conservatives were being their usual narrow-minded selves, using quotas to block certain immigrants while allowing others unfettered access to Earth."

"Their policies weren't right. They had two sets of standards. That's no way to rule a planet—with fear and discrimination."

"But they were right. More off-worlders, more foreign health issues."

Iman shook her head again. "Earth couldn't exist in a bubble. We gained from opening our borders to many. And we suffered, just as other planets suffered who admitted humans into their population. It's a risk every planet took."

"But—"

"Bad things happen. I didn't want to die, didn't want to leave you alone." Tears formed but didn't fall. "We can't outrun our fate. We can run, we can hide, we can pretend and ignore. But in the end, it comes for us, whether we're ready or willing. As cruel as it was, my fate took me from you and my parents much sooner than I would have liked. I wanted our baby, to see her born and to raise our little girl with you. But it wasn't meant to be."

Tears trickled down her face, and she let them fall.

They hadn't even decided on a name. Zion had known, even then, that Iman's uncertainty as to what to name their daughter came from a place deep inside of her that silently feared how much more Zion would mourn their daughter if she died with a name, a personhood beyond Iman's body.

It was all there, in her tear-streaked face, how hard she fought to stay alive long enough for their daughter to develop to the point of being able to survive outside of her mother's dying body. But it wasn't to be. The Fates not kind to the Grace family back then.

Iman wiped away her tears, then gifted Zion with a watery smile. "I chose you. And you made me so happy. I lived. I laughed. I loved."

She kissed his cheek and wrapped Zion in a consoling embrace. "And you love her. More than you ever loved me."

Zion made to protest, but Iman shook her head. "Like I said, there isn't much to do here but think."

She stepped out of his embrace, and Zion waited for the sense of loss to overcome him. It didn't. That feeling, that warmth she used to evoke by her mere presence was gone, apparently never to return.

"I learned to cope with my death, Zion, and so must you. You can't continue to blame yourself for my death no more than I could continue to hate you for binding your soul to another."

Hate him? He didn't know she'd felt that way. But damn if he didn't understand.

Zion ran a hand through his hair—thick and dark the way it was when he was a young man wooing a pretty college student.

But Zion didn't hate Lela. He could never hate her. She'd loved him. Gave him a son. Mourned him. For too long. Far too long. Then she'd moved on, gave her heart to someone else. The same way he'd tucked his memories of Iman away, freeing his heart to love again, opening his soul to Lela.

No, he could never hate Lela. But he was angry. At her, him, and Ammon. At life. At death.

"I love you, Iman."

Zion did. He'd never stopped. Never would. But…

She clasped her hands around his. "I know, and I love you. When we married, I thought that existence was all there was for us. That once we died that was it, our time together would be over."

So had he.

"You never promised me forever, and I never expected it."

Her hands were so warm, her words even warmer, thawing the edges of his heart.

"But you and Lela are different. You two are connected in a way I could never fathom. Beyond time. Beyond death."

Iman's hand found his chest, the placement over a heart that beat only when he thought of Lela.

"Beyond regret. Beyond grief. Beyond anger."

One finger rested on his chin.

"Let go of the anger, and claim the other half of your soul."

She stepped away. Her dark hair swirled about her, the shape of Iman fading, melding into blackness, the illusion dissolving around them.

Zion reached for her, suddenly horrified of being alone with his thoughts.

But she was gone, her parting words clipping his conscience before she disconnected their electrical link. "Anger is a lonely fortress, keeping you in and Lela out. Tear it down or be imprisoned there forever."

Connection broken. Zion was once again alone.

But he didn't want to be alone. Zion wanted… He just wanted Lela. But he couldn't have her, didn't know how to escape his so-called fortress.

He wanted to though. God knows he wanted nothing more than to do just that. Time was not his friend. Had never been kind to him.

Time. Limited time.

Screw that.

*****

Zion whirled, his dark-gray suit jacket swinging with his swift movement. He walked and walked, his mind unconsciously forming the images around him. But he paid the landscape no attention—his need to walk, to clear his head, to get away from himself far more important than the manifestation of an illusion.

When Zion finally glanced up, he stood in front of his childhood home. A two-story, brick house loomed before him, positioned at the end of a cul-de-sac in a quiet neighborhood with more asphalt than naturally growing trees. Unwilling to probe either his heart or his mind to the reasoning behind this particular illusion, Zion strolled down the short driveway, up four steps and to the front wraparound porch.

With a weary sigh, Zion sat in the closest of three wicker chairs on the porch, propping his dress leather shoes on the matching ottoman in front of him. And sighed again, his hands settling behind his head and his eyes closing.

Tired. So tired.

"I've never known you to nap in the middle of the day since you were a boy of four, telling your mother, 'Big boys don't need naps.'"

Zion's eyes snapped open, his feet thudding to the porch floor, and a half-smile, half-frown forming, a perfect mirror of his conflicted feelings about the new arrival.

"I didn't invite you here, Dad."

Elijah William Grace Jr. stared down at Zion, tall body, broad shoulders, and bald head casting a shadow over Zion and blocking out the light from the imagined sun.

"That's no way to greet your father, son. Your mother and I taught you better than that.

Yeah, they had, his father undeserving of the attitude. Zion shifted one seat down, allowing his father to claim the chair where Zion had been deep in thought—not napping, despite appearances and his utter fatigue of the soul.

"You're right, Dad. I'm sorry." Zion patted his father's shoulder in apology, when he sat. "I have a lot on my mind and would be grateful if you told me why you're here."

Zion didn't like this. Perhaps he could've shrugged Iman's demanding call off to former wife concern. But Elijah appearing, out of the blue, well, that was stretching coincidence a bit far.

"Just thought we could talk. You know."

No, Zion didn't know. But he was beginning to feel manipulated.

"Did Purpose send you here?"

Elijah crossed one leg over his knee. "Not Purpose exactly."

Zion gave his father a sidelong glance, noticing, for the first time, that the man wore his old black-and-blue sentinel detective uniform. Elijah's gold shield and weapon belt were absent, conjuring an overlaying image of his father when he'd returned home from the precinct one day, informing the family of his impromptu retirement.

He'd simply gone into work that day, as he'd done for over thirty years, and turned in his shield and firearm. That had been it, no explanation to his supervisor, no goodbyes to his brothers and sisters in blue, no box of mementos from his desk he dragged home. He'd left it all behind—all except the nightmares.

"Give me the Fate's message and then let me have a bit of peace and quiet, Dad. I'm not in the right frame of mind today to have a nice father-son visit with you."

Elijah's smile said he understood but that he wouldn't be leaving just yet. "It doesn't work that way, son, I'm sorry."

Of course it didn't.

Zion leaned back in his chair, waiting for whatever lesson the Fates wanted him to learn. Why not? He had nothing better to do than lament eternity without Lela.

Elijah conjured a tall glass of iced tea and took a sip, closing his eyes then sighing his enjoyment when half the drink was gone, ice clicking when he placed the glass on the ottoman in front of him. "Do you know how many times I swore I'd never take another drink only to find myself hoarding booze and lying to family and friends?"

Zion sat up straight. He knew his father struggled with his addiction to alcohol. Hell, it had caused more than one fight between them, threatened their family and Zion's faith and trust in his father.

After the child serial killer case, Elijah had turned to the bottle, finding no true comfort but temporary states of oblivion instead. Yet the signs of Elijah's downward spiral had been there before the killer's death lair had been found.

Missing children.

Mourning parents.

A frightened and angry public.

Too much. It had all proven to be too much for Elijah to handle—so he didn't.

"More than I'd like to admit," Elijah confessed, not waiting for Zion's reply. "The Twelve-Step Program," he huffed, "easier said than done."

Yeah, Zion could only imagine. Elijah Grace had one of the strongest personalities he'd ever known. The man was tough, but alcohol addiction wasn't a foe defeated easily. Elijah had fought that battle and lost—repeatedly.

"The first step is admitting that you can't control your addiction or compulsion. That was a hard one for me."

It would've been for Zion as well. Negotiators were taught to always be in control. If they ever lost control, that spelled death. For them. For others.

"But you made it, Dad, found your way to the other side."

"I was lucky."

Zion disagreed. Elijah worked hard to regain control, to be something other than the scared, hopeless drunk he'd become.

"Not luck. You beat it. You were stronger than your addiction."

Elijah shook his head. "I had good friends. And an even better family who looked past the irresponsible drunk I'd become and remembered the man I used to be. And then there was Jasmine."

Jasmine, Elijah's wife and soulmate. Zion envied him, that unbreakable bond—the one that drew Elijah's soul to Jasmine's eleven years after a stroke claimed his life. They were together in death as they had been in life, alcohol addiction no longer a daily battle.

"None of us can do it alone, Zion. I tried, and I failed."

"What are you trying to tell me? You no longer have to deal with your old addiction."

"True," he smiled with self-satisfaction. His mother used to say she fell in love with Elijah because his smile was like glimpsing a rainbow after a hearty downpour. Their marriage had weathered many rainstorms—none of which dampened their love for each other and commitment to their family. "But I never forgot the steps. And when I look at you, all stone-faced and sad, I'm reminded of one."

Zion didn't bother with the obvious question. He knew his father would tell him. At least when he did, Elijah's fatherly visit would be over.

"One important step is to help others who suffer from the same addiction."

Zion shifted in his chair to better see his father. "I'm not an alcoholic—never have been. You know that."

"I know. It's not exactly the same, but you do need my help. Hell, you need someone's help."

No, he didn't. He only needed to be left the hell alone.

"I believe Iman already beat you to the punch. She came, she talked, she left. Apparently, I have anger issues."

"That's obvious, but that's not what I'm talking about."

"No? What are you talking about then?"

Elijah picked up the glass of iced tea and drowned the rest of the contents before continuing. "I can never get it just right—you know, the way your mother used to make it, with just the right amount of loose tea, mint leaves, honey, and ice. Anyway," he sat the glass on the porch beside his chair, "alcoholics have the Twelve-Step Program. I lived and breathed that program, accepted my addiction and the fact that I would have to deal with it for the rest of my life. But you, son, you've never truly accepted your fate."

"What fate? I'm dead, if you haven't noticed. We're both dead, what fate is left for us?"

"Kubler-Ross, the Five Stages of Grief."

Zion's hands balled into fists, but he remained seated, forcing himself to listen despite the urge to end the link with his father.

"I always thought you handled your death and rebirth a little too easily. I mean, you actually died, Zion. The Fates, from what you told me, brought you back to life."

That wasn't exactly what had happened, but it was close enough.

"Thirty years." He shrugged. "It's better than nothing, but it couldn't have been an easy pill to swallow."

No, it hadn't. But I had no choice.

Zion had enough psychology classes in college to know of Elisabeth Kubler-Ross' theoretical stages of coping and dying.

"Denial, anger, bargaining, depression, acceptance." Elijah ticked each one off with a finger.

Zion had never felt so tired. He wanted nothing more than to curl up and sleep the rest of his existence away. Kubler-Ross was long since dead, so why did he feel like she had been haunting him for years, staying quiet and out of sight—but there, always there with her damn stages.

"How far did you get? Did you even make it past bargaining?"

He had. In truth, he'd flown right past denial, shoved over anger, and slammed right into bargaining. He'd wanted to live, no matter how long, if he could see Lela again, have her in his arms and his life. Denial, anger, and bargaining were the easy stages. While the last two…

"Depression." Zion stood and walked away from the wicker chair, unable to stay seated and feign a calm he didn't feel.

Elijah stood as well.

"You never made it to acceptance, did you?"

It wasn't truly a question. That was the reason why Elijah Grace, above all others, was there. Who better to understand than a repentant alcoholic?

"If I didn't accept my fate, then how could I expect Lela and Xavier to? It wasn't fair to them. I got my bargain, my Lela, my family, my three decades."

But it still hadn't been enough. The more he got, the more he wanted. The happier his life with Lela was, the longer he wanted to experience it. It wasn't fair. It simply wasn't fair. He had everything and nothing. How could he ever accept that?

"You pretended, tried to prepare them as best you could. But you never prepared yourself, accepted that you would get no more time with them, with Lela."

Zion's knees buckled. Elijah's strong arms caught him, held him and provided the strength Zion no longer possessed.

He helped him back to his seat, careful eyes watching.

"Thanks. I'm fine now."

No, he wasn't. More pretending. More lying. More denial. Perhaps he never made his way through stage one. Zion almost laughed at the frightening realization.

Anger and acceptance. Coping and dying. How could he manage it all in the limited time Lela had before her soul was lost to him forever?

Zion closed his eyes, cutting off the route of his burning tears.

"I always knew Lela would be the one."

"How?" How could Elijah know what had taken him so long to realize?

Elijah scratched his head and smiled. "You had to see your face, your eyes when you spoke of her. All of those long-distance calls to Earth and all you could talk about was the Asiyan peace negotiator—Lela this and Lela that. It was as if you were a kid again with his first crush. Honestly, I was relieved. I didn't think I would see you speak like that about another woman after Iman's death."

Neither had he.

"She was good for you, drew you out of your shell. You know, I never believed in this whole business of soulmates or even the idea of life after death."

Obviously convinced Zion wouldn't fall out of his chair, Elijah let him go and sat on the ottoman where Zion's feet had been propped earlier.

"I thought I would die and that would be all Elijah William Grace Jr wrote—nothing more. No me. No Jasmine. No nothing."

"But the Asiyans had it right."

"Yeah, who would've thought it? And I'm glad they did. I wouldn't trade more time with your mother for all the vodka and whiskey in the cosmos." Elijah leaned forward, his sober eyes so very brown and clear. "But you, son you're throwing it all away. Lela loves you. For a while, I was allowed to watch over her after you died."

He hadn't known that either. The Fates were full of surprises, their level of investment in Lela's well-being unexplainable.

"I saw how your death ripped her apart. I couldn't offer her much, but I was able to comfort her when she slept, helped push back some of her more terrible nightmares."

Elijah's hand came up to rest on Zion's knee, a reassuring weight that did nothing to soften his words.

"She mourned you for a damn long time, and it hurt like hell to watch her pain. And I was allowed to be there when she took vows with Chief Magistrate Ammon. She loved him, too. He was good for her, made Lela smile, something she'd deprived herself of after your death."

Zion wanted to scoot away, to shut out Elijah's words, but he couldn't. He knew this was something he needed to hear.

Had that been the reason why his father's star had been permitted to watch over Lela? For this very moment of doubt, jealousy, and insecurity? Had the Fates foreseen all of this?

"She was happy with him. You must accept that. She deserved that happiness and Ammon gave it to her. But she didn't give him all of her."

Zion's spine stiffened. She had given all of herself to Ammon. Like Elijah said, she'd loved him, was happy with him.

"I think—"

"She didn't, Zion, trust me. I know."

How could he possibly know? Unless…

"She told you? In her dreams…?"

"Hell no. She never knew about that. Never knew my soul watched over her."

"Then how?"

"Sage. She told Sage. Sage told Jasmine," Elijah waved his hand in an odd gesture, "and well, you know, the whole trickle-down Grace effect."

Zion pondered his father's words, a slight smile forming at the edges of his mouth.

"Lela would never say something like that unless it were true." Zion felt the first embers of hope.

Elijah slapped his knee, then pulled back his hand. "Sage was the holder of Lela's secrets—the sister she never had growing up."

So his father, mother, and sister had known Lela, despite her long marriage to Ammon, hadn't decided to break their soul bond and bind herself to the Paladin. "One of you guys should've told me. Enlightened me and instead of allowing me to think the worst."

"You have to learn your own lessons, son. Knowing is only part of the battle. You have to earn the rest. We're all here for you, but you have to want the connection more than you want to hold onto the pain of death, the sense of betrayal at Lela's marriage, the guilt over Iman's death and the misguided notion that you need to suffer as a result."

Elijah stood, ran a hand around the collar of his shirt, and walked around the chairs and toward the end of the porch.

"Move past depression, Zion, so you can accept your death. Only then can you live. Only then will Lela see your star as the beacon she needs. You can bring her home if your star is bright enough to show her the way."

Elijah walked down the porch steps. "Is your star, your love bright enough to guide Lela home?

Was it?

Zion jumped from his chair. He had some thinking to do. No, he corrected himself, he had some healing to do.

"Is your star, your love bright enough?"

God, he hoped so.

CHAPTER TWENTY-FOUR

If I Shall Die Before I Wake

The concept of time no longer had any meaning to Lela. There was no sun or moon to guide her from one hour to the next, from one day to the next. No stars, no tides, no time, no Lela. Just endless blackness, unbearable bleakness, indefinable shadows of lost loves, corrosive bonds, and shattered promises.

And while Lela had chosen this fate, a part of her, the shadow of hope yet to be obliterated by the other shadows, hadn't quite abandoned her. No, its' flicker, a tiny, dying flame remained, a symbol of a yet known future.

But Lela had long since turned her back on Mother Cosmos, believing it had shied from her first, taking all she loved, all she would die to protect and keep with her. Irrational, unfair, she knew. Yet the heart didn't always make sense. The heart did as it wished, leaving the mind to catch up or be left immeasurably behind.

So where did that leave the soul? Abandoned? Lost? Confused?

Perhaps the soul was swept away in the current, pulled by a force it couldn't name or define. Kidnapped by emotions so deep, so complex, that it only existed at the atomic level. Neutrons, protons, and electrons circling the magnetic core, drawn to the pulsing heat, bending and manipulating, fusing and forming bonds meant to last.

Or so Lela had thought. Some bonds, apparently, only lasted the breadth of a cycle. In Lela and Zion's case, thirty cycles.

Lela drifted, surrounded by ghosts of her making, ghosts that offered no quarter. Specters that had become leeches sustaining themselves off her misery and guilt, becoming bloated while Lela's soul slowly withered, taking her closer to her final death.

How in the midst of such a frontal assault, Lela could find hope, she did not know. But for the first time since arriving in the desolate place, Lela sensed a presence other than her own.

Having not enough soul energy to create an image of herself, Lela remained in her electrical state. She didn't require yet another reminder of the woman she'd been, of the body that had lived too long, experienced too much. Nor was a body necessary, for the presence she sensed didn't take physical form either. Yet she knew who had joined her, although she knew not how.

"*It's been a long time.*"

Ah, that voice of old. So long ago. Too many years to count, but Lela hadn't forgotten. She would never forget, her electrical spirit lifting, if even a tiny bit.

"*You shouldn't be here, Sage.*"

A laugh, strong and bittersweet. "*No, it is you, my stubborn Asiyan, who shouldn't be here.*"

A familiar charge. Asiyans, according to most other races, were indeed stubborn. Lela found it a prevalent trait among her people, and yes, even within herself.

"*Perhaps that is the reason why we became friends, for I've never known a human stubborner than you, my friend.*"

"*Am I?*" Sage asked, her electrical spirit drawing closer, so close Lela could feel the force of the woman's star, her own meager in comparison.

"*Stubborn?*"

"*No, your friend? Am I, Lela?*"

It was a pointless question from a woman too intelligent to pose such a query. The answer a given.

Instead of answering the question, Lela responded to the unasked one. "*It's not our bond of friendship and sisterhood that set me on this path. Indeed, for many years it was the only evidence that my heart remained."*

"Zion then? Ammon?"

Lela didn't immediately respond. It had been too long since she'd had anyone in which to confide. Sage's death had taken a toll on Lela she would never share with her friend. Sage, like so many others, had grown old and died. And Lela remained. She always remained.

"Both." A simple but complex answer. Lela's life, even her death, fell into both categories, a duality of want and guilt. Always guilt. *"If you're here to tell me to move on, to go to the Realm of Thuraya, I can't."*

"I'm here only as your friend. No lectures. No arguments. Just friendship. What is it you need from me?"

Lela thought, not able to remember the last time she wanted anything other than a quick death. Shameful, dishonorable, but death of the heart often preceded death of the mind and of the body.

"Just your company, sister of my heart. I've missed you so."

"You've never asked for much."

Sage was wrong. Lela asked, she'd prayed and pleaded. And she'd received Zion then Ammon. No, asking was never Lela's issue, dealing with the consequences of the cosmos' response had been.

"I don't know how long I can stay, but whatever time I have is yours."

Lela didn't expect more than that. Sage really shouldn't be in this place of ever-encroaching specters of despair. She belonged in the light, even though she'd known moments of darkness in her life.

"Who will come after you?" Lela knew there would be two others. Powers greater than Sage Grace were at work here, and Lela believed she knew the engineers of this reunion. For an Asiyan, life and death could be traced to the three Fates—Purpose, Faith, Truth. But what they wanted from Lela, she couldn't fathom.

"I'm friendship. That's all I know. But I suspect you're right. Friendship alone won't convince you. You're far too stubborn for that. For once I just wish—"

"I thought you said no lectures, no arguments."

Sage laughed, a wonderful sound Lela had missed. *"I did promise that, didn't I?"*

"You did, and I intend to hold you to your promise."

Silence drifted between the old friends, a companionable hush of understanding and trust.

Lela had forgotten how good it felt to have a true friend and not the worshippers that had flocked to her over the years. Nice, well-meaning people with gracious respect and exuberant questions, people who only saw her as Regent Lela of the House of Asheema instead of simply Lela, only ever Lela.

From one timeless moment to the next, Sage's energy was replaced by one much more aligned with Lela's own.

Waking her from her lethargy, it wrapped around her. Invisible arms pulled Lela close, holding her the way he always did when she was lost and alone.

Her rock. Her son. Her Xavier.

Tears that shouldn't exist began to fall. And fall. And fall.

They, too, were absorbed, combining with the electrical current running from Lela and to Xavier, a safety net for her soul.

Xavier held Lela, her nonexistent face pressed to his nonexistent heart. But she heard… felt the beats, the thumping, the flow of blood and oxygen—his strength. The life that had seeped from his body three years ago, a mother's sorrow that had yet to heal.

There were no words to describe such grief. A mother forced to give last rites to her only child. A boy that had grown into a magnificent man, proving in his own quiet way that he was not a mistake of the cosmos but a miracle for future generations.

His death, Lela's last reason to live, his presence there an incalculable motivator to fight the ghosts within her conflicted soul.

"A 'bra." Mother.

The word crashed over her, silken waves of love. Her tears came that much more, her heart forming and pounding a ragged symphony of discordant notes. But her blistered heart beat in time with Xavier's, melding and mixing, crystallizing and clarifying the edges of her battered soul.

"A'bra." Xavier said again, stroking newly grown hair, whispering in freshly formed ears, kissing tear-streaked cheeks. *"I need you. Ab'ba, father, needs you. Please come home. Ky'na."*

Ky'na. Yes, Zion and Xavier were her family. And Lela understood Xavier's plea, his pain. If Lela stayed there, in the Realm of Drogo, they would never be a family again. Zion and Xavier had gone to Thuraya. As had Sage, and probably all of Lela's family and friends.

Friendship. Family.

But there was still something missing, something keeping her tethered to the cold, wretched darkness of doom and despair. Something she couldn't let go of—or perhaps it was something that wouldn't let go of her.

From one exhale to the next, Xavier vanished, leaving a physically formed Lela in his wake. And with the body came all the emotional aches she'd tried to dislodge. Wraiths of guilt swarmed in and surrounded her. A vagrant shroud lapped at the star begging for birth, for release, grabbing at the glowing embers of renewed hope, tearing at flesh made whole by a son's love, a son's need, a son's prayer to A'bra.

More wraiths came. More. More. Suffocating. Gorging themselves on fear made manifest. And just when Lela thought she would succumb, when her slither of hope would be no more, strong hands found her, reaching through the pitiless miasma and taking hold of her waist.

The tug-of-war only lasted three screams of, "No, you cannot have her. Release my shaibya or face my wrath."

By slow miraculous degrees, the soul-hungry wraiths slithered away, freeing Lela from their tentacles of death and leaving her body crushed against the hard chest of… Ammon.

"My shaibya," he'd said. His wife.

Yes, she was. Or rather, she had been.

Ammon was Lela's third. From the moment Sage arrived, she'd known the third would be him. Her *shami*—her mate, her husband.

He hugged her, Ammon's embrace warm and possessive. Lela hugged him in return, holding him just as fiercely, guilt and longing blinding her as tears formed and fell.

He continued to hold her, whispering words of love in her ear, his own tears just as plentiful

"You shouldn't be here," he said, voice thick with emotion, body as solidly comforting as she remembered.

"So I've been told."

"Yet you remain. Why?"

Ammon released her, stepping back just far enough so they could see each other clearly. And while Lela knew not how she appeared to him, from her vantage point, Ammon was the embodiment of the man she'd married decades ago—healthy, strong, and spirited, a Paladin with the heart of a Devdas—a servant of God. The man who'd carried the soul of her Zion.

Because of you. Because of him, Lela silently answered. *Because I could never give you what you desired most. Because you deserved so much better than me.*

Lela had loved Ammon with all the heart she had to give. But he had loved her completely, unconditionally.

When Ammon rested on his deathbed, his brain tumor no longer in remission, he'd gazed at her with both love and anguish. The question he'd never voiced shone as bright in his eyes as a shooting star. "Will you forsake your promise to Zion Grace and be my soulmate?" his dying eyes whispered.

When she'd stared back at him, Lela knew what her own revealed. "I'm sorry. I'm so very sorry."

God, she had been. A part of Lela wanted to give Ammon what he'd desired. Her heart cried out to fulfill his dying wish, to take away his pain, to ease his transition into death.

But she couldn't. As much as Lela loved Ammon, as happy as he'd made her, the pledge she'd made to Zion held her heart and soul in a vice she couldn't and didn't want to be freed from. She was forever Zion Grace's, no matter the lifetime, no matter the place.

Her guilt. But not her shame.

Ammon leaned down and kissed her, a soft, gentle press of lips against lips. Not sensual or demanding, but sweet and unbearably loving.

"You never lied to me, Lela. I always knew your soul would one day seek out Grace's."

"But you'd hoped." Lela knew he had. Sometimes she'd feel his yearning eyes on her when Ammon believed her to be asleep. Sensed his urgency to have her change her mind the more the tumor spread, tainting his brain but never his heart.

"A foolish dream unbecoming of a Chief Magistrate." Ammon shook his head as if to scold himself.

Lela grasped his hard-knuckled hand and kissed the soft palm. "Dreams are never foolish, Ammon. Those who fail to dream… well, they're the foolish ones."

"And what is it you dream, Lela? Of ghosts and darkness? Of family and friends? Of happiness and Zion Grace?"

Like Sage earlier, Ammon knew the answer to his question. Even still, Lela had to admit, there was something in the posing, in the hearing, in the mutual understanding.

"Be not afraid, Lela, to reach for that dream. Be not guilty for seeking the happiness you promised yourself so long ago. You made no such vow to me. There is no dishonor between us."

Ammon kissed her again, more passionate this time but with a taste of something more, something final. "No broken promises or half-truths. Just love and trust and friendship." He tilted her head higher, her eyes unable to see anything other than him. "Just forgiveness where none is needed. But if you think you do, then you have mine. I forgive you for any perceived wrong you think you've committed against me."

The hand on her chin remained, keeping her face firmly in place, eyes riveted to the man who still held her heart, a heart swiftly rising from the ashes.

Hope.

"I love you. I've loved you since the first day I saw you in the Hall of Concord, walking beside Regent Etemaad with an aura of innocence and the scent of purpose. And I love you now. Don't dishonor that love, the years we spent together in mated harmony by imagining wrongs where there are none. Don't punish yourself."

One finger wiped away a stray tear, staying to catch the others as they descended. "And don't punish those who love you by staying here, by committing yourself to a fate you don't merit."

Ammon stepped away from Lela, his star brighter and even warmer than before—blinding her with its loving potency. But she couldn't look away, the majesty of the glow captivating, intoxicating, and blissful.

He pivoted to the right, and Lela saw it was not his star that radiated so magnificently, but another. A beacon of light, a ray of unprecedented illumination cut through the ghosts of her mind, her heart, and her rec-ollected soul.

It called to her, hypnotic and all-consuming.

"Go."

"Sage?" she asked.

"Yes, friendship."

"Xavier?"

"Family."

"And you?" Her voice sounded faint, fading, yielding to the force, her star preparing to take flight.

"Friendship. Family. Forgiveness. Your three fates. Step into the light, and find your way home. To him."

"Zion's light, Zion's star?"

"Yes, but also those who love you."

"It's so bright. So. Bright."

No more sound, just the light. Only ever the light.

It beckoned. And Lela went.
Into the light.

CHAPTER TWENTY-FIVE

I Pray to Lord My Soul to Take

Zion felt like he'd been pacing and waiting and worrying for a century. His stomach was all balled into knots, despite having no true stomach or body. But he did have a soul… and memories and needs and wants. And what Zion wanted, what he desperately needed was for Lela to return to him.

He'd done all he could to make the reunion happen, to light her path from the depths of darkness and despair to the light awaiting her just beyond her sorrow.

Zion could do no more. Lela would have to do the rest. She'd have to want as much as he did—to meet him halfway, to bridge the chasm between their lost souls.

She's capable, but is she willing? God, I hope so. I don't want to live an eternity without her.

"Are you sure she's coming?"

Zion stopped pacing long enough to meet Sage's annoyed gaze. She was as young and beautiful as she'd been when she joined the New York Sentinel Police Academy, all dark hair, fit body, and youthful arrogance. Right now, though, his sister had the fatigued, put-upon look of a woman who was battling her inner self that screamed for her to commit bloody murder.

Zion shrugged. Sure, he'd asked her the same question twenty times over the last ten minutes. At least a dozen more times before that. And eight more before that.

"Do you think Lela understood why you and the others were sent to her?" Yeah, he'd asked her that question just as many times.

Sage growled and ran a frustrated hand through her beautifully loose hair.

"This is Lela we're talking about—bright, capable, Regent Lela. I've never known her not to understand something so obvious. Death hasn't affected the woman's brain cells."

She sighed, and rolled her eyes at Zion as if he were the most exasperating moron she'd met this side of death.

Maybe he was. But, dammit, what was taking Lela so long?

Everyone was there, in this place between time and space. A fabricated reality where family and friends had gathered, their individual stars of light blending together in a majestic lighthouse of love and wonder.

It had to be enough. It had to—

Just when Zion was beginning to doubt the radiance of his yellow brick road, a star tumbled out of the darkness.

Spiraling out of control, its trajectory headed right for them. Zion's body braced for impact, the collision inevitable.

But as the star tumbled end over end, it began to slow and circle. And finally, it came to a complete stop. Hovering above them.

The other stars looked upon the new arrival and then at Zion.

He didn't move. Couldn't breathe. Wouldn't dare hope.

The other stars shifted, widening the space between them until they'd created a large, empty circle. A vacant spot, an offering, an invitation.

All eyes went back to the trembling, hovering star—expectant but unsure.

Long minutes past, but the circle of life, the circle of love remained strong. No one moving, the vacant spot beckoning, wanting to be filled.

Cautiously, the hovering star began its descent. Controlled and steady.

It landed, claiming the spot that was always its right.

Then the crowd converged on the star, swallowing her light but creating a more radiant one in return.

In the midst of the emotional cavern stood a bewildered, teary-eyed Lela.

Beautiful.

"She came." Hoarsely spoken but deeply felt.

Up until the moment she'd come barreling through space, Zion wasn't quite sure the intervention had worked. *But did she make the trek for me, herself, or the others?*

And there were many others, so many Zion could barely make out his tiny Asiyan in the crowd. But she was there, a humble purple dress covering her slim form, thick ivory locks streaming down her back and to her bare feet. Demure and unassuming, with a hint of fragility.

Not Regent Lela of the House of Asheema, but simply Lela. His Lela.

"I told you she would come." Sage gave Zion a reassuring squeeze to his hand. A hand he hadn't realized had reached for his sister when he'd first spotted what Zion knew had to be Lela's shooting star, needing her silent strength.

"I was afraid to hope. To believe," he admitted, his eyes never leaving the ever-growing crowd, and the woman in the center.

"She never stopped loving you."

"She also loves Ammon." It was a hard truth, but one Zion couldn't ignore, could no longer hold against her. She had a right to that love, the companionship Ammon offered, the life and happiness the Paladin had brought her. Anything less would've been a heartless fate Lela did not deserve.

"Ammon was worthy of her love and devotion." His grip tightened, understanding the painful heat of her honest words. "But she has always been more devoted to you. You must understand this. Understand and accept that Lela… well, just look."

Sage pointed to the scene before them—bright, vibrant points of light everywhere.

Lela was smiling and crying, silent sobs that shook thin shoulders.

Her parents were there. So were his. Lela's sister and her family as well. Bayden. Bartek. Regent Etemaad and his wife. Chief Magistrates. Ammon. Xavier and his wife stood behind Lela, Xavier's fingers wrapped in his mother's hair the way he used to do when he was a boy of five, clinging to her when she returned from a long day of work.

There were many others. Diplomats. Friends. Allies. And too many Asiyans to count. Most Zion didn't recognize, was sure he never knew. But they were there, adding their brilliance to the moment, paying homage to a long-lived life.

Watching them all, Zion truly saw, really understood. His heart went out to Lela, his throat constricting, a visceral reaction to all his wife had loved and lost.

"So many." A whisper.

"Too many. She's endured much."

Yes, he hadn't understood. Couldn't see past his limited lifespan, while shamefully envying Lela her long life.

But at what cost? Well, Zion could see the cost. The stars surrounding her attested to the price she'd paid.

"She knew them, loved them, and had to go on when they died. One by one by one. Family, friends, lovers, all extinguished lights in Lela's world."

The evidence was there, greeting Lela and welcoming her home.

The Fates were there as well, off to the side, eyes on Lela, uncharacteristic smiles making them appear more mortal and less mystical, less divine. Yet there was something in the way they took in Lela, their gaze of approval calculating not just pleased. Then Faith's regard turned to Zion, Truth appeared behind Ammon, and Purpose's eyes never wavered from Lela—her descendant.

Sage released his hand and started to walk toward the crowd. A moment later, she stopped and looked at him over her shoulder. "Are you coming?"

Zion shook his head. He couldn't. Not just yet. Not with everyone around.

Sage shrugged. "Suit yourself."

When Sage reached the crowd, his sister enveloped Lela into a big bear of a hug, her tall frame dwarfing the much smaller woman. But Lela didn't seem to mind, her small but strong arms coming up to wrap around Sage's waist, holding as much as she was being held.

As the minutes faded, so did the circle of lights, growing dimmer and dimmer. Slowly, they all slipped away, until only two remained.

Lela and Zion.

Finally.

They stared at each other, neither moving, a hush of time and uncertainty between them.

Lela smiled, radiant and heartwarming, then placed one foot in front of the other, walking then running toward him, eyes bright with a solar system of tears. Zion kicked himself for not using the last hour to come up with some great first line. But all he'd done during that time was stare at his lovely wife, dreaming of taking her in his arms and kissing her senseless.

Skidding to a stop, she was right before him, head tilted up, lips quivering and eyes beseeching.

"Zion."

God, one word and his whole world fell into place.

"Zion I—"

He crushed her to him, lips hungry, mouth needy, and hands seeking.

Yes, she was finally there. Where she belonged. With him, only ever with him.

Mine.

He devoured her sobs and moans, trailing hot kisses over lips, face, neck, and lower.

They fell, and a luscious bed caught them.

Zion cradled Lela to him, hugging her, kissing her, and exploring her body with teeth and tongue and lips and hands.

She explored too, her mouth sunshine against his thirsty lips, her arms forget-me-nots around his aching, needy body.

Eager hands and a ravenous mouth caressed and claimed. Hips lifted, rubbed, swiveled, and brought tears of joy to his eyes and shouts of pleasure from his mouth.

God, he'd forgotten, but it was all coming back to Zion. Their first kiss, their honeymoon, and all the intimate nights—and days—they'd shared in each other's arms.

He wanted to experience it all again. Wanted more than old, recycled memories. Wanted passion and pleasure and warmth and wetness.

Wanted Lela.

And yes, thank the Fates, he had her, in his arms and under his naked, heaving body.

Moving as one. Crying as two.

Making love.

Cherishing the past. Welcoming the future.

When the wave of sexual euphoria finally released Zion and Lela from its soul-merging talons, they floated back to themselves.

Sweaty.

Breathless.

Sated.

Lela settled in the crook of Zion's arm, his chest her willing pillow.

"Well, he said," swallowing hard to catch his breath, "that was one hell of a hello."

Lela laughed, a sexy sound that went straight to Zion's heart.

"After so long apart, Zion, when I finally saw you, I found my mind had gone completely blank." Lela looked chagrined, brow furrowing when she looked up at him. "That has never happened to me before. Perhaps death has affected my ability to think and reason."

Zion chuckled, reminded exactly why he'd fallen in love with Lela. The woman was so damn adorable.

"So you decided to jump my bones instead?"

She laughed again, throaty and sensual.

"I believe it was you who did all the jumping." Lela raised up on her elbows and looked down at Zion, Picasso marble eyes shimmering with flickers of repressed naughtiness. "Our less than graceful reunion put me in the mind of an old-fashioned boat, rocking and rolling. Not exactly the proper execution of the Unity of Hearts, although I have no complaint with your very human variation on the ritual."

Oh, yes, most definitely adorable.

"Well," Zion plucked a stray strand of hair out of Lela's face, "we are soulmates, captains of each other's ships."

"Soulmates." Lela smiled. "We are." She pressed her lips to his. "You've always been that to me." Another kiss. "Always."

All the humor and sexiness was gone from her voice, Lela's words healing a wound deep within him.

With a seriousness that bordered on sorrow, she caressed his cheek and stared deeply into his eyes.

So much time had passed since they'd last been together like this, since she'd seen him in any form she could touch. And it was all there, in the eyes that held his, in the fingers that stroked and soothed, in the tears that fell.

"I love you. Missed you." Lela shook her head, eyes filling with even more tears. "You can't possibly know how much."

Oh, but he could. For he missed her just as much, and his love for Lela was fathomless and eternal.

"I love you, Lela." The four words carried the weight of a billion stars.

He kissed her. Or perhaps she kissed him. It didn't matter. All that ever mattered, all that ever would matter for Zion and Lela was that they were together.

Bound souls.

Forever hearts.

EPILOGUE

The Fate of Purpose floated in a serene state of electrically-charged bliss. Soon, she could rest. They all could rest—a peaceful slumber, then rebirth their reward for a thousand years of service to Mother Cosmos.

But not just yet.

Lela had only arrived home, reunited with Zion. They would need time to adjust, to acclimate themselves to each other and their final joining as bound souls and stars of light.

Yes, time. Purpose remembered well, despite the years between now and then, between death and Fatehood, between truth and faith.

Fate of Truth.

Fate of Faith.

Her twin souls. In body. In life. In death.

She couldn't see the future, but she could divine the heart and soul of those she birthed. Truth and Faith possessed the same ability. So they had known. From the moment the three had taken their first breaths of life, the Fates had known this day would come.

Providence.

Not without pain, doubt, and heartache. Those emotions and tribulations were part of the process, the cycle of life and death. She could not spare them, their rocky journey of love and loss, guilt and forgiveness, truth and faith.

Yes, truth and faith all too often resulted in truth versus faith. Yet it was purpose that served as a bridge, a bond, a link between the two.

Not infallible.

Not simple.

Not easy.

But open, critical, determined.

Lela—Purpose's light and legacy.

Familiar sparks joined her, encircling her energy within the protective embrace of their love.

"How is Ammon?"

"He has accepted what he believes to be the truth, but he does not yet understand his purpose." Truth drew nearer. *"But he will. In time, he will."*

Ammon—Truth's champion and commander.

"They all will." A truth from her Faith. *"Faith is strongest in those who are most tested, even when they think they have none to buttress their spirit."*

Zion—Faith's zeal and zenith.

"They are bound souls." Purpose smiled. *"More than they now know."*

"As we are." Truth.

"As we were meant to be." Faith.

"But they are not us. They will trod their own path, become the Fates Mother Cosmos needs. Purpose.

As three. As one.

Fate.

THE END

Now that you've seen how it ends, want to know how it all began?
Stay tuned for the next book in the Forever Yours Series.

THE GARDEN

Bonus Story

I wrote "The Garden" a couple of years ago but never published the short story. When writing *Bound Souls,* I used the basic premise of "The Garden," with the dying husband and devoted wife. From there, the two stories diverge—different characters, planet, and ending, but the same forever kind of love. Enjoy the love story of Monifa and Akin.

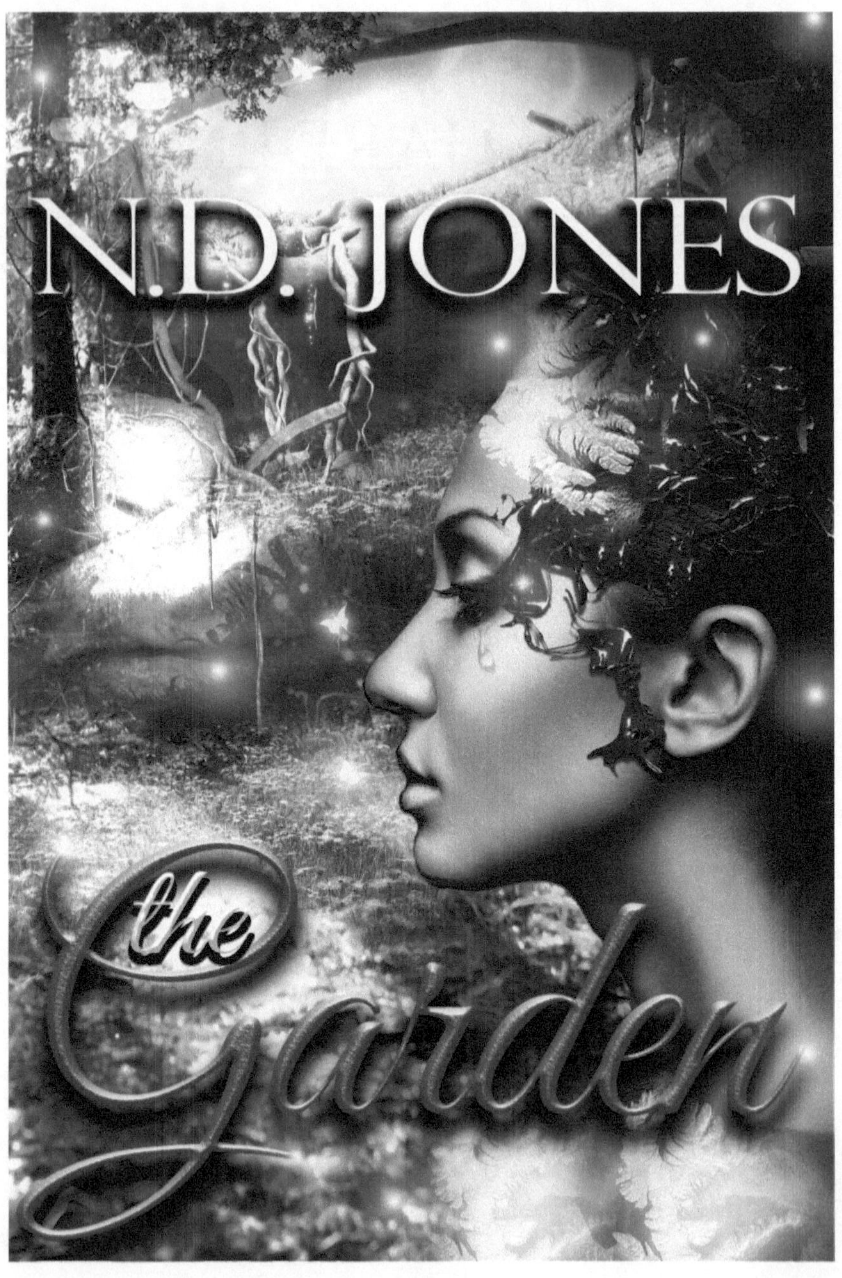

N.D. JONES
the
Garden

"I am not having this discussion with you," Monifa said, face contorted in an annoyed grimace, voice echoing the same emotion. "You are being ridiculous, Akin, and I wish you would just calm down and think rationally."

"Rationally?" Akin repeated, following her into their bedroom and slamming the door behind them. "Rationally?" he asked again, grim-faced and angry.

Monifa went to her closet and swung the glass doors open, trying her best to stay her anger. Akin had been on a verbal rampage the entire ride home from the healer induction ceremony. Her youngest sister ascended to the first rank of Mganga wa Kienyeji and could now perform basic herbal treatments. In time, like Monifa, her sister would gain more knowledge, more magic, and her repertoire of treatments would increase, as would her clan status and rank within the tribe. Yet, her mate's sour disposition had cast a dark shadow over the tribal rite of passage.

"I should've knocked Matata on his healer clan punda. He hopes to seduce you to get your support for him on the Healers Council of Zande. He thinks he's charming and virile and..." Akin punched the closed door, his warrior's flesh no match for the durable metal. Blood sprung forth in a deep, vibrant green, oozing from the open slits between his knuckles.

"Gungu dichtu," he swore, pulling back his right hand to survey the damage.

She ran to him then, quickly grabbing a towel from the master bathroom first.

"Let it be, Monifa," he growled when she took possession of his battered and bleeding hand.

"Let me see." It was a low but firm command. She lightly wrapped the towel around Akin's knuckles, then gently patted to absorb the blood. "You are acting like a complete maniac. Or perhaps as'shtu would be a more appropriate descriptor," she corrected, ignoring her mate's raised eyebrows at her uncharacteristic vocabulary choice. "And do not tell me I got it wrong because you have used that word enough times over the last eighteen cycles for me to know precisely the meaning."

Of the four tribes that called the planet Zande home, only the warriors had such coarse words, and informal speech, as part of their language. Before meeting Akin, she would have never dared to use such vulgarity, but two decades, three daughters, and a second language later, there was not a syllable in the warrior tribe's language of X'bilu Monifa she did not know.

To say Monifa was upset would be an understatement, to say she was concerned about her mate's state of mind would be as accurate as concocting the perfect medicinal remedy. This was not the first time Akin had overreacted to what he perceived to be an insult.

"Monifa," he started, "Matata was flirting with you. It was as clear as the nose on his face, which, by the way, I should've bloodied for him. A healer cannot heal himself, you know."

"Akin Tunde, there will be no more talk of punching or bloodying or any other form of fighting. This is not like you." She removed the towel to get a better look at his hand. "You are lucky. It does not appear to be so bad as to require sutures. A thorough cleansing, bandage, and treated ice should be all that is required."

Monifa stood, narrowed her eyes at her mate, and walked out of their bedroom, opening the door almost as forcefully as Akin had closed it. He said nothing, and for that, she was grateful. She hated his mood swings. And to her dismay, the occurrences between them had increased over the last six months.

She moved into the kitchen, opened the refrigeration unit, and shoveled two handfuls of ice into a bowl. Monifa located a small clear vile from an overhead cabinet and dropped two ounces of a green fluid into the bowl. She covered the dish with her right hand, recited a brief incantation, and looked down to see the ice glowing. The medicinal fluid was being absorbed into the cold blocks. She blew on the ice, dispersing the magical glow into an evaporating mist.

Monifa plucked out the pins that held her hair aloft, permitting the locks to fall in thick gold-and-black curls about her shoulders. She then sighed with exasperation. Akin had always been a level-headed person. As a tenth-degree Kamau Njia warrior and clan leader, he could not be anything but even-tempered. Yet something was going on with him, and she did not know what.

She made her way back to the bedroom. Akin was still sitting on the bed, nursing his hand, frown firmly fixed and unwavering.

"I can't believe you called me an as'shtu," he complained, lifting his eyes to her when she entered. "You never use such language, Monifa, and in defense of Matata, of all people."

She sighed, indeed regretting her word choice, no matter how accurate or well-deserved. "I apologize." She inserted his hand in the bowl of ice. "I was upset. I should not have spoken to you the way I did." She paused then, met his gaze, and returned frown for frown. "Regardless of the word, the sentiment remains the same. I do *not* apologize for that part."

"What kind of apology is that?"

"An honest one and the only one you will receive." She stalked away from him and to her closet. Monifa slipped out of her red-and- white ceremonial robe, replacing it with a delicately woven blue sleeveless shift. She sat on the edge of the bed, removed her shoes and stockings, all the while ignoring her brooding mate.

Still seething, Akin renewed his argument. "Matata was flirting with you."

"Healers do not flirt," Monifa answered with a note of annoyed finality.

Akin abruptly twisted to face her, nearly dropping the bowl of magically-treated ice in his irritated state. "You can't be serious. I distinctively remember you flirting with me when we were on the Healing Isle."

"I never flirted. I was being friendly, helpful. I had to get to know you in order to administer the appropriate medicinal treatment. That is the way my healing magic works. It is much more effective if I know something of my patient's soul, mind, and heart."

Akin snorted. "Like the dinner in your personal chamber was my idea or the sexy black gown you wore when you came to mine was just an expression of your healer curiosity about warrior women's fashion."

"Do not mock me, and do not presume to have known my mind or intentions back then. If I say I was not flirting, then I was not." Monifa thought about it for a moment, moving to rest her back against the headboard. "I am not even sure if I know how to flirt."

"Oh, you know, Monifa." His frown gave way to the briefest of smiles. "All females know how to flirt. It's part of your genetic makeup or something." Akin's frown returned as quickly as it had vanished. "And Matata knows how to flirt as well. Sure, healers are subtler than warriors and use tribal ceremonies to justify their actions, but the intention is the same."

She pulled her legs to her chest and gave her mate a long, considering look. "What is this really about, Akin?" she asked, her voice deliberately soft, placating.

"What's wrong is that I don't like other men directing their pheromonal attractants at my mate. I don't appreciate you being eyed as if you're a Grade A piece of prime meat in a farmer's market full of carnivores."

Even after so many years of marriage, Monifa still hadn't heard all of Akin's regional sayings and, like now, he could still pull a new one out of his cloak and leave her stumped. Yet, she'd had much practice at uncovering the rose hidden in the weeds. And right now, Akin's garden was chock full of the wild plant.

"Whatever Matata did that upset you so, I am sure he did not mean it the way you took it. We have known each other for a very long time. He is a good friend. But you know that already. In fact, he has been here for dinner on several occasions, and you never expressed any ill feelings toward him before now."

Monifa was taking a page out of the spiritualist's tribal training guide for beginners, yielding and redirecting a strong force with a seemingly weaker one. She didn't want to fight with her mate, especially when he was in such an irrational frame of mind, and when she had no clue as to the source of his anger.

"You're naïve, Monifa." Akin swung his bad hand from the bowl of ice. "You never notice such things. You think everyone is all good and light. Well, they aren't." He stood and placed the bowl on the nightstand on his side of the bed.

"I am not naïve. I just do not agree with your assessment of Matata. I would know if he or someone else was interested in me in a romantic way. Perhaps there is some kind of miscommunication going on and we simply need to think about it and figure it out."

Still yielding, trying to reflect his anger.

"Like with Baruti," he spat, whirling on her, face set in granite. "How long did it take you to figure that little one out? That jealous mentor of yours almost succeeded in poisoning me with a batch of deadly herbal tea before you realized he coveted more than your healing herbs and friendship. It was your *healing touch* he most desired, your *cunchu*," Akin stated crassly. "No, healers may not flirt, Monifa, but they sure know how to squirm themselves into the lives of the person to whom they're interested."

Prudence and strategy gave way to anger. Immovable force would meet immovable force.

Monifa moved swiftly, quicker than her trained but aging warrior could track. Her magic and anger propelled her forward until she was standing squarely in front of him. Her finger poked Akin in his solid chest, her chin lifted and set.

"Listen here, Akin, you have been in a foul mood for the last six months, and I have no idea why. I have tried ignoring it and talking to you about it. Nothing works. You have just become angrier and grumpier as the days go by, and frankly, I am sick of it. This is not like you and if you insist on continuing this paranoia and disrespectful behavior..."

She trailed off, unwilling to issue the ultimatum she felt coming. In her mate's current mood, he would be just foolish enough to challenge her, and she was feeling just stubborn enough to follow-through. Instead, Monifa said, "We both need time to cool off before we say something we will regret. You can stay here." She moved toward the bedroom door. "I will sleep in the guest room for the night. Perhaps in the morning we can have a more dignified conversation without insults and name calling."

Monifa opened the door only a few inches before she saw a tawny hand with swelling blotches push it back into place. Akin's bruised hand rested on the door above her head, the front of his body pressed firmly against the back of hers, his breath warming the gold dangling loop in her pointy ear—a tenth mate season gift.

"I overheard him," Akin said. "Six months ago I overheard Matata ask your father if you would consider having a healer after being mated so long to a warrior and if your clan would approve such a union. He said since he was one of only a dozen healers who fought beside the warriors in the great Emancipation War that he could offer you something no other could—a healer with a warrior's heart."

She stiffened, hand on the door dropping.

"He said in spite of you breaking tribal law and mating with a lowly warrior, you were more healer in heart and soul than any woman of your tribe." If possible, Akin leaned in even closer, his lips slightly brushing her ear. "Your father told him he didn't think you would mate yourself to anyone else and Matata said, unlike me, he had plenty of time. And in three years the goddess would take me, leaving you alone, no mate. 'Monifa of Alur of the healer tribe, Monifa Tunde will be alone and lonely. But she won't have to be forever, and once she emerges from the requisite season of mourning, I will be there to show her how much more living there is to do.' And that my dear, naïve mate, is an exact quote."

Akin pushed from the door and staggered to the bed, dropping his tall frame like a safum after a long farming season. He looked old, Monifa thought, watching him through sorrowful eyes. So much older than he had only a few minutes ago. She at least now knew the reason for his strange behavior. She thought knowing the source of Akin's anger would make her feel better, give her a stronger angle from which to deal with her mate.

How foolish I have been. How terribly, terribly foolish.

Monifa joined him on their bed, sitting next to Akin and grasping his unharmed hand in her own. They sat like that for several minutes, neither willing to fill the silence, an uncomfortable bubble of realization having settled over them.

It was true. Akin only had three years left on his lifecycle—perhaps less. He was tired and felt even more so as the years crept by. He felt like he was on a Class C war cruiser, barreling through hyperspace, making its final descent into oblivion. And the ride would soon be over, much quicker than he'd thought, the g-force hammering against his aging body.

Warriors weren't meant to live to see many sunrises and sunsets. Goddess Mawu didn't create them that way. As goddess of night, joy, and motherhood, she buried her hands deep within the planet's core and forged life out of clay and water. She first birthed the spiritualists and gave them East Zande, naming them Spiritualists of Shona. She granted them long life so they could worship her for many years. As well as the power of soul mysticism, this was necessary for delivering the souls of her followers from the physical plane to the spiritual one.

Next, she created the healers and bestowed upon them a home in West Zande. She anointed them Healers of Alur, giving them long life, a loving heart, and the power of herbal mysticism necessary for communing with nature and all her creatures therein.

She then looked to the north and dug even deeper, extracting the most fertile soil from the planet's depths. From the rich, northern red soil, hearts thumped, neuro-pathways pulsed, and she called them

Builders of Kamba. With the power of welder mysticism and a long lifespan, they would construct cities, spacecrafts, machines, and temples to the goddess from which all her children could sing her praises.

Finally, she looked to the south, its soil rocky and hard. Her precious creations needed protecting, so she whispered, and the sky parted under her command, bringing rain, softening the terrain. She swept her hands over the southern silt, blew on it, and decreed they would be the Warriors of Maasai. They weren't her finest creations. The soil too untamed to form a truly cultured being, their lives thus mirrored the ground from which they were harvested—hard, rough, resilient. But finite in form. Yet, they were gifted with the power of steel mysticism, necessary for waging and winning any battle, every war.

Akin spared a sidelong glance at his mate, whose head was down, eyes closed, hand still fiercely gripping his own. She wasn't ready for the ride to end either. Yet they both knew it was slowing, preparing to grind to its final halt and he would have to disembark, leaving her behind.

This situation with Matata had been eating away at him for the last several months. But if he were honest with himself, he would admit that Matata was simply an outlet for his own anger, fear, and depression. He was growing older, his reflexes slower, Fist of Power weaker, and his stomach… well, let's just say he'd had to use the services of a good seamstress over the seasons. Yet, Monifa was still as beautiful and fit as when he'd first met her on the Healing Isle. Sure, her hair wasn't as dark and vibrant as it once was, black coils giving way to gold, but she still took his breath away, Akin's attraction to his mate as strong as ever.

However, he didn't begrudge Monifa her slow aging or fine, alluring features. In fact, he loved that about her. What did bother him was that other men could see what he saw. Everything about his mate exuded intelligence, grace, dignity, strength, and beauty. Yet he learned a long time ago she could never see herself the way others did, especially men.

While Akin rarely entertained such jealous thoughts before or cared much when he caught a male giving his mate an approving look, now he saw nothing but. And such recognition, under the circumstances, en-raged him, an insult to his masculinity, his pride.

"I'm sorry, sweetu," he finally said, lifting her chin with his injured hand.

Tears flooded her golden-emerald eyes. She wasn't ready for this conversation. How could she be?

"No, it is me who should apologize, Akin. I thought you were being paranoid, seeing things that did not exist."

"I acted like an as'shtu, a brute, nearly dragging you out of the temple before the ceremony was over. I might as well have hoisted you over my shoulder and beat my chest. You were right."

He rubbed his thumb gently across her right cheek then lips. "You're an incredible woman, Monifa." Akin paused, nearly biting his tongue on his next words. The ones his heart screamed to not utter. "You're one of the chosen, created from the best of this planet, created for a higher purpose. For a healer, you'll be in your prime when the spiritualists guide my soul home." His voice cracked when the held tears dropped from Monifa's eyes. She knew where he was going with this.

"You'll have to go on without me. I don't want you to spend the next century by yourself."

The voice of her father, Monifa's clan leader echoed in his head.

"I know you may love my daughter, and I have no fear you will pro-tect and watch over her. Yet your life is fleeting, a mere grain of sand in the unyielding winds of time. We have our traditions for a reason, Akin. Tribes were never meant to commingle in this way. If you mate with my Monifa, you will do so at your benefit but her peril. She will mourn you for the rest of her days, after the Goddess calls you to sanctuary."

"I will not be by myself, Akin. I will have our daughters," Monifa said, standing and walking away from him.

She moved toward the window, refusing to acknowledge the true meaning of his words. Akin followed, viewing her stern but sad image in the window-wall, the reflection of Zande's twin moons glistening off the crystal ocean below. He wrapped his arms around her waist and pulled her to him.

"The thought of another man being this close to you," he whispered, stirring her hair with the silvery pulse of his magic, "makes me want to commit murder. When I heard Matata offering for you, it took all of my self-control not to take a battle-ax to his pretentious skull. The only thing I kept thinking was that he couldn't have you, you're mine and mine alone."

"Is that why you have been so angry these past few months?" She turned in his arms, resting her head against his resilient shoulder.

"Yes and something else."

"What?"

Akin lifted her chin, forcing Monifa to meet his eyes.

"I didn't want to acknowledge how selfish I was being." Leaning down, he placed a tender kiss on her lips. "I want you to be happy in that century, or so you have left. But I don't want you to find happiness in the arms of another man."

"I have no desire to mate with anyone else or to take a lover." Her words were reassuring, as was her kiss, a desperate one full of a mate's integrity and denial. "I cannot imagine being with anyone other than you. I love you. I could never love another."

Akin knew she spoke the truth. He believed her, but she didn't understand. He did. He'd been through it before.

"When Thema died, a part of me died with her. Like you, I thought there would never be anyone else for me. And that was true for a long while."

Monifa shook her head in protest. "Do not, Akin," she pleaded. "Do not say such things. There will never be anyone else for me."

He saw the near panic in her face, her haunted golden eyes brilliant with resolution and despair.

"It is not the same."

It was exactly the same. Yes, what he felt for his first mate was different from the love he had for Monifa. But it was love all the same.

Loving Monifa didn't mean Thema ceased to occupy a special place in his heart and mind. A warm memory of his first mate and their life together would always be a part of him, as he would always be a part of Monifa. But she couldn't see it, not now. But someday. Akin didn't want to think about that and clearly, neither did Monifa.

"All right, sweetu," he soothed, bringing her face to his own. "Enough talk for tonight. We still have plenty of time."

"I do not need time. I know my mind. It will not change. I will not have Matata or any other."

Akin smiled at his devoted mate. She was indeed naïve, and blessedly so. The selfish part of him pleased at her defiance.

"Come to bed, sweetu," he said, wrapping his left arm around her small waist and leading her away from the window and the bleakness of the late night sky and their conversation.

He undressed in silence, Monifa watching, studying him. He knew what she was doing, her rational mind battling her heart, considering his words, and the long years ahead of her without him. She grimaced, turned away from him, and hid herself beneath the improbable security of the bed covering.

He slid into bed, scooting until he was where he wanted to be. The perfect spot, body spooned against that of his mate's. Akin's left hand found Monifa's hip and his mouth her bare shoulder. He caressed both with slow, smooth, and practiced movements, creating an old rhythm and a familiar heat.

"Akin," she said, her voice low and throaty.

"Shh, sweetu, no more talking, no more thinking, no more anger, no more fear. Let's just enjoy each other while we still can. Please, Monifa, I need that. I need you."

He did, so very much. Akin didn't want to think about the future any more than his mate.

And when they made love, it was slow, so heartbreakingly slow and exhaustingly delicious. Akin worshipped at Monifa's temple, whispering prayers and bestowing gifts, hoarding her essence, her light, for the dark, lonely journey to come.

Though fatigued, he didn't sleep. He watched Monifa, the rise and fall of her chest, the anguished expressions that marred her features, telling him she wasn't peacefully sleeping, unable to let go of her anxiety over his impending death.

Akin moved her hair from her face and gracefully, purposefully, massaged the tips of her pointy ears, helping her relax. Her tense body melted under his war-roughened fingers, taking on a more natural posture, breathing growing deep and heavy.

He smiled at his mate and wrapped himself around her, using his left arm to pull Monifa close to him, claiming her as his. She was still his, he reminded himself. For the next three seasons and another for mourning, she would be his in mind, heart, and body. But after that… well, life went on, even for the most loving and dedicated of spouses. Akin was sure Thema had forgiven him for finding love and happiness with someone else. And he could… would do the same for Monifa. But not now, not tonight, not yet. He still had time. They still had time. She was his, yes, his and his alone. For now, until Goddess Mawu called him home.

*****

"Wake, my child, and come to me."

The feather-soft voice glided over her body, prodding her awake. Groggily, Monifa opened her eyes.

"Wake my child and come to me," the willowy voice came again. "We have much to discuss."

Monifa sat up in bed and looked over at her mate. Akin slept soundly, breathing even, aura peaceful. His long, thick, ash gray dreaded hair coiled around his neck like a scaled beast of prey, marking him as warrior tribesmen. The vivid illumination from the moons cast a singular glow on Akin's slumbering form, his naked body a testament to his many battles, his many wins. There wasn't an inch of his strong form Monifa did not know. Not an inch she wouldn't coat in every herbal treatment she could conjure if it meant extending his life, keeping him with her and their girls.

"Come, Monifa, the time draws late. Come to me, the beauty of the night awaits."

Monifa gave her mate a wistful look, grazed his temple with the gentlest of lips, and slipped from their bed. She quickly donned an ankle-length, fern green robe, the color symbolic of the healing nature of the Alur tribe, the color of Zande's bountiful land.

She peered over her shoulder once to make sure Akin was still asleep. He was, and she proceeded out the door on the east side of the bedroom. The door led to a balcony, and from the enclosed structure, she walked down four flights of steps. At the end of the last flight was a narrow, fortified passageway designed by her mate for emergencies. It led to the sparkling granules of the beach over which their personal sanctuary resided.

Five minutes of walking, Monifa emerged from the red clay tunnel, her eyes alighting on the greenish-blue rolling waves of the Pride'ntu Ocean. The air was mid-summer thick with a hint of relief wafting from the cool, calm giver of life, giver of hope.

Monifa moved further onto the beach, her long robe gliding behind her, the hood catching the untamed spill of locks. She reached the shore's edge, bent down, and rescued a pebble from the pull of the ocean's currents. The pebble was hard and flat. Its shape was indefinable but strangely familiar. Monifa held onto the speck of nothingness, its safety of sudden importance.

The voice came again, as gentle and loving as before. It always was, Monifa reminded herself, but she hadn't heard it for a very long time. Why was she hearing it now?

"Why have you called me to this place, Goddess Mawu?" Monifa's voice was strong but respectful, her eyes focused on the ever-moving undersea shadows of the ocean, where she sensed the mystical energy of her goddess.

"You have not been to temple in far too many seasons, my child. Do you no longer need or desire the guidance of your mother?"

It was a non-question. Bait only a child or fool would find appetizing. She was neither.

"You know my heart and my mind, Goddess, for you have given me both."

"And so I have, my child, but your faith has wavered."

An eager wave washed close to Monifa's feet, her toes digging firmly into the sticky, wet sand, the edge of her robe lightly dusted with both.

"Not wavered, my Goddess, at least not in the way I think you mean."

"Explain, child of Alur."

So, she would make her speak the words she could so easily read in her heart. The truth that was as cold, dark, and deep as the ocean before her.

"He does not deserve to die." A soft admission. "Akin and his kin fought bravely for our planet when the Destroyers came to imprison and enslave our people. And they have done so over thousands of years. Yet they are destined to live only half the seasons granted to the other three tribes."

"And you think this unfair?"

"Yes."

"And you blame me?"

"I think," Monifa started cautiously, "the caste system is indeed unfair to the warrior tribe. They protect our home. Yet, they reap few benefits of their toil."

"And you blame me?"

"Will you force me to say the words, Goddess, or will you accept my silence as answer enough?"

A warm breeze encircled Monifa, billowing her hair and robe.

"I created four tribes, my child, not a caste system," the goddess said, the reassuring warmth of the breeze increasing. "I gave you all intelligence, a loving heart, but most importantly, free will. How you decided to use that free will is what created the caste system."

Monifa took hold of her unruly hair, tucked the ends in her robe, and pondered the goddesses' words.

"But you created four distinct tribes. Even our appearance and ability varies. I do not understand."

"Yes, none of you have ever understood. I created four tribes but only one race of people. Appearance and ability are shallow indicators of true difference. Besides, omnipotence, my dear Monifa, is as much a curse as it is a blessing."

"But you are a goddess, how can you then argue against the very supreme power you possess?"

This conversation had taken an odd turn. Monifa thought she would come down to the beach and pray, if not beg, for Akin's life. In spite of her own absence from temple and growing anger at his fate, Akin had always been a faithful servant of the goddess, never questioning, always accepting. Yet, Monifa stubbornly questioned, and absolutely refused to accept his fate.

"It is the fact that I am a god that allows me to make such declarations. My sweet, naïve, Monifa, gods have been known to get drunk on their power and become the cruelest of beings."

"But you are not cruel."

"Do you not think me cruel, my child, when you watch your mate grow old and weak?"

Monifa's head dropped. Shame and the truth pulling it downward.

"I thought it unfair…and, yes, perhaps even cruel."

The wind swirled, encouraging her chin upward.

"When Gods fail to understand the importance of self-control and balance, they tend to create beings that are too powerful, never content, and lust for power, even at the expense of others."

"Like the Destroyers?"

"Yes, like the Destroyers. They came to your Homeworld, blanketed your sky with their great ships, their hunger for expansion and dominance, vulgar and unquenchable."

"Many of us died, but we fought and drove them from here and back under the rock from which they slithered."

"Yes, and how did you all manage that admirable feat?"

"We worked together, of course, my Goddess."

Monifa could've sworn she heard laughter emanate from the watery depths of the swooning tide. This wasn't time for laughter but action. She needed the goddess to save Akin before the last grain of sand in the hourglass of time slipped through the neck and landed with a silent cry of finality.

"I breathed life into four tribes, Monifa, but one incredibly complete being. The spiritualists are the soul, the healers the heart and mind, the builders the hands, legs, and arms, and the warriors the sword and shield. None of you can exist without the other. Four pieces of a brilliant jigsaw— independent, unique, powerful—ONE."

She had never thought of the tribes in those terms, such were the strict rules of Zandian society—four tribes, four regions, four languages, four cultures… but one people…?

"So, we complete each other," she said, unsure whether it was a statement or a question.

"Yes."

"Does that also mean that where one is weak, the others are strong?"

"Yes."

The ocean started to stir as Monifa worked out in her mind what this new knowledge could mean for her family, for her mate. Her heart started to soar, but she squelched the embers of hope, too afraid to entertain the bazaar possibility.

"Do healers have the answer to the rapid aging of the warriors? Do I?" she asked, unable to keep the tremor from her voice.

She heard the laughter again, deeper, and more satisfied this time. The water plowed in, wetting her robe and pushing her backward.

"Yes."

Her heart tightened at the simple yet explosive response. It couldn't be that straightforward. Could it?

"How?"

"Your magic, your healing hands. His magic, his protective nature makes for a powerful herbal remedy. And the love you share will make it even the more potent."

"But—"

"Go now, my child, your mate awaits."

"But—"

"Go and trust in the magic I have given you both. Go and trust in the love that erased the artificial tribal lines that have separated my children for far too long. Go and trust in me, your goddess."

Monifa parted her mouth to speak, but the mystical energy flowing from the ocean was gone. Only roughly moving rapids were left and the dawning of a new day. She turned and hurried down the beach and to the door leading into the passageway, her mind reeling.

Sweaty and soiled from the spray of the ocean and the grainy, fine sand, Monifa made her way into the bedroom. Akin was still asleep. Good. She hurried to the bathroom, removed her clothing, and bathed. Thirty minutes later, she was back in bed beside her mate, his hard, masculine presence reassuringly familiar.

He turned over, his eyes opening, and the joy she felt came across in her smile.

"Good morning, sweetu." Akin pulled her close. "Where have you been?"

She gave him a surprised look, and he laughed.

"Just because I'm dying, it doesn't mean I've lost all my warrior senses."

She winced at his casual acceptance of his death. Warriors didn't live past fifty seasons and Akin was already in his forty-seventh.

"Tonight, on the beach, the goddess came to me, Akin. She said I harbor the power to cure you in my hands."

Monifa studied her hands and then placed one on her mate's beautifully bronzed cheek. "I never even considered the possibility. I assumed it was beyond a healer's ability. It never occurred to me to think of a warrior's short lifespan as a medical condition like any other."

Akin sat up in bed, his fawn-soft eyes radiant and hopeful. She hadn't seen that emotion in them for far too long.

"Is it possible? Do I dare hope, Monifa?"

"The goddess does not make false claims. I do not have the answer yet, my love, but together we will find the cure."

"Together?"

"Yes, your power to my power." She held both of his hands in hers. "My love to your love. My heart to your soul. We will do this together."

"Together," Akin repeated, a silver of his warrior's magical energy forming a warming circle around them.

"Together," Monifa echoed, her own magical energy merging with that of her mate's. "You are mine, and I am yours. For many tomorrows and beyond."

*****

From the threshold of his mate's medical lab, Akin stared in astonishment. Ten minutes ago, their youngest daughter summoned him in a panic of rushed words and teary eyes. Now he knew why.

Monifa, his articulate, tranquil, and immaculate mate was on the floor of her lab staring at a bland, beige ceiling as if it held the cryptic answers she sought. And all around her defeated form were broken beakers and crystal jars, ripped medical files and reports, and an assortment of herbs and candles in a hodgepodge arrangement of smells and chaos.

Debris cracking under Akin's boots, he waded through the carnage, peering down at his unseeing mate once he'd reached her. Splayed in her green healer's robe in a sacrificial pose, Monifa would've made for an exquisite offering to the Destroyers, a stratocracy where men preferred their women weak and submissive. But Goddess help him, Akin had never seen his mate this dejected. The fact that she'd demolished her beloved lab was an undeniable testament to her wretched state of mind.

"I got you, sweetu." Akin bent over, taking extreme care to lift his mate just right so she wouldn't cut herself. But he needn't have worried, Monifa didn't stir, not even to scold him for "overexerting" himself. She rest limp in his large arms, her slim form no more taxing than bench pressing a medium-class battle ax. True, he was dying, had months left—probably—but Akin still had enough strength of body, mind, and magic to carry his distraught mate from her lab of emotional horrors.

On silent booted feet, Akin walked through the house, whispering a soft, "She will be fine," to his worried girls. At fourteen, eleven, and eight, their concerned, bright gazes roamed over their mother's lost form. Akin understood. They were afraid. So was he.

It was bad enough they had to cope with the knowledge of their father's impending death. Abena, his youngest daughter, had assigned herself the role of his personal nurse, while her older sisters worked beside their mother in the lab. But Monifa was the cuphea hyssopifolia of the Tunde family, the strongest, most resilient annual on Zande. The plant could survive the overbearing weight of the sun, the overpowering moisture of flooded soil, and the underwhelming lack of rain. While in bloom, the pink-purple heathers were radiant, casting a demure aroma. Monifa was like that, her spirit strong but not overpowering. Like the annual, Monifa's essence never died, even when the seasons changed.

Except now.

Except today.

Akin settled Monifa on their bed, the crème bed sheets a backdrop against her green robe, making his mate to appear more like a chrysanthemum shamrock than summer heather. Her golden eyes were glassy, lovely skin taut, body unresponsive to his touch, his words.

He hated seeing her like this. Today's destruction of her lab was the apex of Monifa's declining mental state. This couldn't go on. He must put a stop to her downward spiral. Monifa must be made to understand, there was simply nothing else she could do for him. Over two seasons, she'd done nothing but research, experiments, testing, meditation, and endless rituals that drained the entire family. And for what?

No cure. Only disappointment.

Grief.

Tears.

And while Akin didn't want to die, he would rather end his life tomorrow than watch his mate kill herself trying to save him. There was no longer light in Monifa. The sparkle she'd always exuded lost in her pursuit to find the elusive magical concoction that would stave off an early death for him and his fellow warriors.

Monifa had tried everything, combining herbs and their magic into a thousand possible remedies. He'd drank mystical brews, covered himself in glowing potions, and ate fruit and vegetables that apparently only grew in his mate's private garden. She had done her best, no man could ask for a more devoted partner. It was enough for him, to be loved so deeply and completely. Akin could die and truly rest in peace.

But Akin knew Monifa would find no peace after his passing. No, to Monifa, Akin's death would mean she failed as a mate, as a healer, and as a mother.

Akin reclined beside her, cradling Monifa to him. Breathing shallow, her eyes filled with tears. She turned into his chest, face warm against his black tunic. Cold hands came up to his cheek, stroking with aching gentleness. A silhouette of healer energy skated along his shaven chin, around his neck, and down his back. He'd never felt this particular magical energy from his mate before, the immense melancholia in it pillaging his senses and stirring his magic into action.

While Monifa's tears wet his tunic, he detected the hint of cherry blossoms suffused with the rich, intoxicating scent of the lotus.

Ancient stories passed down from griot to griot told of magic so old, so mystical, so powerful that the goddess hid it away in a cavern deep in the Ma'xambo Forest. No light, heat, or even cold could breach its antechamber. Yet within the blackened quiet of the forbidden, sacred place, a spectacular tree existed that combined the best properties of a cherry blossom and lotus.

No one dared create a word for such a godly creation, but all knew that only the most dedicated and deserving healer would be granted access to the divine tree. Such a person would have to embody every aspect of both the cherry blossom and lotus—purity, beauty, knowledge, grace, female strength, and love.

The sweet aroma grew, Monifa's tears running down his neck. Akin's chest absorbed the wet, wild magic each tear droplet made, forming a circle of pink lotus petals around his heart. The delicate petals vibrated. The thrumming pulse majestic and musical, a symphony of enchantment coursing through him. Sinking deep, it reached for his soul, his faith.

In a flash, Akin was on his back, Monifa astride him. She'd flipped him over and tore his tunic in the process, exposing his hard chest and petal-covered heart. Monifa placed one hand over her heart, the other over his. And her eyes. Dear goddess, his mate's eyes were a hypnotizing hue of green, glittering poignant with rejuvenation.

Monifa focused those eyes of wonder on him, her right hand warming the petals on his chest, sending them deep within. His skin no barrier to the potency. As each petal melted into his heaving chest, Monifa's eyes glowed even brighter, becoming more vibrant, chilling Akin with her forceful gaze.

He'd never seen her like this, both frightening and enthralling. Following the path of the petals, her magic glided from her fingers, the power of an erupting volcano without the danger and fear. Healing lava swam through his body, the scent of cherry blossoms and lotus mauling his senses. Monifa's softly muttered spell soothing.

Under the weight of her healing touch, Akin's body convulsed. His chest was stretched tight from an invisible force, a determined line running from Monifa and into him.

Then Monifa spoke in the tongue of the ancients. A long ago and lost language. One neither of them should have known, but they did.

His mind transcribed effortlessly, keeping pace with Monifa's precise utterances. What began as a prayer, a plea, morphed into an archaic incantation.

Clarity surrounded Akin, a winter fog dispersing. He now knew what to do. The warrior gave his mate what she demanded, what she needed—a key to unlock the gate to the ancient garden.

Power surged through him—untamed warrior power, magic bestowed by the goddess Mawu. She loved him.

The words from the incantation felt wonderful mingled with his magical energy. Monifa accepted it all—uncivilized and unfiltered—twirling it in a massive ball of raw power built on their shared love and commitment to each other, their daughters, and their goddess.

Monifa's mind opened to him. This once, Akin glimpsed the world through a healer's unique vision. If he'd ever doubted the magnitude of his mate's ability to find a cure for him, he doubted no longer. For what he saw made him want to drop to his knees in supplication.

In a place where no life should exist, rows of cherry blossom trees grew. A horde of white blooms flowed from one tree to the next, creating a panoramic cloud for the eyes to feast upon and adore. From an improbable muddy swamp ensconced in a dreary cave, white lotus flowers meandered throughout the garden, their purity of color, form, and potency mixing deliciously with the overhanging cherry blossoms.

Akin felt a breeze, saw it in fact. A spiral of colors—red, green, and yellow slithered through cracks in the cave's walls, growing as it approached the bounty. It was the key. To Akin's surprise, the flowers parted, opening their sanctuary and accepting the hushed request for entrance.

With the speed of a warrior raising his battle ax to defend home and hearth, the spiral of colors flung itself into the cave floor, circling and growing with each rotation. Drilling deep until it hit bottom. With a crack, thud, and boom, roots clawed their way to freedom, bringing forth rich, life-affirming soil.

As Akin watched, what was once an unfathomable hole of worthless rock, transformed into a magnificent habitat for a mature tree. A tree pregnant with branches heavy with red, green, and yellow flowers.

His flowers.

Their flowers.

His cure.

Her gift.

Another breeze and the image began to fade. The divinity of the garden in a cave drifted further and further away. Akin lost focus, unable to hold on. He let go and fell, his body weightless and free—freer than he'd ever been. But he knew she would catch him, she already had.

When he awoke, red, green, and yellow flowers decorated their bed, the aroma familiar, heady.

Monifa sat beside him smiling, eyes focused, free, unforgettable. She reached for him. Steady fingers slid over his bare chest where the petals had been. Akin peered down at those healing fingers and saw it. The tree. Their tree. On his chest. Over the heart that beat triumphantly for his soulmate.

"You did it," Akin choked, unable to keep the tears at bay. His much larger hand grasped his mate's, holding it hostage, the way she held his strongly beating heart.

"*We* did it." Monifa leaned over and kissed him. "In my delirium, when I thought I had nothing else to draw upon but my faith in our goddess and my love for you, I saw it."

"The ancient garden?"

She nodded before giving him another tender kiss.

"I saw it and reached for a petal. Just one. I only needed one. But it was too far away and unreal, a shimmering oasis in a vast desert." Monifa stroked Akin's broad chin. "Then you came to me, drew me into your arms and wrapped your magic and love around me. It was then I knew."

"Knew what?"

"That the answer was inside us this entire time. But we had to dig deep, plant the seed, and allow it to grow. And it did." She unzipped her robe, slid it off her left shoulder. And there, over her heart were two flowers—a cherry blossom and a white lotus.

THE END

Thank you for reading "The Garden." To read more books by N.D. Jones, go to ndjonesparanormalpleasure.com.

ABOUT THE AUTHOR

N. D. Jones is a USA Today Bestselling author who lives in Maryland with her husband and two children. A desire to see more novels with positive, sexy, and three-dimensional African American characters as soul mates, friends, and lovers, inspired the author to take on the challenge of penning such romantic reads. She is the author of two paranormal romance series: Winged Warriors and Death and Destiny. She's also embarked on a science fiction romance series, Forever Yours. N.D. likes to read historical and paranormal romance novels, as well as comics and manga.

OTHER BOOKS BY N.D. JONES

PARANORMAL ROMANCE

Winged Warriors Series: (Angels and Demons)
Fire, Fury, Faith (Book 1)
Heat, Hunt, Hope (Book 2)

Death and Destiny Trilogy (Witches and Were-Cat Shifters)
Of *Fear and Faith* (Book 1)
Of *Beasts and Bonds* (Book 2)
Of *Deception and Divinity* (Book 3)

Stones of Dracontias: The Bloodstone Dragon (Dragon Shifters)

Dragon Lore and Love: Isis and Osiris (Dragon Shifters)

CONTEMPORARY ROMANCE

Styles of Love Trilogy
The Perks of Higher Ed (Book 1)
The Wish of Xmas Present (Book 2)
The Gift of Second Chances (Book 3)
Styles of Love Complete Series (Books 1-3)